TEA LEAVES

MAHZI KANE

DEDICATION

This is dedicated to everything and everyone with whom I have come in contact. Each interaction and observation is inspiring; it sparks something in my imagination and creative self to tell a story … to share my voice. Thank you for helping me to have something to say.

ACKNOWLEDGMENTS

My mother, Kathryn Outting, for encouraging me since the day she found out I could write.

My suns, Ishine and Noble, for giving me two more reasons to push.

Chapter One

S iSter ' S K eeper : i r i S

PEOPLE TELL ME THAT I THINK that I can say whatever I want without a care or thought for feelings other than mine. Now while this may have been true in the past, age and experience have taught me that I have got to control my tongue because every single thought coursing through my brain does not have to be spoken. Which brings me to a present thought of deciding whether or not telling one of my dear sister-friends, Sage, that she is being a silly b-i-t-c-h. But how do you tell a good friend something like that without hurting her feelings? You'd think that with a name like Sage she'd be all wise and prudent and what not. Wrong!

"I just don't understand why Lamar thinks he can act like my man. When we first started kicking it, he made it understood that he was not looking for a commitment. His seven-year relationship ended, leaving him bitter and with a string of bad credit. Nobody said anything about being his woman. And he knows that I still see other people but now it's like he wants me to play the wife role."

"Well, Sage, maybe it's the months you've spent shacking up at his crib, screwing his brains out and making four-star meals for him and his boahs, not to mention the impeccable job you've done of changing his stank bachelor pad into something off of MTV cribs."

"But from the jump, we knew that this was not going to develop into a serious relationship: merely the comfort and convenience of having someone to kick it with. We have a great time when we're together and some of the best sex this side of the rainbow."

"Basically good dick and no complications."

"Our goals seem so attainable, don't they?

Sage and I are in the King of Prussia Mall, which is huge. I could spend my entire life away here in its 200 stores, but right now I'm on a quest for the perfect pair of shoes to set off the dress I'm wearing to my fiancé's office party tonight. His web design company, Ideas Made Concrete, is celebrating a stellar year. They were rated as a business on the rise in *Entrepreneur Magazine,* plus the books show a great profit gain for the quarter.

"I can't believe that he got caught up after all the trash he talked. I'm usually the one pressing the relationship issue, but this guy won't let it rest. So you know I'ma have to card him."

The perfect way to get rid of a guy: send him a greeting card pointing out all the things that he did to ruin the pseudo relationship you had etched out in your mind, but that lost its zeal in real life. And oh, by the way, can we still be friends?

"How do you think he will take it?"

"I don't care, as long as he leaves me the fuck alone. That fool had the audacity to show up at my apartment at 6 in the morning with croissants and cinnamon-apple spice herbal tea, my favorite. At first it seemed charming until he started roaming around, peaking in and out of every room. Then it was clear that he was only there to make sure another dude wasn't, like he pays my bills. I was too outdone."

Sage and her soap opera drama can be life-draining at times, but I endure it and finally lay my hands on a black pair of Kenneth Cole stilettos with soft leather and a pointy toe. Grooving to *Who Is Jill Scott?* on Route 76 in my white Malibu and puffing on hydro, I drop Sage off at her apartment and then head home. As a Philadelphia native, my stomping ground was and still is the north side. It has a reputation for being dirty and riddled with violence, ignorance and poverty, but that's not what it's like where I'm from. The neighborhood I grew up in is like a small piece of suburbia surrounded by high-rise project buildings. Try imagining a diamond placed in a pile of shit. That's where I grew up.

Malcolm and I live in the Art Museum Heights section of the city. Our duplex has large windows, spacious rooms with walk-in closets, a fireplace and serves as our cozy hideaway from the rest of the world. A home is supposed to be peaceful, filled with culture, art and a love for your lineage, and that is what we have. Our walls are covered with African and Indian pieces, sculptures and masks from Nigeria and the Congo. One of my favorites is a Native American Kwakiutl Mask from the mid1800s. The facial features are distinct and regal. Pretty swirls of indigo and orange finishes make the entire mask stand out. It doesn't match a thing in here, but I love the enchantment it brings. There are several pieces of art that we've purchased from artist friends, like a painting of a bare-breasted sister rocking an Afro and a peace sign. One of my many hobbies is photography, and I hang pictures everywhere. Photographs are living pieces of history for future and present generations. It's like catching moments of time in the palm of your hand like a pretty butterfly.

After I check our messages and return a couple phone calls, I go to the bathroom to shower. Finished, I dress in no time and call Malcolm to see when he'll be home to pick me up.

"Hey, how are you?"

"Fine, Iris. How are you?"

"Divine as usual. What time are you coming to get me?"

"I'll be there in about 15 to 20 minutes. Do you need me to bring you something?

"No. I'll see you when you get here."

I hang up and do one last check to make sure I look gorgeous. The stunning black halter, A-Line Donna Karan makes my small frame, nice rack and ass pop like the fireworks at a Fourth of July picnic. And of course we can't forget the shoes. To top it all off, I added a cute little clutch purse with diamond studs that Malcolm gave me for our one-year anniversary and my signature scent, Indian Sandalwood. I wear oils because they mix with the pheromones in your body so no scent smells the same on any two people. Before I know it, the bell rings, I grab my wrap and am out the door. I get into Malcolm's silver Lexus GS 300, then lean over and kiss him long and soft on the lips.

"How has your day been?"

"Ummm, kinda mediocre, but it's getting great at the end."

He leans over to pull me close, and we kiss for what seems like forever. I can feel the energy of his lips after our embrace ends.

"OK, OK, let's get going before you make me miss my own damn party."

"I take it you like what you see."

"Yes, and don't act like you don't know it."

"This old thang? I found this dress in the back of the closet, but the shoes are brand spanking new. Sage and I spent hours searching King of Prussia, but I found them."

"And how is Sage?"

"Let's not even go there. You know how my crew can be at times. Tonight, the only two people that I care about are right here."

Mahzi Kane   Tea Leaves

"I like the sound of that."

We arrive at the DoubleTree hotel and ride the elevator up to the Grand Ballroom. Huge chandeliers drizzle from the ceiling like clustered icicles. Diamond-cut mirrors line the walls and blanket the room with an elegance that can definitely be felt. A jazz band is in a far corner playing "If Only for One Night" by Luther Vandross while the caterers set up along the sidewall serve appetizers. Invited guests laugh, mingle and look as though they are having a good time.

"Well, well, well, look what the cat drug in."

It was Malcolm's right-hand man, Dennis. He is a self-proclaimed ladies' man slash comedian, but I find no humor in the dry jokes he insists on telling over and over and over again.

"How are you, Dennis?"

"Damn, girl, you look so good, I'd drink your daddy's bathwater."

See what I mean? They chuckle and lean in as they shake hands.

"Hey, hey, hey. Watch who you talking to, partner, or I'll take you outside and whip yo' ass.

"Malcolm, this party is off the hook, I mean for an office thing. Everyone is having fun, and the food is excellent. What is the name of the catering company?"

"Roots & Culture. It's owned by a very close friend of Iris'."

"My compliments go to the chef. If you don't mind, I'd like to steal you for a minute. There are a few important people that I want you to rub elbows with."

I give Malcolm one last look and then they go, leaving me to search the room looking for a familiar face, or should I say, one I feel like talking to. I spot two women whom I recognize from Malcolm's office and make my way over to them, stopping to exchange pleasantries along the way. Suddenly I feel a pair of eyes burning into me like hot coals. I turn around to see a man who looks to be in his late 50s ogling me as he strokes his goatee. Within seconds he is on me like flies on shit.

"Can I have one-millionth of a second of your lifetime, sweetness?"

"Unfortunately, I see a couple of people I need to speak with, so no."

"I'm sure you can squeeze me in, my dear."

"Sorry, but like I said, I see some folks I'd like to acknowledge before they leave or before I take my seat next to my fiancé."

"Fiancé? Is that supposed to scare me away? How about I give you the number to my cellular phone and you call me as soon as you get a free moment?"

"I am not interested. Bye-bye now."

"So you're trying to tell me that in my Armani suit, Botticelli shoes and authentic Rolex, I can't get the chance to wine, dine and 69 you?"

"Fool, I wouldn't let you scratch at the raggedy tag inside the old piece of drawers that my great-grandmama used to clean the silver. I suggest you get a grip. I'd hate to have to knee you in the nuts for being a jerk."

If pupils were daggers, the best neurosurgeon in these United States wouldn't be able to save him from my crookeye glare as I walk off in my finest diva stroll. Obviously, he does not know that he is in the presence of royalty. Mr. Armani Suit stays away from me, and before I know it, Malcolm and I take our seats, get through dinner service and his speech, and say our good nights.

By the time we get in the front door, I am almost naked and we are all over each other.

Mahzi Kane   Tea Leaves

Champagne goes straight to my head to unlock the freak in me, and with that in mind, I was sure to have five glasses at the party. We make love in the vestibule up against the wall, back-alley style. It was enough to make my eyes cross. We shower and I whip up two sandwiches while Malcolm rolls a blunt. I am a lover of Cannabis sativa. In blunts, bongs, pipes, joints, natural leaf, cornstalk — roll that shit, light that shit, smoke that shit. Next thing I know, we are ready for round two.

*

I sit in my office plugging away at a poem that I've been struggling to finish when Clarke calls me. Clarke and I have been friends since high school. We met at the Philadelphia High School for Girls in 1990 and have been very close ever since. We would choreograph dance steps for school performances and house parties with four other girls. So much of our time was spent together that people started saying we looked alike. After high school, we shared apartment: a hole-in-the-wall with one-bedroom over top of a deli. The rent was cheap, it was ours, and we loved it, but eventually one bedroom proved to be too little space for two women to peacefully occupy.

Clarke is highly intelligent and drop-dead gorgeous, and she uses both of these qualities to her advantage. Clarke works but only when and for however long Clarke deems necessary. Must be nice, right? But the girl never wants for a thing. That's where her stable comes in — her faithful stable of hoes, as she affectionately calls them. Clarke uses men, gets them all dirty, and then throws them out. One after the other. Don't get me wrong, the men are well-aware of her intentions as well as her character, but they always think that they will be the great Mandingo Warrior to tame Clarke. Silly rabbits.

"Wassup, girl?!"

"Hey, Clarke, how are you doing?"

"Moving and grooving, you know me. Keeping busy with my stable as usual, but I called to tell you how I had to walk off the plantation yesterday."

"Dag, Clarke, didn't you just start working there like last month?"

"Something like that. I don't even remember when I started. But anyway, the District Manager is a total bitch. She'd been at my store for a couple of weeks to work with a trainee, and she was working my last nerve. Becky is unprofessional, especially when it comes to speaking to people in the proper manner. She's the type who thinks that the world is supposed to kiss her ass 'cause she has a title. Sorry, she found the right one 'cause I'm nobody's kiss-ass."

"Get to the part where you quit."

"I was changing the back wall displays when Becky got a call about an upcoming floor move. She then tried to get me to start the floor move, as if I wasn't already in the middle of a project. You know I was not even hearing that. Not to mention there were two other managers at the store, so why she tried to work me like a field hand, I don't know. Then she's like, 'Clarke, I need to speak with you in the back.' So whatever, I follow her and I'm like, OK, what's up? She goes into how she runs a tight ship and she gets the feeling that we aren't meshing. I just stared at her 'cause I was waiting for her to make her point. Then she started this spiel about respect for the chain of command and being a team player. Next, she went into my attitude and personal phone calls, and that's when I stopped her mid-sentence and said, 'Look, Becky, this is only a gig to me; it's not my life. I enjoy shopping. I enjoy creating displays. That is why I am here, not for you and your bullshit. I could be finishing my work right now, which would allow me to possibly start the floor move, but instead I'm standing here listening to you go on and on about nothing. Let's get to the issue. This is really about the fact that I don't need you to hold my hand through this shit and truth be told, I could do your job blindfolded, and you know it. There is nothing you can teach me, got it? That's why I don't respect you and your so-called tight ship. I quit and good luck with that floor move.' And I rolled out. Fuck that, I don't need some poor white trash up in my face about dumb shit when I have a whole degree in visual marketing. Damn that! They a trip, ain't they?"

"Clarke, you are sooooo crazy. You change jobs the way most people change underwear."

"Yeah, that's why I don't wear any, ha!"

"You nasty. What are you gonna do about your rent and bills?"

"Now you know one of my hoes has that covered. I called Solomon all upset about having to quit my job, and he told me not worry 'cause Big Daddy got me until I get back on my feet. Speaking of which, I am in desperate need a new pair of shoes. I got to shop when I get upset. Feel like rolling out to the mall for some retail therapy?"

"That sounds like a ball of fun, but I am working. I know it's a foreign concept to you, but I have to finish this so I can get this manuscript to my publisher. Sasha has been waiting for two weeks so I gotta take a rain check. How about we go to Cabana's tonight for margaritas?"

"That's wassup. I'll scoop you up around 7."

"Cool, I'll call the rest of the squad, and we can make it Girls' Night Out."

Mahzi Kane   Tea Leaves

"All right, holla."

"Peace."

Now back to this poem. I want a sharp finish, and it's not flowing properly. Even though I write poetry and various works of fiction, and once in a while I do freelance articles for *The Daily, The Philadelphia News* and *The City Weekly,* I know when I've been beat. I leave the office and call Malcolm to let him know about my plans for the evening. After that I whip up a dish of vegetarian pepper steak over brown rice with corn muffins. Most people frown on not eating meat, but I've found that I have more energy, my thoughts and ideas are clearer, and I feel healthier. I've been a vegetarian for six years and Malcolm for eight. The one drawback about being a vegetarian is that it's expensive as hell. Plus whenever we go to someone's home for dinner, they always serve flaccid vegetables and bland tofu. I hate tofu.

I shower and put on a snug pair of boot-cut jeans, a white tee and shoe boots, and call my girls. By 6:00 everybody is confirmed, but Rashida couldn't get a babysitter, so she wouldn't be able to join us. Back in the office, I finally write an ending I like, and then the phone interrupts my joy. It is Clarke.

When I get into her black Mazda 929, she is on her cellphone, and I can tell she is talking to a man by the expression on her face. Instead of going to college she should have tried out for the WNBA, 'cause this chick got mad game. I start shuffling through her CDs until I find 2Pac's *Makaveli* and insert it into the player.

"I swear guys stay wanting to lay up. Damn, let a playa play!"

"Girl, you are too much! What do you think that they should expect in return for paying your bills, your car note, your insurance, your rent and funding your shopping sprees? A Thank You card and a fucking Peppermint Pattie? You are being a bit naïve, don't you think?"

"I don't make any of them do anything that they don't want to do. Grown people do grown things. Being my friend and having the privilege of sexual contact should suffice. They need to recognize that I ain't about laying up under a man all day and all night. I have things to do."

"I'm not getting into this discussion with you again because, as I've stated before, it's your life. But I will say this, instead of opting for being grown all the time, try being an adult that is mature and responsible. But onto a different subject, Rashida can't come out, but everybody else will meet us at Cabana's."

"Let me guess, no babysitter? Erik needs to be ashamed of himself for not helping out with his son."

"He gets away with doing nothing, and even when Rashida took him to court, Erik kicked that out-of-work song. Then the judge gave him 30 days to find work, but he ain't got the good sense to care about a court order. They awarded Rashida $20 a week until he could produce pay stubs."

"What the hell is $20 a week gonna do for a 15-month-old child? That barely covers the cost of pampers. This system is a joke. In order to get welfare, you gotta file for child support, even if you're with the daddy, or you gotta be poor as hell, rubbing two nickels together. Trying to get one of these sorry-ass fathers to play their part and not just send money is like pulling teeth. Then you see this nigga out in the street and he got a fresh pair of Timberland boots, a sharp-ass cut and banging the latest CDs. I swear I'm never having kids 'cause I can't deal with the baby-daddy drama. I'll cut a nigga in a minute. Girl, there's something in the ashtray. Please spark it up before I really get to ramming."

"Miss Blunt Mobile, you need to empty your ashtray because if you ever get pulled over, you're goin' down and not the way you like."

We park and walk down to Cabana's at Fourth and South Streets, located on the corner of the block. South Street is a hot spot in Philly, especially for eating and shopping. In the summertime it's packed with fly cars with state-of-the-art systems blasting the latest hits, and the sidewalks are mobbed with guys trying to holla at chicks strolling up and down the block in their hottest outfit acting like they don't want the attention. There is always a weirdo or an unconventional sight to feast your eyes on — I once saw a guy shooting heroin in the middle of the block. South Street also has a variety of the best restaurants around. Ishkabibble's and Pat's King of Steaks are legendary, and Cabana's is known for having the best margaritas in town. It's a nice-sized restaurant, and it's always packed, especially on weekends. When we get to Cabana's, it isn't hard to find our crew. I hear Ila's loud mouth as soon as we hit the front door.

"Party over herrrrre, ain't shit over theerrrre!"

"Oh Lord, I sure don't feel like fighting tonight. Ila better calm down. I can't stand that rowdy, drunk shit."

"Relax, Clarke, she'll be fine. Peace, sistahs."

We all exchange hugs, and Clarke and I join Sage, Ila and Toya at the bar. We order a round of margaritas and start to catch up.

"How was Malcolm's party, Iris?"

"It was cool, Sage. Of course I was the cutest thing there, and those shoes are very comfortable. Malcolm and I danced all night. The low point of the evening came in the form of an old, corny dude trying to pick me up with a lame-ass wine, dine and 69 line."

"No, he didn't! Did Malcolm hear him?"

"Hell no, he was off taking care of business, but I handled the situation with ease. Beautiful women cause some men to lose their got-damn minds. Little do they know that this beautiful woman can go from queen to bitch in 2.5 seconds."

"Ain't that the truth? Strange men have paid for my lunch, offered to take me on island getaways, and even buy me cars — all before they know how to spell my name right."

"Toya, I have been at clubs and guys will offer to give me head right there on the dance floor. For all they know I could be the nastiest skank walking, but they're eager to wear my thighs like earmuffs."

"Well, Sage, you are the unofficial Luke dancer of the squad, so I can't much blame them."

"Clarke, I don't care if a dude stands on his head and recites the alphabet backwards in Español, sucking his dick is the last offer I'm throwing out there."

"I hear that!"

"Ila, I don't get how you even have an opinion about something you've never experienced."

"Sage, I know how I feel. I don't know what it is, but the mere thought of putting a sweaty penis in my mouth after it's been swinging in the wind all day makes me sick to my stomach. I can't get with that. I gag on bananas, so that hardly makes me the deep-throating kind, feel me?"

"Girl, you don't know what you are missing. That's how I turn my worthy hoes out: fellatio like a muthafucka!"

Clarke is clutch-the-pearls vulgar at times, but that's one of the things that I love. She is as real as real gets about everything, especially her sexuality.

She goes for what she wants and couldn't care less what people think. You have to respect that about a single woman trying to make her way in a man's world. I might understand Ila's refusal to give oral sex if she wasn't adamant about receiving it on a regular basis. Her infamous line is that if he ain't licking it, then he ain't sticking it. Hypocritical, right? I don't know what man she thinks is going for that in a healthy relationship. As our laughter subsides, I spot three brave souls headed in our direction.

"Don't look now, ladies, but we are about to be macked."

"I'm taken so I'm not worried."

"Toya, I will never understand how or why you choose to commit yourself to a man with a wife."

"Can't explain it Clarke, but when it's me and him, nothing else matters. I mean nothing, including his wife."

"That Lauryn Hill shit got you slipping on your pimp game. You see where it got her."

"Everybody can't be like you."

"The world would be a much better place if they could."

"Hmmm, a bunch of out-of-work, fellatio-giving broads that don't wear panties … that is hardly the utopia we've been waiting for."

"Excuse me, ladies, next round on us?"

"Sure. Bartender, another round of margaritas. My name is Clarke; this is Iris, that's Sage, Ila, and Toya's on the end."

The brothers introduce themselves as Ed, Don and Corey. I can feel them size us up to see which one of us they are most attracted to, but Toya turns her back to us and fiddles with the straw in her drink. Clarke, Sage and Ila are eager participants in the race to see who will make a connection this evening. Ila is in a semi-monogamous relationship: Justice is totally committed to her, but her commitment to him depends on whatever cutie happens to be sending compliments her way. Even if I wasn't rocking my 2-karat engagement ring, none of them are my type— not that I have an actual type. Ed is about 6 feet tall, 200 and some-odd pounds, very fair-skinned, and has the nerve to have a tail with a bead on the end. I guess he thinks he's preserving what he perceives to be "good hair." Don, on the other hand, is caramel-colored, skinny and has some kind of acne thing going on that is way unattractive, but he has personality and a great sense of humor. Corey is the cutest with a deep-chocolate complexion, the sexiest eyes you ever did want to see, a kinky Afro, nicely groomed mustache and full beard. By the time the fourth round of drinks comes, Clarke and Corey are all up in each other's faces like they are on a romantic date while the rest of us get drunk and engage in typical bar etiquette: party and bullshit.

"All righty, I'ma holla at y'all tomorrow."

"Clarke, where are you going?"

"Iris, Corey and I are gonna go catch a bite to eat at The Diner. We can hardly hear what the hell the other person is saying in here."

"How am I supposed to get home? You are my ride, remember?"

"Can't you call Malcolm to come get you? Or Ila can drop you off, right?"

"Whatever. It's no big deal for me to take Iris home, but all I know is that I was raised to leave with the people I arrived with. Plus they serve food here, so that bite-to-eat shit ain't flying with me."

"What the fuck is this, hate on Clarke night? I'm trying to pimp this nigga, maybe get my freak on if he's lucky, and y'all tripping. It ain't like I'm leaving you with a bunch of strangers, Iris. We're all crew here."

"If you say so, Clarke. Go do you. I'll get home."

"You're my sister for life, Iris. I'll call you in the a.m. and let you know what happened. Holla!"

And like that, Clarke and Corey are gone. Ed makes a half-ass attempt to get Sage's phone number, but she sinks his battleship quick. Defeated and outdone, Ed and Don finish one last round with us and then depart. Once it is all crew, Sage and Ila rip into Clarke, which I expect.

"Can you believe that whore?"

"Sage, don't trip. We know how Clarke is. She's all about her — all of the time."

"I don't see how or why we entertain her. I'm ready to be done with her trick ass."

"Ila, because she's good peoples when she wants to be. She and I go way back."

"All I know is that's slimy and I'ma keep my distance from her before I end up laying her ass out … wayyyyyy back."

"Ila, it ain't that deep."

"It is to me, Iris. Real friends don't act the way she does."

"Don't get all riled up because you will hurt her. I remember when … what's the guy you used to mess with and he had that girlfriend who followed us to the store?"

"Toya, if you gonna tell the story at least have all the details. It was the movies. His name was Ahmad, and his bitch, Tammy I think, called herself stalking me. It was a sorry crack at it because we saw her and her cousin following us from the jump. We dipped back to Toya's, and I filled a sock with pennies and tucked it in my inside jacket pocket. We were walking and bussing it up like it wasn't nothing. Girl, we get in the movie, and as Toya and I were going up the ramp to find seats, here come these bitches."

"Then the one chick says to Ila, 'I thought I told you to leave Ahmad the fuck alone, can't you get your own man?'"

"Then Toya looked at me and was like, 'Do you know this chick?' and I was like, 'I don't think so, but she don't know who she's stepping to 'cause not too many can fuck with these hands.'"

"And before I could blink, Ila had whipped out the sock of pennies and was beating that girl all upside the head and face. Pennies were everywhere! Ila tossed that girl back and forth like a raggedy old baby doll. The whole thing lasted about five minutes, and then the chick's cousin broke it up. We ducked out the theater quick fast before security came. We laughed all night about that mess."

"That's right, I don't play that."

"But, Ila, you were fucking her man. How does she deserve to get beat down with a sock of pennies?"

"Sage, I didn't say I was right, but I'm still not going out like a chump. She shoulda been 'bout it. Anytime she's following me in broad daylight, her fight game should be tight. And for the record, I wasn't fucking her man. He was eating my pussy and giving me money."

"If she was handling her business at home, then her man would have had no reason to go elsewhere."

"If that ain't the most quoted page out of the other woman's handbook, then I don't know what is! Toya, that is the lamest cop-out ever invented. If he was a man, he should have been straight up with how he felt about both women. That is what responsible people do. You don't sneak around behind someone's back whom you claim to love, telling lies and breaking your word. If you want out, then you say that shit and roll."

"Iris, it's not that simple. There could be other things involved."

"Like what? Please enlighten us."

"There may be children involved. Like in my situation, Lamont doesn't love his wife anymore, but they have two young children. He wants to remain in the household that his children are raised in, and I don't blame him for that. As a matter of fact, I think that's a very good thing. His wife knows that he is unhappy, and she doesn't try to make things better. All she does is nag."

Sage looks at Toya as if she has uttered the dumbest thing ever said and snaps back with:

"Maybe she knows that he's fucking somebody else after she done gave him two got-damn babies, worked her ass off and made a home for them, and on top of it all, he doesn't even have the balls to tell her that he wants to leave. You and Lamont are selfish.

"Sensing that your husband is unhappy and knowing that he's cheating are two different things. Perhaps she's nagging because something isn't feeling right, but she can't fix it by herself, especially when that doesn't seem to be his focus. I'd cut Malcolm's dick off and dump his ass in the nearest river if I ever found out he cheated. Then I'd have it bronzed and display it on my mantle so the next one knows that I don't play. If being with another man is a viable option for me, then I'd leave Malcolm, and I tell him to have the same respect for me. I can deal with being hurt by the truth, but I refuse to live a bunch of lies."

"But Lamont is in a bad situation. It's not all his fault. How can love be selfish? He's trying to do the right thing for his kids and make a good exit plan. If that's not thinking about his wife, then I don't know what else he can do. I'm doing my part and being patient because when he and I get married, I will make him happy and nothing like this will happen."

Ila looks at Toya like she is not only crazy but downright stupid and asks:

"What's your assurance? I'm sure that Lamont's wife didn't see adultery in the forecast when they stood before God and their families and took vows."

"He complains that she's like an old woman, just set in her ways and doesn't like to embrace new things. Lamont says that she let herself go — barely keeps her hair and nails done. She's bossy and controlling and is always on his back about something. I'm younger, I know what makes him happy and I'm submissive."

"Dippy is more like it."

"I'm not dippy, Ila. Just ready to please my man. Chile, he can do whatever he wants to me in the bedroom. His wife is such a square; they never even did it doggy-style! And she wonders why he's not happy. When you add all that up, I think I'm doing a much better job of being his wife."

"Toya, does he talk to her about these issues? 'Cause you seem to know everything he wants you to know about their marriage."

"What is that supposed to mean, Sage?"

"What it means, Toya, is that Lamont's mouth ain't no prayer book! You're so eager to believe everything he tells you. Sounds to me like he loves that he can control and manipulate you, but his wife ain't going for it."

"Everybody acts like I'm dumb! I know what I am doing. God!! I'm the one living it and with the exception of Iris, nobody else got a man, so why should I take y'all advice? For the record, I don't care what he tells his wife. All I know is what he tells me, and I know that he loves me and when his kids are older, he's getting a divorce and we're getting married."

"And live happily ever after with a white picket fence, a dog and two and a half kids, right? Girl, you better wake up and smell the bullshit you swimming in."

"On that note, I'm going to the ladies' room."

"Wait for me, Ila."

Toya is shaking as Ila and Sage get up.

"Are you OK?"

"I am tired of people telling me how to run my life. I hear the same thing from Pia and Danielle. Nobody knows how Lamont makes me feel. When you're in love with a person, giving up is not an option. All he's asking is for me to stick by him while he works through this."

"We don't want to see you get hurt or waste time, energy and love living in a dream world. Just think — she has invested a lot in that marriage. What makes you think she'll give him up, considering that she has much more to lose than you do? She's his wife and the mother of his children. All you are is his mistress. In your heart, do you believe that Lamont will divorce his wife, leave his family, and come build one with you and everything will be peachy keen?"

"Yes, Iris, I do. I have faith in love, and I have faith in him. What else am I supposed to do?"

Just then, Toya's phone goes off.

"That's Lamont; I have to check in."

Check in? I'm engaged, and the last time I checked in, I was 12 years old. I can see that nothing good will come from this Lamont situation. Unfortunately, Toya has to walk those miles alone. People make learning the hard way the norm. The old me would have given a lecture about self-esteem, not settling and upholding the unwritten laws of sisterhood. Fuck all that. People don't want to hear it, and then I get pegged as the preachy friend. My new motto is, "Say nothing." Life is short, opportunities are few, and I only have so much energy. I refuse to waste any of those or my peace of mind on the affairs of others, even if they are my dear sisters.

*

I stumble into the apartment about 2:30 a.m. As I anticipate, Malcolm is up going over paperwork and listening to Bob Marley. I take my shoes off at the door, hang up my jacket and head up to the bathroom. I brush my teeth, wash my face and put on my nightgown. I stop off at the bedroom to dig in the stash. I walk into the office rolling a blunt and lean over to plant a seductive kiss on the back of Malcolm's neck.

"You giving me chills with those kisses."

"What are you doing up so late?"

"Waiting for you. I take it that you enjoyed yourself?"

"You know it. We kinda got into it with Toya though."

"Over Lamont?"

"Yup. She swears that love will save the day. It makes me sad, but there's nothing else for me to say or do. All I know is that the next time she calls me boo-hooing over him, I don't want to hear it. Choices have consequences."

"He's only gonna break her heart. Toya thinks his wife is what's holding him back, but it's not. It's never about the women. If it wasn't Toya that he was cheating with, it would be someone else because he has unresolved issues. He is a control freak, and they give him all the power. Peep it: He decides who he wants to be with, when he wants to be with them, and they jump at his every beck and call."

"That's all very true, but all Toya can see is that his wife is what's stopping them from being a happy couple."

"Like I said many times, he's going to break her heart. Clarke called you about 45 minutes ago. I thought she was with y'all?"

"Miss Thang was with us, but then she left with a dude she picked up at the bar, talking about they going to The Diner to get something to eat."

"Hold up, how did you get home?"

"Ila."

"Why didn't you call me?"

"Because Ila had to drop off Toya anyway, so I rode with them."

"How is Clarke OK with leaving the person she went with for a chump at the bar? The food at The Diner is nasty as hell, and she ditched you for that?"

"That's Clarke, take her or leave her."

"Sounds to me like she's the one doing the leaving. If you insist on maintaining this so-called friendship, I suggest you take your own car from now on. That's some real slimy shit, and I don't like it."

"I guess I'm used to her. But you are right. I do need to take my own car. How are things at IMC?"

"It's all good, baby. Brother Sayid said he wants to meet with me, something about a few discrepancies in the books, but other than that, it's all good. Brother Sayid is a sharp cat and we are really benefiting from his consulting. Dennis fired another secretary."

"What happened this time?"

"Typical Dennis shit. Promised the woman a raise while he was nailing her, and then wouldn't follow through with it after the deed was done. I was in my office, and all I heard was an irate woman yelling and screaming about how she ain't lick brown sugar out the crack of his ass for nothing, and the entire time Dennis was politely packing all of her things into a box."

"How do you think that makes the other female employees feel? He is making it seem like that type of behavior is cool, like it's acceptable. He better watch it because he's gonna mess around and get shanked or even worse."

"I tell him all the time that he is too old for the stunts he pulls. He should have a better regard for women and how he acts at work. I'm going to have to sit him down again because soon one of these ladies will sue his black ass, and that's when it really will become my business. I can't have the other associates trying to pull the same shit."

"At this rate, the ladies will think they need to give blow jobs just to get a good parking space."

"Speaking of which … "

And with a sly grin, Malcolm eases his hands under my nightgown. He slips his fingers between my thighs and gradually pushes them apart, the entire time staring into my eyes. I watch in awe as he lowers himself to taste me. My legs spread as he does the same with my lips. His wetness kisses mine and time stops. I exhale smoke and ecstasy. I feel him going deeper inside of me, savoring my juices. I bury his face into my center and wonder how he causes me to feel this way. It seems as if he reads my thoughts, doing everything I want, all that I need and exactly the way I like it. He's trapped as my legs lock him in, showing how desperately I need for him to continue. My back arches and my toes stiffen. Stars come out and my body fills with tingles that evolve into a noisy outburst. First convulsions and then a stream of orgasm confirm that he delivers total satisfaction. Once I am able to open my eyes, I mount Malcolm and ride him into the wee hours of the morning.

I roll over at 11 a.m., groggy, sore and smiling. Malcolm has left for work. Taped to the dresser mirror is a long-stemmed rose and a note that reads, "They call me egotistical, but I blame you 'cause it's your love that has me feeling like the world is mine to do with as I please to please us...Have a lovely day, my love." That man is too good to be true. It's sad to say, but I find myself looking for flaws or waiting for a horrible ordeal to occur. I have this daydream of surprising him at his office with an afternoon picnic. As I turn the knob to his office, I see him tonguing down some thick-bodied woman with a long, curly weave, and I shriek at the top of my lungs for her to get off of my husband. Funny how society has us so conditioned and addicted to drama that when there is none, we seek it out. I mean, I've had my fair share of heartbreaks, but ever since Malcolm proposed and I accepted, I've been doing a lot of thinking about men and women and what I expect to give and get out of marriage. I've come up with many soul-searching truths, one of which is that I am scared to death of failing. At what? At being the wife that I know Malcolm deserves. My parents have been married for 26 years, which is no easy feat by a long shot. People are not as surprised to hear of divorce and multiple marriages, and it makes me wonder if a lasting marriage is realistic in this day and age. I am petrified of having him leave me, not only in the physical sense, but emotionally, mentally or spiritually. There's another vision I have of coming home one day and finding all of his things cleaned out of our apartment and a "Dear Iris" letter tacked to the refrigerator. In the letter, he explains that it's not him, it's me, and everything that I am is not anything that he wants. And then I fall to the floor weeping hysterically. I'm striving to deal with these abandonment issues. I mean, I am a very strong-willed and independent person, except where Malcolm is concerned. He's my lover, my light, my protector and my soulmate. He is intelligent, ambitious, handsome and passionate. I fear that I may not be good enough for him. Yes, I have the pretty face, the body and the brains, but what if those things aren't enough to keep us connected for all eternity? What will I do then? Who is this ringing my phone?

"Peace and blessings."

"Girl, let me tell you what happened last night."

"Who is this? I know it's not the broad who ditched me on Girls' Night for some dude and now has the nerve to call me up to brag."

"Iris, I'm sorry. You know I didn't mean nothing by it. If I made you feel a certain way, that's just me. Am I forgiven?

"I guess. It is in the nature of the righteous to forgive transgressions. So what happened with this Corey fellow?"

"At Cabana's we had a nice vibe going, laughing and getting along splendidly. I found out that he graduated from Temple Law and just accepted an offer from Mason & O'Connor. That didn't impress me much since I know that firm has the lowest percentage of minority attorneys. Maybe he'll be the trailblazer, who knows? Then he mentioned his brand-new Escalade, and that's when bells went off. I suggested a more private place to talk. We went to The Diner, and girl, that jeep is the truth! I got in it and it felt like my ass became one with the plush leather interior. We talked over appetizers, blah, blah, blah, and I decided it was time for me to put it on him."

"Clarke, I thought one of your rules was to never give it up on the first night?"

"I know but he had a smile that made the back of my knees sweat! I couldn't resist my curiosity to see how our vibe translated in the bedroom, and you know me, I was determined to be pushing that truck like it was mine. I convinced him to come back to my apartment for a drink. We got there, and all of a sudden it was like I was 16 again and taking a nigga's virginity. First he sat way at the other end of the couch, and I had to play inchworm to get closer because I wanted to kiss him. The kiss says it all because if stars don't come out the first time a dude kisses me, I show him the door. He kissed me, and oh my god, his lips were like two huge cushions all over me. Slowly we got into foreplay, and I'm trying to tell you, he had me climbing the wall. We moved the party to my bedroom so I could create the mood. I knew I had him when I stripped butt-naked and his eyes almost popped out. Corey got undressed, and as he put it in, I felt material brush against the inside of my legs.

"What?"

"Yes, it was his boxers, girl. He was trying to quick-and-through-the-slit fuck me. I asked him what was up with the underwear, and he had the nerve to play nonchalant, like he didn't know what I was talking about. I told him that there was no way he was fucking we with boxers on like we were in a college dorm room with his roommate and buddies around."

"Call me crazy, but it sounds like you speak from experience."

Mahzi Kane   Tea Leaves

"Heyyy, different time, different place, but let me finish this story. He went on to say that he had a complex, and it shouldn't matter, that all I needed to worry about was laying back to take this dick."

"Y'all were in the privacy of your home, not a soul to be found, and he wanted to keep his boxers on?

"Yes! I sat up, turned on the light and told him it was time for him and his Superman cape to go. I'm 26 years old, and I'll be damned if I put up with the dumb shit, not even for the chance to push his truck."

"That is exactly what your fast ass get."

"I knew you would say that. You need to get that hate out your blood."

"You need to get dick off your brain."

"Anyway, I was pissed and horny as hell, so I called Damien, and he rushed right over to put it on me. The night wasn't a total wash after all.

"Hold on, that's my other line."

"Collect call from … TOYA! Will you accept the charges?"

"Yes. Toya, what the hell is wrong?"

"Iris, I'm in jail! I need $500 dollars to get out."

"What?! Where at?"

"I'm at the roundhouse on Race Street. Can you please come and get me out? I swear to God I will pay you right back."

"OK, OK, I'm on my way."

"Clarke, that was Toya on the other line. Her ass is in the joint!"

"Wait, what? Jail? What the hell?! What happened?"

"I didn't even ask. I'm about to go bail her out. You coming?"

"Nah, man, I have to get ready for brunch with Brian, but call me and let me know she's all right."

"See what I mean? Dick on the brain. I'm out."

I can only imagine the kind of foolishness that has gotten Toya locked up. I love her to death, but she is one of the silliest women I have ever met. On the outside, everything looks good: She rents a house with her cousin Pia; she doesn't have any kids; and she has a good job at Compensation Technologies. But when it comes to men, she is as stupid as a fucking rock. My gut is telling me that in some way, shape or form, Lamont is behind whatever is going on. I jump in my car and speed to the roundhouse, which is only like 10 minutes away on a normal day. Today I make it there in five. I walk up to the front desk, and there are two overweight, white police officers sitting there. One has his feet propped up on the desk, nibbling at the remains of a powdered doughnut, and the other officer sits in front of a computer screen with a blank look on his face, picking his nose.

"Pardon me, officer, I'm here to post bail for Toya Haddad."

He punches in her name, and the information appears on the computer screen.

"Here we are, Toya Haddad. That will be $500 dollars."

I pay the bail and take a seat on the rusty old bench to wait for them to bring Toya out. Malcolm would have a fit if he knew I was bailing her out. Not because of the money but because I'm always saving her from herself, it seems. I admit that her being the youngest of us all makes me feel somewhat responsible for her. I am my sister's keeper. We are not physical sisters in the sense that we were born to the same parents, but we walk through life together, which gives us a relationship that goes much deeper than being girlfriends. When life gets unbearable, we carry one another. When we get unbearable, we drop one another back to reality. When we become despaired, depressed or desperate, we pick one another up. It's all a part of accepting people for who they are. After 30 minutes, Toya finally comes out of the holding cell dressed as if she is going to work, but her face is flushed, a dead giveaway that she has been crying.

"Toya, what happened?"

"Thank you so much, Iris. I really appreciate this. I can go tap MAC right now to give you back the money. I can't believe this is really happening to me!"

"What happened?"

"I have to get back to work! I was only out to lunch. I can't afford to lose my job."

"I'm only gonna ask you one more time, and then I'm gonna punch you in the fucking mouth! Toya, what happened?!"

"I'll tell you in the car. I want to get out of here. This has been the most embarrassing day of my life."

That statement carries plenty of weight coming from a person who's screwing another woman's husband. Toya scurries out of the roundhouse and I follow. Finally, inside the car, I turn to her and cross my arms.

"I'm not starting this car until you tell me what is going on."

"OK, OK. I don't know if I ever told you, but Lamont doesn't have his license because of some old stuff from when was younger. He and I are planning a weekend vacation to Martha's Vineyard, Oak Bluffs actually, you know the place where they filmed the movie *The Inkwell?* Larenz Tate was in it, remember, him and Jada Pinkett? Oak Bluffs was one of the first resorts for black folks and … "

"Enough with the history lesson. Get to the part where you get arrested."

"We needed a way to get there because Lamont and I can't be seen driving together in his family car. He suggested that I go to the DMV and get a license, and then we could rent a car."

"Toya, your license is suspended, and it won't be reinstated for another year. You can't get a new one."

"I wasn't getting it in my name."

"You mean to tell me that you went to the Department of Motor Vehicles and tried to get a license under another name?"

"The way Lamont explained it to me, it seemed like it would work. All I had to do was get a name, a social security number, and go in and apply."

"Everything in the DMV is computerized now. When they put in your social, a picture comes up."

"Now you tell me. We were sitting there, and it didn't feel right. I told Lamont that we should leave. He said that I was being paranoid and to be easy. The next thing I knew two cops were walking over toward us, and I knew that we were caught."

"You keep saying we. Where is Lamont, still in jail?"

"No, he didn't get arrested. When the cops got close, Lamont played it off like we weren't together. I don't know where he is."

"His harebrained scheme got your dumb ass locked up, and I'm the one who had to come bail you out in the middle of my fucking day? What kind of bullshit is this?"

"I know, Iris, and I am extremely thankful for your help. You always come through for me, and I have no idea what I would do if you didn't have my back. Please don't give me a big lecture. I feel stupid enough."

"Listen here, I'm the one who feels like a fucking idiot. I come rushing to your rescue on the presumption that some real shit went down, and once again it's just you being a dim-witted bitch over somebody's half a piece of husband! I am so tired of trying to save you. I can't and won't do it anymore. Tell me this: Why didn't you call him to rescue you since he's so fucking fantastic?"

"I tried but he didn't answer his phone."

"Ain't like he didn't know where you would be! Did you see his black ass rushing in to bail you out? Hell no. He's probably too busy running up in another dummy with her legs wide open and her brain tightly shut."

"He can't come bail me out. How would he explain that to his wife?"

"The same way he would explain not only funding a weekend getaway to Martha's Vineyard, but a reason why he was there without his family! But then again, your gullible ass is probably paying for that too."

Toya is crying and I am fuming mad. Her tears only make me angrier, acting like she has no fault in this, as if she didn't play a major role in this entire mess. Women allow themselves to be put in certain situations and then cry victim. Not this time. Not on my watch. And certainly not on my dime.

"You can kill the crocodile tears because they don't mean a thing. Let's go tap MAC so I can get my fucking money and go home."

We drive in silence, and Toya stares aimlessly out her window, struggling to pull it together. I think of the first time Toya and I met. It was about eight years ago. She was working in a drugstore stocking shelves, and I happened to be in there when the shelf she was refilling collapsed and packages of ramen noodles flew everywhere. I spent the next 20 minutes helping her restock. We found out that we had similar interests in music and spoken word. It turned out that she used to date one of my cousins. The rest, they say, is history. I should have known then that that would be the formula for our friendship: Toya makes a mess, and Iris helps clean it up. We pull up to the bank on 17th and JFK Boulevard. She exits, makes her transaction and returns to the car. She gets in and hands me $600. I guess she thinks that I will be softened by the extra money, but I put it right in my pocket without saying a word because $100 is the least she can do for me.

"I know you don't expect me to take you to work."

"We are only three blocks away."

"Exactly."

Shock spreads across her face. I am never this brutal with her, but I have had enough. The days of cleaning up and owning other people's shit are over. Toya collects herself and slowly leaves the car. I speed off before she can barely close the passenger door.

Chapter Two

W here i ' m F rom : r A S h i D A

"RASHIDA, WHERE'S JADEN?"

"Out with his dad, Iris."

"No wonder, it's scorching hot today, another rarity for this time of year."

"I know, right? This is one of those weeks where Erik is actually being civilized. He's had Jaden since yesterday, and he's not bringing him back until tomorrow evening. I'm off for a couple of days, and I am thankful for the break."

"First I have to pick up my grandma's prescription and drop it off. Then I was thinking we could get some platters and chill at the park or something."

"Sounds good to me. You know I love me a good fish platter. While I was off yesterday, I registered for school, and I am feeling good. I have to make changes so I can move forward, and that was the first step. No kid, no baby-daddy drama and no crazy-ass passengers — girl, I feel like I'm on vacation."

"All you need is the sandy beach and Dexter Saint Jock."

"Swinging his big dick."

After the nightmare yesterday with Toya, and Clarke prior to that, I need to return to my roots, so to speak, and kick it with Rashida. We have known each other since forever. Rashida and I are the same age, and growing up in the same neighborhood, we became more like sisters than friends. I lived on Turner Street until my parents moved us to the northeast, and she lived on Newport Place. We were on the Double Dutch team at the local recreation center, but on different teams, and that meant more time together walking to practice and traveling to the state finals. Whenever we would battle girls from the projects, as long as she was around, victory was in the bag, and soon our reputation made it so that we didn't battle at all because nobody could beat Ra-Ra, as she was called. She has always had this knack for being not good, but great, at whatever she set her mind to do. She takes talent to the next level. Her mom wasn't really attentive, so Rashida saw and heard a lot at a young age. She taught me how to dress to impress boys, what a period was, all about foreplay and sex, how to dance - I mean everything. She always stood up for me because I was the skinny, quiet girl, but later on she helped me get the fear out of my heart and develop the ability to hold my own. She still lives at home with her mom and older brother, Tommy, which is not an ideal situation when raising a child, especially for somebody like Rashida who values independence. Hard work and determination, not handouts, she says, will get her where she wants to be, and driving buses is temporary until she saves enough for an apartment. I love my godson to death, and it hurts to see them struggling but Rashida is strong, and I know for sure that she's making a good life for her and her son.

Rashida and I go to what has to be the slowest pharmacy in the free world. The pharmacist tells me that there's a 45-minute wait because they're backed up. How does that happen? All they're doing is putting pills from one big bottle into a smaller bottle and printing out a label. I will never understand. With Grandma still at dialysis, we head uptown to Soul Food Sanctuary while her medicine is prepared.

"What school are you going to?"

"Main Line Academy for 12 months. I'll take evening classes four times a week, and in two weeks I'm going to cut back on my hours at work. It's less money, but school is a priority right now that will bring in more money later. Jaden is getting big as hell, walking and getting into everything. My baby needs his own space, his own room, you know?"

"I feel you. I mean if you need a loan — "

"Iris, no. You aren't the one that got pregnant. I did. I have to suck it up and deal. I know it will be hard, and I'm going to have to make sacrifices, but it'll all be worth it in the end. I never pictured myself here, that my life would be this single-mom, baby-father shit. That's what I get for thinking Erik was my black prince."

"We're programmed as little girls to think a man will save us. Every story ends with the handsome prince rescuing the beautiful princess and sweeping her off to a world with no troubles. We buy into that shit and look for a man to do damn near everything for us except bleed every twenty-eight days. I even find myself looking for Malcolm to be my hero."

"He's your fiancé. Isn't that what being married is about, being able to depend on the other person to be your ride-or-die partner for life? To have your back and fight your battles?"

"That's partially true, but in other ways, it is unfair. Why should he do anything to help me if I am not willing to do it for myself first? Of course I want his support, and it is comforting to know he's there, but I can't expect him to have all the answers to all my problems. That's added stress and pressure to be responsible for another person's troubles."

"You should know, Miss Save-a-Hoe."

"Why you say that?"

"Bailing out Toya, always forgiving Clarke, and you were just offering me money. Iris, worry about you and the man you are about to spend the rest of your life with. That is the new life waiting for you, and the squad gotta see that and start taking care of our own problems, no matter how tempting it may be to lean on you instead of dealing with our own mistakes."

"Huh?"

"Sometimes one mistake can end up causing problem after problem, but you can't see it until it's too late. I never told a single soul this, but I had Jaden to try to keep Erik and it haunts me every day."

A sadness that I didn't recognize came over Rashida. I never thought of her as the co-dependent type, and her confession has me stunned.

"But how? Why? I remember you were thinking about abortion, but you said you couldn't go through with it and have it on your conscious."

"I made it seem like it was for fear of being punished by God. The truth is, I wasn't thinking about God. I was thinking about me. Thinking about the things I wanted. I felt like if I got rid of the baby, Erik would leave me for sure and I would be damaged goods after that. He was already cheating on me, and if I was able to get pregnant once, it could happen again and he wouldn't allow abortion money to keep cutting into his tricking budget. When I didn't go through with it, we talked about getting married and raising our son as a family. I didn't have a job, but Erik hustled and did construction from time to time, so I figured what better time since it was already done. We didn't have our own place, but I thought it would all work out as long as we were together. I didn't have that real family environment – it was just ma, Tommy and that awful Mr. Jenkins not to mention my dad in jail with a life sentence and no chance of parole. My family life ain't shit, Iris, and I wanted better for Jaden, so I decided to have a baby to try to make a boy into a man … to make our bullshit into a family … but by the time I was six months pregnant, I knew I had made the biggest mistake of my life. Erik stopped going to doctor's appointments with me because he always had to take care of business and when he did come to birthing class, he slept. We barely had sex at all because he said he didn't want to hurt the baby. I told him I needed his love and affection; he told me that wasn't important. When Jaden was born, Erik turned around though and became everything I wanted. He took care of us, bought pampers, food and even paid my ma the rent she is always hounding me about. He came to see us every day, and I stopped finding phone numbers and condoms in his pockets. We talked about moving, and he checked out a few places on his own. I finally had him — or so I thought. One night, he called and said he was on his way. It was late, past midnight, so I asked where he was coming from, and he said the strip club."

"That used to piss me off, how he would go to see strippers while you were at home pregnant, and then even after you had Jaden. He out waving dollars at some random twat instead of being home with the family he claimed to care so much about."

"I remember his little sermon to try to justify it like it was yesterday. He'd say, 'See, there's nothing wrong with a man wanting to see that form of entertainment, it's normal.' But let me say I'm going out to the bar or to the club. Then it became, why did I need to go out, who or what was I looking for, and why in a club of all places? He'd say that only freaks go to the club. I told him, funny, seems to me that all the freaks would be at the titty bar."

"Priceless."

"That night, I went to the living room to wait since I didn't want the bell waking up my ma. Erik came in reeking of alcohol and tried to give me a sloppy kiss, but I pushed him away in disgust. I flopped down on the couch, and he stumbled his drunken ass over and asked what was wrong. That's when I saw it."

"Saw what?"

"Cum. There were white, crusty spots all over the front of his black jeans."

I knew that Rashida and Erik broke up because of his cheating, but I didn't know it was like that. Talk about messy.

"What did you say? What did you do?"

"Nothing. I sat there. I couldn't yell, I couldn't cry, I couldn't talk. It was my fault. I knew what he was about, yet I made the choice to not only stay with him, but to have his child. The first time he cheated, shame on him; the second time, shame on me."

"You didn't say anything the entire night?"

"Nope. We sat there watching videos for a while and then he passed out. I thought about all the things I had put up with just to be with him, all in the name of having this wonderful family, and I had to ask myself if I was happy. The next morning, when he woke up, I told him it was over and I wouldn't compete for his love anymore. Not with strippers or homegirls or play cousins that he just happened to have fucked. That's the night I started to hate him."

"What did he say?"

"That I was tripping again and he didn't know what was on the front of his jeans or how it got there. Said it might have been icing from the cake because some guy was having a bachelor party. I told him I didn't believe him, and then he said I couldn't keep our son from him. I told him that he knew it was not about Jaden and that it was a typical asshole move for him to even bring that up, like I'd really do that. I condemned him for never really loving me and mocked him for even claiming that he did because how could he truly love me when he didn't try to make me happy? Finally, I told him I wouldn't be a good mother if I allowed our son to grow up seeing him disrespect me."

"That was it? He left? Tommy didn't have to put him out?"

"No, he got out on his own, but he said one thing to me that I will never forget."

"What's that?"

"He promised from that day forward, that as long as we are both alive and our family is apart because of me, he is going to make my life a living hell."

"Wow" is all I manage to say. My mind races to come up with something insightful or poetic to bring to the moment, but all I keep thinking about is why she kept this from me. But I thought it would be selfish to inquire about something so trivial when she had just shared something so monumental.

"At least you have a beautiful son to show for your heartache and troubles."

"Very true. I just wish I had the beautiful husband to go along with him."

Mahzi Kane   Tea Leaves

After stopping off to get my grandma's medicine, we pull up in front of her house, and she is sitting on the steps. Grandma Rue loves to sit on the front step and eat peanuts. Really she loves seeing what is going on in the neighborhood, like a self-contained town watch. Grandma Rue is 4 feet, 9 inches, with long, gray hair that stops at the middle of her back. Her eyes seem to look straight into your soul, and her smile is like a Caribbean sunrise. When I was younger, my great-grandmother Mary, may she rest in peace, babysat me, and when Grandma Rue came home from her job as a seamstress, it was our private time. Every afternoon she would have a bag of roasted peanuts, and we would sit on the step and talk and talk about nothing at all. She never married, although she did have a longtime love, Mr. Ray. Unfortunately, both Mr. Ray and Grandma Rue were slaves to their mothers. My great-grandmother Mary couldn't stand Mr. Ray, and she forbade Grandma Rue to see him to the point that he wasn't even allowed to step foot in the house. Mr. Ray's mother wasn't any better because she kept him busy running her errands and fixing things around her apartment that weren't broken. Mr. Ray passed away four years ago, and I think he took a piece of my grandma with him when he left.

"Hey, Grandma Rue."

"Hey, kitten. Thanks for my medicine."

"Anything for my favorite grandma."

"Gal, don't try and sweet talk me. I'm ya only grandma. Rashida, come on over here and give me a hug, you ain't too big to hug an old lady, are you?"

"Show me an old lady."

Rashida leans over to hug Mamie Rue, a pet name between them since grandma said they were way past the "Ms." stage.

Mahzi Kane   Tea Leaves

"How's that fine little rascal of yours doing?"

"He's doing real good, Mamie Rue. He's walking, saying little words like "mommy," "daddy" and "stop.""

"I see you out here eating peanuts in your pretty dress. You trying to catch yourself a little something, Grandma?"

"Gal, please. Ain't no man studdin' me, and I sho' ain't in the market for a new headache. I'm out here catching a breeze and enjoying this lovely day the Lord has blessed us with."

"All right then, Grandma. I'll come to take you grocery shopping tomorrow. Is 10 good for you?"

"Yes, kitten. Me and my coupons will be waitin'."

"See you then, Grandma Rue."

"Love you, kitten. Rashida, bring that little rascal by to see me sometimes."

"I will, Mamie Rue, I promise."

"And don't let that no-good daddy of his drive you crazy, 'cause a man a have ya acting like an ass if ya let him."

"OK, Mamie Rue, I won't."

Grandma Rue is a riot. There is always something to laugh at if she's within speaking range. She's where I get a lot of my speak-your-mind attitude. She is my father's mother and the matriarch of the Isan family, owning cherished mementos, newspaper clippings, celebratory diplomas and degrees of almost every relative, near or far, close or distant. On many an afternoon, she would tell me about her great-great-granddaddy Willie Isan and how he migrated from the South.

"Willie Isan was considered an uppity nigra'," Grandma Rue would say, "'cause he gave us the name Isan. Said he ain't calling hisself or the fruit of his loins afta the white man who was the source of black folks' grief anyhow. He came to Philadelphia and took odd jobs. From there, his hard and diligent work, not to mention the savings in the Mason jar in the cellar, helped to open his own five-and-dime shop, Willie's Silver Dime. He ran his business based on two thangs: own ya own and do it witcha own people. And that was the start of the Isan tradition of self-sufficiency and ownership."

Rashida and I drive by the playground on Oxford Avenue. It is 1:30 p.m. and the basketball courts are bare, but children scatter the playground. This used to be our major hangout for many years. At any given time, there was something going on in the playground. Whether it was summer basketball leagues, pool parties or cookouts, there was always a good time waiting on the Ave, not to mention eye candy, some of which we've tasted and re-tasted, double-dipped and shared. It is a pleasant day, and the Rock Garden is the perfect secluded spot to put us in a free space where we can talk. Nestled inside Fairmount Park with weeping willow tree limbs that seem to reach out to touch you in a soft place, it has Ginger and English Ivy, streams and ponds that sparkle and blades of maiden grass that tickle our toes. I am still reeling from Rashida's confession. How in the world did she think that a baby was gonna keep a man? Seems to me that's more reason for him to run off. Why would she do that to herself for a person who treated her so poorly? What gave her any indication that what she was doing would end well? Now she has to deal with the effects forever.

We carry the food, blanket and radio to a shady spot where I spread out the blanket, set up the food and put our favorite rapper's recent release in the CD player.

"Why you so quiet, Iris? Usually you've got a zillion funny stories, anecdotes or wedding ideas to ramble on about. What's up, you all out of things to say?"

"Nope. I'm just thinking if I … I mean if you … I mean."

"Oh shit, the great novelist is stumbling over words?"

"I'm trying to pick them very carefully because I do not want to offend you."

"Now you know we go back like school gym suits and penny candy. I could never be offended by something you say so spill it."

"Do you regret having Jaden?"

"Of course not. I regret the circumstances, sometimes his father and the bad choices we made in our relationship, but never my son."

"Don't you think it was dumb to use a baby to try to keep a man? Not like you're a strange experiment gone wrong, I know women do it all the time but … "

"I know that shit now, but at the time, I guess I believed what I wanted to believe instead of seeing what it actually was. I loved Erik and practically ate, slept and drank that nigga. I would have given anything for him to love me back the way I loved him. I was a fool in love, and so I made a foolish decision."

"Remember the red Honda Civic?"

"Here you go drudging up old memoirs of my days as a dizzy broad."

"Girl, please. I'm never letting you live that shit down. Against your better judgment and my good advice, you lent your car to Erik on a Friday morning, ain't hear from his ass until Sunday, and when he walked into his mom's house and we were posted up on the couch waiting, he looked like he was about to faint. Between all the stuttering, he tried to turn it around on you … why you didn't trust him … why were we staking out his mom's crib."

"I know, Iris, I know. I was there, and completely delusional. Why didn't you slap me?"

"A head-on collision with a brick wall wouldn't have been able to smack you out of whatever spell he had you under."

"He kept telling lie after lie after lie every time I asked him where he had been with my car all weekend and why he didn't return any of my pages. If his mom wouldn't have come in, I would have never found out that he took some young, bucktoothed girl on her prom in my car, which he was passing off as his, and then had the balls to go to Atlantic City for the fucking after-prom weekend."

We look at each other and burst into laughter, and tears well up in our eyes by the time we calm down.

"I can laugh now, but it wasn't funny that day. I tried to kill his ass. His mom was about to call the cops. And after all that, I still took him back. All I can do is shake my head and pray I'm smarter now."

The sun dances across our faces as we lay back on the red and white checkered blanket. The sky is peaceful with pretty blues stretching as far as the eye can see; the horizon sprinkled with specks of blue and orange as sparrows flitter about and drink from the streams. Far off, seagulls glide through the air with the ease of a sharpened knife slicing into hot butter. I am overcome with a tremendous sense of gratitude for the beauty nature offers yet never asks for anything in return, except that we treat this earth with the utmost respect. Three hours later, Rashida and I pack up and head back down the way. After I drop her off, I plan to stop by my parents' and then head home to start dinner. I have an intimate dinner planned for Malcolm and I because our schedules are so hectic, it feels like I never see him. The sun begins to set, and the sky is streaked in orange. Rashida seems less stressed, like all her bad decisions have tucked themselves away like a squirrel storing nuts for winter, but the expression on her face leads me to believe that these won't be back. Her honey-brown skin glows, assuring me that the confident glint I see in her eyes is real: She is in control and everything is going to be fine. I smile, thankful to have a sister like Rashida.

"All right, it's been real. We gotta do this more often."

"Who you telling? Next time I want to see my godson."

"Yeah, well, it'd be nice if he had a cousin to play with, hint, hint."

"Now it's really time for me to go."

"For real though, I'll call you on Sunday after church."

"Church? I didn't know you still go to church."

"Once in a while. You should … "

"Ah, ah, ah. Respect my shit, please."

"My bad. Anyway, we'll talk … plus you have to tell me what new ideas you have for the ceremony."

"All right, see ya later."

Religion is one of those topics I tend to steer clear of. Telling people that I follow principles that state that the kingdom of God is within, and that makes us God, triggers long and rather unproductive debates. I can't criticize something if it's making someone a positive force in society, even if it's a dogma that I can't personally accept, but I find that there aren't too many people who share my sentiment. How can any person wholeheartedly uphold the tenets of a particular faith and not be tolerant of another person's view? Respect is a universal law, an automatic right that we all should expect as an extension of the divine. I have knowledge of who I am in this world, and I live it out, but not through religion or rituals: no prayer, church, mosque or holidays. My actions are my testament to my awareness, connection and adherence to any supreme power, and that's all I need to be at peace.

*

Visiting my parents is always an adventure, primarily because they are hilarious. Queen and Martin Isan have been married for 26 years, and it shows. They have this comedic repertoire that reeks of understanding and true friendship. A thing beyond the immature practice of falling in and out of love on a whim, but that "we've built a family, seen struggle and success, learned something from each other and grown as people" kind of love. They are not perfect by any means, but that is what I admire most about them: they argue, cuss and fight, but there's an invisible line that they never cross. That's what I want for Malcolm and I. My parents live in the Northeast, off Rhawn and Roosevelt Boulevards. The house is like something out of a magazine. Every time I visit, there's a home improvement project in full swing. It hardly resembles the place where I spent my teenage years. My parents moved here when I was about 16. The majority of my time was still spent around the way, staying at Grandma Rue or Rashida's house on the weekends. Not that this modern house and upstanding suburb weren't lovely upgrades, but I longed for the old sights and sounds of my neighborhood. Moving into a lavish home was my parents' dream, not mine. In turn, it did give me an appreciation for hard work, ambition and dedication. My father retired four years ago from the gas company, where he worked as lead photographer. He took photos of gas explosions and company events, and he even dug ditches when money was tight and the overtime was available. Grandma Rue was mad enough to spit out her teeth when she found out my father got a job: "Oh, Martin, how could you?! How could you take up working fo' those people knowin' the history of our family, the work they did, the danger they faced, and all they done to give us our own, built wit' they own hands and a pride that was untouchable 'cause nobody could just toss 'em outta a job one day or tell'em it wasn't no work and turn right 'round and hire a white man or an immigrant. Naaaaah, we was the boss, and the boss make the rules, and the rules help you play the damn game, Martin … you can't go forgettin' that … hmph, I guess some thangs just ain't sacred no more."

I must have heard that speech 100 times. Finally, one day Grandma Rue let it go. I think that was around the time Mr. Ray died. Queen Isan is the epitome of grace and femininity. It is present in all that she does, from her petite frame of 5 feet, 6 inches to the strands of gray that stand out in her perfectly cropped short haircut; even her walk has an unmistakable air of sophistication and flair.

"You don't need a $12 dollar jar of cold cream," she would preach. "All I've ever used is soap and petroleum jelly."

And boy, can she burn! This is one of the many reasons my dad plunged all of his earnings into buying her a restaurant. For 10 years, Soul Food Sanctuary has been run like a fine-oiled machine. With a menu ranging from fried fish platters and barbecued ribs to clams over linguine and seafood fettuccine with alfredo sauce, it has everything a hungry belly could want. My mom is always trying to get me to come back into the kitchen, to keep the legacy going, but writing is my passion. I can cook, but I'm moved to write because to have the guts, maybe even the arrogance, to think something, and write it down for the whole world to see and never take it back is the most spellbinding thing that I have ever experienced.

"Anybody home?"

"Hey, hey, who's that?"

"It's me, Daddy. It ain't been that long, so don't try to act like you don't recognize my voice."

His embrace is tight, the way a protective daddy always hugs his little girl, no matter how old she gets.

"Let me get a look at cha; ooooh weee, girl you looking more and more like your mama every day. How's that soon-to-be son-in-law of mine?"

"Working hard as usual. Where's mom?"

"She ran to get something … oh, wallpaper for the bedroom."

"Which one?"

"I don't know, one of 'em. I can't keep track. Soon as the pension checks come, Queenie spending it up."

"Oooh, Daddy, stop, y'all are so funny."

Mahzi Kane   Tea Leaves

"I'm only poking fun at your mama. What you doing up these parts?"

"I was visiting Grandma Rue and Rashida, so I figured I might as well see all my family."

"How's Ra-Ra doing?"

"Good, she's going to school to be a paralegal."

"That's good, real good. She's always been smart, and that'll give her a nice foundation to start something strong for that boy of hers. I know how Grandma's doing 'cause I spoke to her ornery ass yesterday."

"She didn't mention it to me. Too busy eating peanuts and watching the neighborhood, I suppose."

"Maybe. Wanted me to go with her on a trip down South to visit Aunt who-gives-a-damn. I ain't stepping foot down South - too many bad memories. Why would I go down South when I can go to an island in the sun and get me a drink with an um-ber-rel-la in it? Why in the hell would I wanna go down South, tell me that?"

I know it's time for me to go. Listening to one of dad's "down South" tirades is not on today's schedule. For all of my dad's rants and outbursts, I'm still not clear on what's the big deal about him taking a trip to the South, but this is not the night I plan to find out.

"All right, Daddy, I'm about to be on my way."

"Leaving so soon? I knew your mama was always your favorite."

"Now stop it, you know that's not true, it's just I have to get dinner started. We hardly spend any time together with Malcolm working hard at his business and me at mine. So tonight I'm making red snapper, his favorite."

Mahzi Kane   Tea Leaves

"Go 'head, girl. One of the quickest ways to a man's heart is through his stomach. I'm living proof of that."

Daddy lets out a loud laugh as he rubs his Buddha-like belly.

"I'll tell your mama that you were by, and you tell Malcolm I said hello and not to be a stranger 'cause my chessboard is waitin'. How's the wedding plans going?"

"The best description would be a sea of tedium with all of the details, checklists, vendor contracts - it's never-ending, Daddy, I'm telling you. I meet with the coordinator in three weeks, and I still have plenty of decisions to finalize. It's a joyous occasion, and because of that I've resolved not to stress."

"And you shouldn't. It's your day, and like I always say, do it your way and everything will be perfect, just like you."

"I love you, Daddy."

"Love ya too, Sweet Pea."

"Wow, you haven't called me that in years."

"I know, Sweet Pea, I know."

I arrive at the apartment a little before 8. I put some jazz on to set the mood to mellow. I chill a bottle of White Zinfandel and toss the three-green salad with a light vinaigrette. Soon garlic spinach and grilled red snapper smell up the place something good. After the long-grain rice is complete, I hop in the shower and emerge feeling rejuvenated. I light the last candle and hear Malcolm's key in the door. As I am holding a single yellow tulip behind my back, the big smile I wear soon fades once I see Malcolm's expression.

"Baby, what's wrong?"

"You would not believe the day that I have had, Iris."

I rush him over to the sofa, take his briefcase, pass him the blunt and pour him a glass of wine. I join him on the sofa and take his hand into mine.

"Let me see, where do I begin? … "

"At the beginning."

"My day started as referee. Two grown women, and I use the term loosely, were engaged in a damn death match over jelly."

"Jelly?"

"Yes, JELLY! Kathleen said she saw Tanya take her jelly. Tanya claims she thought it was hers. Whatever the case may have been, it ended in fisticuffs. After breaking it up, mediating and handing out suspensions, the copy machine broke down. The office manager won some kind of trip and is out for the week. I spent nearly an hour on the phone being transferred and put on hold until I finally got a service technician to come out."

"Sounds like the 'S' on your chest really came in handy today, huh, Superman?"

"Man, I've had a pounding migraine since 9, I haven't eaten, and I am fed the fuck up at this point. Then on top of all that, I get here and my thoughtful wife-to-be has all of this waiting, and I come in bitching about work. You must think I'm ungrateful."

"Not at all. I've missed you too much these past weeks to think something like that."

"I have to fire Dennis."

"WHAT?!"

"Maybe even press charges against him."

"Why?!"

"Remember the discrepancies Brother Sayid found? Well they belonged to Dennis. He's been using the company's expense account for his own personal needs and lavish ones at that: extended stays at Four-star hotels; $300 dollar designer shirts, breakfast, brunch, lunch and dinner at all of the expensive restaurants in town. His position does not entail that many business meals or the countless lingerie purchases on his company credit card. I could go on."

"My goodness, Malcolm, I don't believe this."

I pull him to me, wishing I could stop time and make it all go away. Malcolm works his ass off, and to have the guy he's known since college, his roommate for five years - to have that same one take advantage is out of this world. Malcolm should have fired him so many times, but it was this assumed camaraderie and unspoken oath that helped Malcolm to give Dennis chance after chance to redeem his selfish ways.

"This is betrayal like I've never felt. If that bastard was here, I might kill him. I would have done anything for that brother, but now there isn't anything in this world that could make me forgive this. I don't even like thinking these types of thoughts, but that's where I'm at with it. My anger toward him is nothing compared to what I feel toward myself."

"Don't blame yourself for another man's shortcomings."

"I should have picked up on it. That's the first rule of running your business: Watch everyone and trust no one."

"You hire employees that are capable, trustworthy and overall good people, or you would not have them working for you, right? Dennis fucked up, period, and that doesn't have shit to do with rules of business. That has to do with what's inside."

"I knew that Dennis was jealous of me. I always got the girls he wanted, and the grades he wanted. I have the car, the business, the success . . .

you. His actions could have led to our downfall! Man, fuck him forever!"

Chapter Three

t hinKin ' Wit ' Y our A ss : i L A

I AM GETTING TIRED OF JUSTICE'S
ASS. Don't get me wrong, he means well, but
sometimes he is so nice and attentive that I could
stab him in the neck with a spoon. All he does is
work, work, work, and then he wants to be with
me, either at my apartment or he wants me to come
to his house. Where the hell are his friends? What
happened to the basketball games he used to go to?
What about the guys from work? I need evidence
that he has interests outside of our relationship.
Everyone thinks he's such a good catch, and he is
but there's just no excitement. Predictability may be
comforting for other women, but for me it's
boring. I like a man to be spontaneous once in a
while, you know, one who's up for a quickie in the
restaurant bathroom. The things I used to think
were cute make me wanna scream, like the way all
of his cologne bottles are perfectly organized on his
dresser by size and shape. His ties and socks are all
organized by color. Anal-retentive for a man, I
think, and if he eats anything other than chicken, I
think I might pass clear out. Even the way he
chews his food makes me wanna beat his face in. I
don't think it's coincidental that these feelings have
come to a head since I saw Piccolo last week. I
can't stop thinking about him. Fire couldn't burn
away my memories of what we had. I was Piccolo's
girl the entire four years in high school. He was
"the man," which made me "the chick" by
association. Everyone who was anyone wanted to

be down with us. Knowing us was something special; hanging out with us made you elite. Piccolo was the first guy I had sex with; the first to make love to me. After our first time, we walked hand-in-hand and he fingered me, said he wanted to have my smell on as many places as he could so that he could take it home with him. He taught me that a real man doesn't want a girl to just lay there, but at the same time likes to be in control. He showed me how to work my hips, how to do it slow and easy, and how to get buck wild. The first time he licked my kitty cat I jumped from the bed and locked myself in the bathroom and didn't come out for a half-hour. I didn't know what the hell he was doing to my body, but what I felt had me scared, and I needed to pull myself together. Piccolo adored me, and I knew it. He loved and defended me with everything he was at such a tender age, and I messed it up. Senior year had me on my high horse, and I decided that I would step out Piccolo. I hooked up with some guy — I can't even remember his name — from a neighboring prep school. I don't know how Piccolo found out, but when I saw him standing at my locker that Tuesday morning, I knew I was caught. His words had a roughness he'd never used with me, and I could feel his hate. That was the last time he ever looked my way. Seeing him last week awakened an inferno of feelings that in all honesty I didn't know I still had. He was the last person I expected to see on Wayne Avenue, but sure enough it was him. At first I didn't think he would recognize me, and then I wondered if he'd speak to me, even if he did know me by sight. Boy was I blown away when he scooped me up into his arms and wrapped me in the biggest bear hug like a scene out of an old movie where the lost love returns and they go

Mahzi Kane   Tea Leaves

walking off into a pretty sunset. Piccolo still has it
— the power to make my crotch tingle with
anticipation — and I want that man bad.

"Ila, are you gonna fry that chicken for my
lunch tomorrow?"

"Yes, Justice, I said I would, and please don't
bug me about it!"

"I was just making sure. What crawled up your
butt and died?"

"Nothing, it was a long day working with the
children."

*Justice noticed that for the past couple of days, Ila had
been snapping his head off for the smallest things: if he
hadn't screwed the cap tightly on the toothpaste and why his
boxers matched his clothes, just silly shit. After working
hard all day long in a poorly lit, dusty warehouse doing all
kinds of manual labor, the last thing he needed was a petty
argument. She was like sunshine to him — something to
look forward to every day; though lately his sunshine seemed
to be transforming into dark storm clouds.*

"Did I do or not do something to you because
for the past couple of days, I don't know, you've
been moody. Not your usual moody either. What's
the deal?"

I let out a big huff and roll my eyes. Again, he
is getting on my nerves.

"Why you think that it's always about you?
Can't I be in a not-so-great mood every once in a
while? Shit, even Barney takes off that big, dumb
purple suit."

"See what I mean? I am concerned, and you
respond with so much agitation, like I'm getting on
your last nerve!"

"Finally you're getting the hint."

I thought that was a mumble under my
breath, but apparently not.

"Hint? Look here sister-girl, you ain't gotta
hint a damn thing to me. How about I go home

Mahzi Kane   Tea Leaves

and give you time and space to get out of your big, black, bitch suit."

He snatches his hat and jacket off the back of the chair in the kitchen and slams the door behind him.

"He'll be back."

And I continue sitting on the couch watching television and twirling one of my braids.

*

The television show goes off and I decide to go for what I want. I fish Piccolo's card out of my Gucci bag, and after a few minutes of hesitation, I dial his number and am greeted by the sound of his voice. As I hoped, he is not in a relationship, he lives alone and has recently bought a house in Germatown. I desperately want to see his new house, but that would be too much temptation too soon. A few minutes of awkward silence emerge between the small talk and Piccolo suggests we meet for drinks. We decide to meet at a little restaurant on City Avenue at 9:30 p.m. I hang up the phone and do a happy dance around my apartment, and then I go pick out an outfit to hug my thickness just enough to get him drooling. I want him, but I want him to want *me* even more. I settle on a navy blue mini to show off my thighs and the sleekness of my long legs, and a cream, sleeveless mock neck sweater. I throw a denim jacket over top and slip into my navy blue knee boots and do a spin in the full-length mirror on the back of my bedroom door. I look hot and I know it. I walk out the door excited at the possibilities waiting for me and ignore the blinking light of my answering machine.

I arrive and Piccolo is waiting for me in the vestibule area just like we planned. I like a man who keeps his word. Piccolo takes me in from head

Mahzi Kane   Tea Leaves

to toe, savoring on each and every inch of my voluptuous body. He can only begin to imagine the pleasure that awaits him between these luscious thighs but I pretend not to notice. Piccolo is fine as all hell: 6 feet, 7 inches, with shoulders that slump and a tone to his skin like the color of the men that work at the 7-Eleven. His braids are fresh, his shape-up is tight, and the darkness of his eyes makes me want to run naked through his thoughts. Like two huge pillows, his lips call for me to lie between them and allow their comfort to rock me to sleep. Damn, I could suck his dick and like it.

"Smoking or non-smoking?"

The hostess's question shakes me from my daze.

"We'll go to the bar. Thanks, sweetheart."

Piccolo can see that Ila is feeling him and her frazzled state turns him on even more. He had thought about her several times over the years and is very pleased with this chance to catch up on life. She leads him by the arm to a table near the bar. From behind he licks his lips as he watches her ass move like the wind, so seductive and sultry. It is gonna be hard for him not to take her back to his place and sex her like the true stallion he has become.

"So, Piccolo, what have you been doing with yourself besides buying a new house and keeping yourself looking so fine?"

"Don't laugh, but I work as a guidance counselor at a middle school."

"You're lying!"

"Nope, it'll be four years next month."

"I cannot believe that one of the baddest dudes in school is now guiding and molding young adults. I am very impressed. Working with children, especially older ones, is a hard job."

"You have children?"

"Hell no. I work with children at a daycare center. I'm not ready to be a mother, but I love interacting with the babies. Do you have any?"

"Nope. I've been busy establishing my career and trying to make a difference in the lives of these kids, so maintaining a steady, long-term relationship has kind of fallen to the wayside. I am a Big Brother though, and me and my little dude hang every other Saturday."

"It's rare to find that in a person."

"What's that?"

"The ability to step outside of yourself and your own personal needs and wants in order to better someone else's life. That's compassion. I must tell you that it's very, very attractive."

The emphasis that Ila puts on "attractive" and the way her right eyebrow arches when she speaks makes Piccolo's manhood stiffen with excitement. He shifts in his chair in an attempt to tame his third leg.

"I'm glad you like it. Besides your job at the center, what else keeps you busy?"

There is no way in hell that I'm telling this sexy, ambitious, intelligent man sitting before me that I am in a two-year relationship. Infidelity was the reason Piccolo broke up with me in the first place, and I know it wouldn't sit well with him that my faithful boyfriend has no idea that I am out on what would technically be considered a date. Gotta keep my pimp game tight.

"I have a friend, nothing earth-shattering. Besides that, I hang with my girls, Iris, Rashida, Sage, Toya and this chick Clarke that I tolerate 'cause she's Iris' friend. Personally I can't stand the bitch, and I don't trust her, even though Iris swears she is harmless. Iris is a writer and does poetry readings, but once in a while she'll put together a jam session — you should come with me to one."

Mahzi Kane   Tea Leaves

"I dig spoken word. I'll definitely hold you to that invitation."

Shit, that ain't all he can hold me to or up against for that matter. The air between us is so charged with sex that I can cut a piece with my knife and pop it in my mouth. I rub my thighs together to try to stamp out the fire brewing and decide I am going to have this man but first I have unfinished business with Justice.

After drinks, we sit in my car listening to slow jams, reminiscing on old times and expressing newly found goals. I drive him to his charcoal gray Maxima, and he takes my hand and kisses it gently before promising to call me in the morning. I walk in the crib around 1:00 a.m., still high and pull off my knee boots at the fridge. I grab a bottle of juice before I sit down to check my messages.

Beep. "Ila, this is your daddy. I was calling to check on my baby girl and make sure you got the check I sent. Call me tomorrow. One love." Beep.

Beep. "Wassup, Ila? It's Sage. Call me when you get a chance. Just when you thought Toya couldn't get any dumber, wait till you hear this shit. And I wanna tell you about this scrub I went out with last night. Gotta go, here comes my client. Holla." Beep.

Beep. "Whatever the problem is, I am sure we can work it out. I love you and I plan to make you my wife. You have to talk to me and let me know what's going on in that head of yours. There's nothing we can't do but we have to do it together. Call me." Beep.

Justice. What am I gonna tell him? The truth will hurt him, but I can't lie about where I want to be, and I do not want to play games with his emotions. Walking away from him is hard, but trying to make myself stay where my heart is uncertain is pretty much impossible.

Mahzi Kane   Tea Leaves

"Hello."

"Hi, Justice, it's me."

"Yes, I know. Are you feeling better?"

"I was never feeling otherwise."

"Where were you?"

"Out clearing my head and getting my thoughts together."

The silence is heavy as Justice waits for her to speak. He has had enough of playing 20 questions and besides, it seems to get him nowhere.

"Justice, I think we should break up."

He still doesn't speak. He wants to yell, to tell her how ungrateful she is, how her father made her into a spoiled brat and nothing is ever good enough for her, she required more … more of all the things he just can't seem to provide. But instead, he says nothing.

"I don't know. I'm just bored with … no, that's not what I want to say. What I mean is, I don't want a long-term relationship. I've felt this way for some time, but I didn't want to let you go, I mean, what girl would? Justice, please don't ever doubt my love for you … you are a good man."

"Just not good enough to be your man?"

"Please don't make this harder than it already is."

"I'll make it even easier. Tomorrow when you're at work, I'll come get my shit, bring you yours, and we can be done with all of this. Have a nice fucking life."

And he bangs on me. I want to call back to tell him not to be bitter and that we are better this way, but who am I to tell him how he should feel? I'm relieved that he did end it so bluntly — it's never easy trying to drudge up words to say what I mean without really saying how I feel. It was bound

Mahzi Kane   Tea Leaves

to end with us anyway. The lying and cheating is just too much of a hassle. Justice needs a woman who is ready to settle down, and that's not me; at least not with him. Being married to him would have been an epic of the same shit every day, only in different clothes, with me cast as the devoted wife, bored out of my mind, resolved to banging the handy man or pool boy to pass the time. I can't live like that. I know I did the right thing.

*

"Wassup, Sage?"

"Nada, homie, leaving Oasis to meet my young boah, Bo. Wassup with you?"

"Getting off work a little early; three of my kids were out today with the pink eye. Guess who I was out with last night?"

"Justice?"

"How would that be surprising? Piccolo, silly."

"Piccolo! How the hell did you hook up with him?"

"Girl, I was coming out of the drug store on Wayne Avenue and there he was, looking as good as he wanted to look! It don't make no sense for one man to be that fine with all these ugly muthafuckas running 'round here."

"I know that's right. What happened? Did you speak? Did he speak? Did you give him your number? When y'all hooking up?"

"Slow down with the interrogation, and let me tell you the story. We got each other's numbers, and yes, we hooked up last night."

"You aren't wasting any time, huh?"

"Nope. We went out for drinks, and then we sat in the parking lot listening to music and talking. Girl, I want him bad, and it's not just about the sex. I can't wait to have him hold me, oh God!"

"You got it bad."

"I always did have it bad for him. He does something to me that I can't explain. Justice and I broke up."

"WHAT?! You dropping bomb after bomb today. How?"

"I've *been* tired of his ass. Justice is looking for a wife, and I could not spend the rest of my life with him, drowning in boredom."

"I can't believe this. What did he say?"

"He said he'd get his stuff while I was at work and for me to have a nice fucking life, and then he hung up on me."

"Awww, I feel bad for Justice, I always liked him, and you know that man is hurt because, boring or not, he loves you, Ila."

"That's what made it so hard to do, but it was inevitable. Enough about me, who did you go out with last night?"

"This character named Shaky."

"How the hell did you hook up with a dude named Shaky?"

"Katrina, the girl that works in the third chair, he's her cousin, and he came in one day. He got a cute thing going on, so I macked him. Big mistake. This asshole showed up at my apartment in a peach colored jean suit and then tried to tell me it was orange — like that made it any better. Mind you, on the phone he was talking all this Big Willie shit, how he get money and he gonna take me out and have it all, Cristal, lobster, whatever I want. Don't you know he had the nerve, the balls, the audacity to pull up in the motel parking lot on the Boulevard, the one by the breakfast joint we used to go to after clubbing all night. I looked at him like he had a third eye sprouting from his forehead. He saw the look on my face, and then got the stutters, talking about we could chill, order room service and rent movies. I told him that's what restaurants and movie theaters were for, so he could take me home 'cause it was not going down like that and he had me confused with somebody else if he thought it was."

"No, he didn't."

"Girl, yes, he did."

"You shoulda went upstairs with him, got him high off that super hydro and took his fucking money."

"He ain't a baller. It would have been a waste of my time and my weed, and you know we don't do that. I told him to take me home. He better not step foot up in my shop again, I do know that much."

"So who's this Bo dude, and just how young is he?"

"Bo is my sweetheart. He has the sexiest eyes in the world that look right into me and bring out Ms. Superfreak. There's something about him that makes my clothes fall off whenever he's around. I can't explain it but I'm digging it to the fullest."

"You put it on him already? How long y'all been kicking it?"

"We've been dealing with each other for about a month. I had to do the thing to the young boah — he was talking too much shit, but I think I have to slow up; he's starting to catch feelings."

"How old is he?"

"Seventeen."

"Cradle-robber. Next you gonna be down at my job, cruising the pickup."

"Shut up, that's only five years; he'll be 18 next month. Besides, men do it all the time; why can't I?"

"I ain't mad at you 'cause the young boahs these days do have it going on. Be careful 'cause he might not be able to handle it."

"Who you telling? Well, I'm at the mall now, so I'ma call you back later."

"You taking him school shopping, how cute."

"You got jokes, I see. I'll holla."

"Wait. What happened with Toya?"

"Iris had to bail her dumb ass out of jail last week for trying to get a license at the DMV with a fake social security number."

"Let me guess, Lamont put her up to it."

"And you know this. Iris went off."

"Well, Toya's learning the hard way that men ain't shit."

"The main reason we don't love these hoes."

"You better tell her, Sage. Well, enjoy your young fella. I'm out. Holla."

Sage is too much. Leave it to her to be messing around with a 17-year-old boy. I have enough troubles with a man, never mind a boy still living at home with his mama. I hope Justice came to pick up his stuff because I really don't want to see him and do the long, drawn-out, break-up thing about who did what and where did we go wrong and why, blah, blah, blah. I've put that relationship behind me and have hopes and dreams of starting fresh with Piccolo. I was ecstatic when he left me a message this morning, just like he promised he would. I can't wait to see him again and hopefully get the opportunity to do all the things that I've been thinking. Finally, this stud in my tongue might be for more than just show.

Chapter Four

D oing m inor t hAngS : S Ag e

BO IS TOO ADORABLE. I MET him after a basketball tournament at Feldman Hall on a local college campus that hosts youth basketball leagues for kids in the surrounding neighborhoods. He's mature for 17, and we have a great time together, plus he's funny, has goals, is smart, virile, a gentleman and is very nice to look at. He also has the sexiest legs that I've seen on a man in a long time. I call him my little show pony. He's in great shape being that he plays basketball and baseball. I'm attracted to him mostly because he gives balance to my quirky, free spirit and his youthful outlook inspires me, he gives me the tingles, and I get charged whenever he's around. He's waiting for me by the food court to grab a quick bite to eat.

"Sage, you look so good."

"You ain't no slouch yourself, youngin'"

"You wasn't calling me youngin' the other week when I was hitting them walls right."

"I sure wasn't."

He grabs my face and tongues me down in the middle of the mall. One drawback to messing with this young dude is public displays of affection. I can't front though, I like it. I like it a lot.

"What time is your game today?"

"Six-thirty. Are you coming?"

"I don't know, sweetheart, I have a client at 5, and I might not be done. I'll hit you up if I think I'll be able to make it."

"Good deal. How is your day going?"

"Fine, not too busy. Just a couple of clients left for the day."

Mahzi Kane   Tea Leaves

"Do you think I can come to your place tonight? You've been fronting on me lately."

"I have not been fronting. I don't want you getting tired of me too soon."

"The way you work it, I'll never get tired of that."

He smacks me hard on the ass.

"You better stop it. You know I like that rough shit."

"Boy, do I."

And like that we are in the back seat of my Neon getting it on in the parking lot.

"Bo, Bo, Booooooooooo!!!"

"I'm about to cum, Sage … this feels good, girl … you don't know what you be doing to me … ohhhh, gooddddddd dammmmmmmn!"

He moves himself deeper into me, and I open wider to take in all of him. He starts hitting that left wall, and I lose it. We lay in the back seat sweaty, panting and totally breathless.

"Thank you. I needed that to make it through the rest of my day."

"I should be thanking you. It's going to be raining threes tonight. You know I play better after I get some good coochie."

He looks at me and places the softest kiss on my forehead. It makes it impossible to remove the smile off my face. I fix myself up as best I can, drop Bo off at 16th Street and then haul ass back down Center City to my hair salon, Oasis. Oasis is located on the lower level of the Convention Center, on 11th Street between Arch and Race. Steven, a co-worker from my days in the Municipal building, got me the contact, and my rent is a steal for this area. Oasis is my baby — the thing that I've always wanted since forever. My salon offers the total, natural hair-care experience. I have never had

Mahzi Kane   Tea Leaves

a perm, and I encourage every sister I meet to get in tune with the natural dynamics of her hair. Once you take care of your hair, your hair will take care of you. I've been doing hair since I was 13. I practiced on my cousins and girlfriends, and by the time I was 16, I had found a fun way to make a lot of money, and pay my way through cosmetology school and the business courses I took at Peirce College. It also gave me a sense of independence because I didn't have to ask my mother for a dime. The relationship I have with her has always been strained. She never really encourages me to do anything except to not be like my father or make the same mistake she made: have babies.

When I walk into Oasis, Ms. Jane is waiting for me.

"Good afternoon, Ms. Jane, I'll be with you in a minute. I had a few errands to run."

I feel leftovers from our quickie about to ooze down my thigh, so I dash to the bathroom before it leaves a stain on my Capri pants. I know that I should use a condom every time I have sex, but I can't get into that latex feel all of the time. Sometimes I wanna feel every vein pulsating in that dick. Besides, Bo and I have been kicking it pretty steady, and the way I put it on him, I doubt that he's having sex with anyone other than me. The last guy I had sex with before Bo was Jesus, and that was over three months ago. That guy was way too obsessed with getting head. He said he had to have it at least twice a day or he just wasn't right. He was not exaggerating either. Funky attitude was his first, middle and last name when he didn't get his fix. I spent so much time with my face in his lap that he damn near knocked out one of my fillings. He dumped me because he said I wasn't interested in making him feel good. Good riddance, I didn't need that headache anyway, or the dental bills.

Mahzi Kane   Tea Leaves

I do Ms. Jane's press and curl, touch up Stacey's twists and take a seat in my own chair. My body is killing me from putting my back into it during my back-seat episode with Bo and standing on my feet doing hair. There is still time to catch the tail-end of his game, but I am not in the mood to sit on a hard bench or deal with icy stares from 17-year-old girls anxious to know, 'Who that?' when Bo comes off the court to give me a hug.

"Sage, pick up line two."

"Oasis, this is Sage."

"I guess you good at something after all. I see your business hasn't gone belly up."

"Hello to you too, Mother. Always such a pleasure to receive the warmth of your maternal support."

"Don't get smart with me, girl. I'll smack you to the middle of hell."

"Mother, is there something I can do for you?"

"Yes, as a matter of fact there is. Ms. Irene wants to know if she can come in and get her hair updated."

"Mother, Ms. Irene can make an appointment like everyone else."

"No shit. Ms. Irene is broke, just like me, and I told her that she could get a special rate. That's why I was calling, to find out how much to tell her."

"Mother, you can't keep doing this. If I give discounts to all your broke friends, I am not running my business, you are."

"Hussy, I know you can't give discounts to everyone, and I know you running your damn business over there. I'm your mother and a dear friend of mines needs a favor. I hardly ask you for anything."

"When you do, it's always for a discount or money. That's the only time you call me, when you want something. I never see you — you are always doing something with Ms. such and such. You never have time for me, except to remind me that I ain't shit."

"Watch your mouth. You spent your whole life with me. You know what I look like. Talk about seeing me. See me for what? I gave you plenty of my time already. This my time. Are you going to give her the discount or not?"

"Yes, Mother."

"Thank you. I'll tell Ms. Irene to call and make her appointment."

No matter how old I get, I still try to win my mother's love and affection. I'm sure she loves me. How could a mother not love her child? She just can't show it for some odd reason. It's not me, it's not her; it's our past. I've suggested that we go to counseling, but mother says that black folks don't need shrinks; that's why we go to church.

"Oasis, this is Sage."

"Sage, why didn't you come to my game?"

"Bo, I told you that I had clients. Don't trip."

"I ain't. We won. I had a double-double."

"Congrats. You know you're the man."

"How 'bout you giving this man more of what we had earlier. Can you come get me?"

"Yeah, I'll come by your mom's around 8:00."

"If I'm not there, swing by the corner and you'll see me."

"Bye."

"Later."

Tuckered out? Totally how I feel, but I always have the energy to be with a man. I feel more like myself when one is around. I can't wait to be married to my rich, influential husband and live in our expensive mansion where my only duties will

be to make a house into our home, take care of the
children and fuck his brains out whenever he
wants. I'd still run my salon but only when I felt
like it since my husband would fulfill my every need
and want. I'd like to be a hipper version of an old-
fashioned sitcom, but the way the pickings are
looking, I don't know if I'll ever get married. Good
men are hard to find and even harder to keep. It
seems like no man I meet is looking for a
relationship, and the men who are, they're the ones
that I don't want. I tell myself to stop looking, but
all of my girls have men. Shit, even Toya shares
one, and all I have is a resignation to walk the earth
until I hook up with my soul mate and discover a
fly love like Malcolm and Iris'. I would never admit
this to anyone, but I would give my right arm to be
the one getting married. I've been envious of her
since she announced her engagement. Where the
hell is my happy ending? I deserve a man to love
me the way Malcolm loves her, but in the
meantime, Bo will have to do.

Traffic is jammed up, it's started to rain and I
have to pick up the pizza I called in because I am
hardly the one for doing a whole lot of cooking.
When I pull up to Gratz Street, and sure enough
Bo is on the corner. Good, I don't feel like seeing
his mom pretend she likes me or approves of me
being with her son. I don't know why mothers trip
about their sons dating older females. Cut the cord
already! He is far from a little boy, and if she could
see the things he does and hear most of what he
says, she would know exactly where I'm coming
from.

Beep, beep.

I wave to Bo, and he gives his friends a pound
and saunters over to my car, which I purchased last
month. I was tired of depending on my girls for

rides, and the bus is not my style. Ila said since I own my own business I should be pushing an E-Class or a Q45 — anything other than my Neon. I like to stay within my means and not be bitter and broke when it comes time to pay bills. I can afford my car note, insurance and everything else with ease. My car will be paid for in two years, and that'll be one more thing that I earned for myself, by myself. If I had a father who spoiled me like crazy, I'd be driving a Millenia too.

"Wassup, sexy?"

"Not much cutie. I'm glad you were out here because I want to pick up the pizza, go home and get out of these clothes."

"I like the sound of that."

"Don't think we gonna be at it like porn stars tonight. I'm tired as shit."

"You say that now, but once I start eating that thang, it's gonna be whatever I want."

I smile and say nothing because I know that he is absolutely correct.

Chapter Five

L ove ' s S ucKer : t o YA

TWO WEEKS HAVE PASSED SINCE MY arrest, and I have not heard one peep from Lamont. He hasn't been at our special meeting place on Thursdays, nor has he returned any of my messages. I've gotten the urge to call him at home, but I'm too scared to actually do it. I miss him - his laugh, the smell of his cologne and the feel of him. His wife must be making it impossible for him to get away. I can't wait until he can finally leave her and come be with me like he promises. I'll be 10 times the wife that she isn't. I'll bring him breakfast in bed, and we'll spend hours talking about nothing and everything all at once. If only he would call.

"Lamont?"

"No, bitch, it's me, Pia."

"Oh. When are you coming home? Your phone has been ringing like crazy, and I'm not answering it."

"I'll be there later on. I've been laid up in the Poconos with Hassan. I guess you still haven't heard from that asshole, huh?"

"Don't talk about him like that. It must be his wife. I'm sure I'll be hearing from him any minute now."

"You wait on that. Let me ask you this: Is the dick really that good?"

"Pia, some things are deeper than sex. We have a connection that only him, God and myself can understand. You wouldn't know anything about that since you base everything about a man on how much he can do for you."

"You damn right 'cause as soon as a man know you got feelings for'im, he pull shit like having you sit up in jail for off-the-wall plans he came up with but you damn near lose your job over, so yeah, you can keep that shit."

"What did you call for anyway?"

"Did my package?"

"Not that I know of. When I leave for work, I'll check to see and put it in your room if it's here."

"I need my shoes. They go perfect with the outfit I picked out for tonight. Aight, I'll see you later, stupid."

"Don't be calling me — "

She hangs up. It baffles me how people can have so much clarity about what I should or shouldn't do with my life when theirs isn't in order. My cousin Pia calls me stupid for being with Lamont. That's a matter of opinion, but the fact is I handle my business. Bad credit is Pia's first, last and middle name, but she makes it a point to look extra fly just to be up in some man's face. She says her bills don't matter because it's all a part of the game plan: Never look busted even if you're broke. I tell her that a man's money isn't everything and that she should follow my lead and make her own. A man has to bring the type of love that makes me feel special just for being in that relationship, for being his partner, his everything worth having.

"Hello."

"Hey, baby, how has my lady love been doing?"

"What do you mean, 'How have I been doing?' How do you think I've been doing? I haven't heard from you since I was locked up."

Mahzi Kane   Tea Leaves

"Don't be that way, girl. You know what that was about. I had to lay low for a bit. Don't take it personal, sweetness."

Whenever Lamont calls me sweetness, I melt into a big ball of mush.

"Can I see you? I miss you."

"I'm still trying to work that out, but you gotta stop blowing me up. It's going to cause suspicion."

"Can I come by your job later?"

"That's cutting it close."

"Please, Lamont. I need to see you. You won't be sorry, I promise. I'll come on my lunch."

"Fine. I can never deny my sweetness. Later."

I knew he would call. I also knew I would see him if I whined long enough. That always works with Lamont.

My boss has been watching me like a hawk since the fiasco of getting arrested, and now I must take exactly one hour for my lunch break, but I keep reminding myself to be thankful that I still have my job. I've been going the extra mile and completing my work ahead of schedule, plus I signed up to help out on a special project to show that I am a team player. Losing my job is not an option, especially since I'd like a promotion, not to mention I'm planning a cruise to Aruba for Lamont and I. I don't quite know how he's going to get away, but we will think of a way. Lamont is always talking about seeing the sun come up over blue and turquoise waters. That sounds wonderful, but I just want to have him all to myself for once — no children, no wife and no secret love to hide. Lunchtime arrives, and I fly out of the building. The bus is nowhere in sight, so I hoof it and my dogs are barking. Clarke says I need to stop buying cheap shoes. Maybe she has a point, but I don't think you have to spend gobs of money to look

Mahzi Kane   Tea Leaves

good. As I turn the corner, Lamont is out front smoking a cigarette - the one habit besides his wife that I wish he would give up, but he's convinced himself that he'd die from stress without them. I tell him not to worry, the tar and nicotine will kill him nonetheless. Then he tells me to be quiet because I'm starting to sound like his wife.

"Hello, handsome."

"Good day to you, sweetness. You look lovely. Do a little spin for me."

I have on my chocolate pants suit, the one he loves because it matches my skin. I turn around little by little, letting him gawk at my full figure, aware of how much he loves to grab my behind. He says he daydreams in traffic, at work, sometimes even at home, about the size of it. I tell him it's impolite to tell a woman that her butt is big, but he says that since I have it I should flaunt it. Before I met Lamont, I was self-conscious about my weight, but he professed how sexy a curvaceous woman is and made me believe it. As our relationship progressed, I bought more revealing clothing - nothing whorish but not the over-sized frocks I had become accustomed to wearing. I never categorize myself as pretty; I think that I'm a wonderful person, and that is what makes me attractive. I think that makes me a catch, yet I rarely seem to get the attention of the men that I want. There are only three relationships in my past and present: Lamont, Scott and Casper. Casper was my very first boyfriend. As his name implied, he was white as a ghost. Rumor had it that his mother was a hooker and her white pimp was his father. My mother used to call us ebony and ivory. Our relationship never became serious, and eventually we grew apart. I think he's married now. Scott was the guy that I gave my virginity. I was head over heels in love from the first day I laid eyes on him.

Mahzi Kane   Tea Leaves

He sang in the church choir and had one of the most melodious voices anyone could be blessed to have. He'd come over after service on Sundays, and we'd read Bible verses, and then he'd serenade me with our favorite hymns. We became close, and he eventually asked me to be his girlfriend. I was stunned because I knew how I felt about Scott, but I never imagined that my crush would have been reciprocated. I wore Scott's class ring, and it felt spectacular to have a boy like me for who I was and not put me down for how much I weighed. I'm a curvaceous woman, but I must admit I was an unpleasantly plump adolescent. I found myself torn between the growing want to express my feelings toward Scott and the ever-present understanding that being loose was something that would cause a young lady to burn in hell. So I kept my legs shut and unsuccessfully tried to ignore the passion that smoldered there. And when we crossed that line, he touched me in such a way that to date has not been paralleled. He planned to marry me as soon as we graduated from high school, but his promises of wedlock never came to be since he ended up going into the Army Reserve. Scott was a sweetie, but not the sharpest pencil in the box. With his grades, college was out of the question, and his father would not hear of him wasting away in a dead-end, low-paying job. Scott wrote me the first six months after he was deployed, but we both agreed that it was too painful to try to sustain our love. If we were meant to be, he'd find me in the future, he said. Then I met Lamont. Lamont, who is so different from any man I have ever known: arrogant, cocky, god-fearing but certainly not religious and Denzel Washington sexy. His honesty is brutal, and his compliments make me feel good about myself. Because of him, I know that I have sex appeal, I believe that I can give a man what he requires from his mate, and I have what it takes to make a relationship work. Just because I sleep with a married man,doesn't mean I have low self-esteem. I'm just willing to look pass a temporary flaw to see the bigger picture. At the end of the day, I want to get what I want — and what I want is him.

I walk into Auto World and follow him to the back. He sells rims and other car amenities. Once in the back room, we are all over each other like wild animals. We cover one another with wet, sloppy kisses while caressing breasts, backs and behinds. He pushes me down to my knees, and I unbuckle his pants so that I am able to put him into my mouth. Lamont lets out a moan of absolute delight. I flick my tongue back and forth and begin easing it down my throat. Lamont uses a shammy cloth to muffle his loudness when the phone starts to ring, and he fumbles to answer.

"No, sweetness, please don't stop. I'm almost there."

I continue to make love to Lamont with my mouth as he presses the talk button in utter agitation.

"Ah, Lamont speaking. Hey, hey, baby, what's up?"

I know it is his wife so I move my head back and forth with the speed of a jackhammer. I want him to scream out my name as proof that I am the best he ever had, I am the one satisfying him in ways that she knows absolutely nothing about, and I am everything that he finds gratifying. Lamont finds support on the wall to keep from falling over as he tries to maintain his composure.

"What? Nothing's wrong. I was out front smoking a cigarette. I had to run to get the phone."

Mahzi Kane   Tea Leaves

Lamont's body shakes, and I know it is a matter of seconds before he explodes.

"Yeah, yeah, I know I said I was going to quit, and I will. Don't start that again. OK, baby, here comes a customer. Call you back."

Lamont slings the phone to the floor, pulls me by the back of my hair and throws me down. He dives into me like the pot of gold at the end of a rainbow. This is beyond screwing. He is making full-on, out-of-this-world love to me. He's coursing through every fiber. I feel him in every one of my nerve endings, and I am alive. My body shutters, and tears of joy stream down my cheeks signifying that it is official: I am so in love with this man.

I get back to my cubicle in the nick of time. My supervisor is making his rounds to make sure people, mainly me, are back from lunch. Meanwhile I wear the biggest Kool-Aid smile and had long since forgotten about my aching feet. I turn on my CD player and snap my fingers when I see my telephone light up and press pause.

"Compensation Technologies, this is Toya. How may I help you?"

"For starters, you can stop fucking my husband!"

"Excuse me?"

"Bitch, you heard me. I said you can stop fucking my husband!"

"I think you have the wrong extension."

"No, I don't. This is Toya, Toya Haddad. You are the one who has been having an affair with my husband, Lamont. It will be a year in July. This is Felicia. You know who I am. I am the one that gave that selfish bastard 10 years of my life and two children."

"I-I-I."

Mahzi Kane   Tea Leaves

"I-I what? You whores never know what to say. Never thought a real woman would call a low-life bitch like yourself out on the scandalous shit you have going on, but you don't know about Felicia. Somebody should have told you. Matter of fact, he should have told you. Felicia don't play games, especially with raggedy sluts who think they can just fuck my husband. You have the right one, trick."

"Felicia, I know this is upsetting, so I understand the name-calling. There is nothing else to say except that Lamont and I love each other, and my joy shouldn't be the source of your pain. But there are some things that can't be controlled. I think you should move on. I assume you love him, and if it is half as much as I do then you want him to be happy, and we both know that is with me. Let him go."

"Bitch, please. Go where? Don't tell me that he's been feeding you that 'I can't leave her right now because I want to be in the household my kids are being raised in' story. Girlie, wake up and smell the bullshit. Lamont is never leaving me, so fuck you and whatever happiness you thought you were going to try to steal from me. Matter fact, we are about to have another baby. Let go of what? What you need to do is hold on to that bit of information, and hold on to it tight, the same way I'm going to do to keep my husband."

"You're lying!"

"Really? Why do I have to lie to you? You are nothing. You are just something to do. I'm the one with the ring. I'm the one he comes home to every night. I don't care what he does to your 21-year-old coochie, he's not going anywhere, and if you believe that he is, you're dumber than I thought. I love Lamont. I don't like him at times, especially when he's messing around, but my vows meant

something when I took them. And they mean
something now, and they damn sure mean enough
that I wouldn't dare lose to a rat-ass bitch who'd
settle for my scraps creeping around in the gutter
like a dirty ho. Our shit is for better or for worse. I
provide him with what none of you silly-ass young
girls can give, and he's never leaving me because of
that, so get over yourself."

"If he's not leaving you, then why are you
calling me, Felicia, just to cuss me out? You know
we've been intimate … is this your way to try to
make me feel cheap?"

"First off, it's not intimacy, it's infidelity. I
wonder how that congregation and pastor at your
mama's church would react if they knew that Sister
Gwen's oldest daughter is breaking one of the Ten
Commandments. But then again, church has the
biggest sinners any damn way. Second, bitch, you
are cheap, cheap as they fucking come with your
turnedover shoes. I told you Felicia knows
everything. Third, you will never know just how
lucky you are that I am pregnant. You better say an
extra prayer tonight to thank God for saving you.
This call is so that you back off before I hurt you.
Enough is enough. We are about to bring another
life into this world. Whatever our problems are,
trust me, you do not want to be a part of it, so be
removed. This is not a request. Ask about me."

I hold the receiver and say nothing. A billion
thoughts and emotions race through me all at once,
and I feel like I am going to pass out.

"I may be silly, but it sounds to me like you're
the real fool. I wouldn't dare stay with a man who
cheated on me."

"You'd just settle for MY HUSBAND
though? Runner-up was never my style. All you get
are the quick fucks and empty promises. Don't you

Mahzi Kane   Tea Leaves

worry about why I stay with my husband, but you better remember that I know everything about you — where you live, where you work, what church you go to. I know it all, and I can fuck your life up whenever the mood strikes. I'm being the bigger woman by calling you and advising you end it now. There will not be a repeat."

The next sound I hear is the dial tone. I run to the bathroom covering my mouth with my right hand. The contents of breakfast and lunch fast approach my throat in unwelcome chunks. I vomit in the first stall I reach, slide down the wall and cry hysterically. I don't worry about who hears me because in this moment I don't care about what people think. I feel like I have been hit in the pit of my stomach with a sledgehammer, and I want to curl up and die. The rest of the day is a daze. Co-workers repeatedly ask what is wrong, but I don't answer. I am unable to reply. Even my supervisor calls me into his office to ask if I am OK. Their inquiries receive nothing more than the same blank stare. I call Lamont at Auto World, but he doesn't pick up. Felicia is having another one of his babies, and all I get is a shot to the back of my throat. I can hear the I-told-you-so's echo around me. I feel like I am going crazy over a man. A man that isn't mine and never was.

I walk into the house, drop everything at the front door and go straight to my bedroom. I shut the curtains, kick off my shoes and am picking up the telephone to page Lamont when it rings. This better be him. On the bus ride home, I envisioned Lamont phoning to say that it was all a sick joke — just Felicia's way of trying to make me upset because he was finally leaving. That there was no baby coming and he would marry me. My mind kept telling me that it was simply a fantasy that I was trying to force myself not to accept the truth that was right in front of my face.

"WHAT?"

"Ummmm, can I speak to Ms. Haddad or Ms. Thompson?"

"This is Ms. Haddad. Who is this, and what do you want?"

"This is Susan from your rental company."

"Regarding what? You should have received the rent check last week."

"That's exactly why we are calling — we've tried to contact you several times through the mail. You are behind $1,200 in rent."

"WHAT?!" How can that be when I pay rent every damn month?"

"We've only received half of the rent for the past three months."

"That means that my roommate has not been paying her rent. I am so sorry for the inconvenience. As soon as she gets in, I'll have her call you to set up a payment arrangement."

"I'm sorry, Ms. Haddad, but there is no arrangement to be made. You are being evicted."

"EVICTED!"

"Yes, if you check your lease, there's a clause that says that unpaid rent in excess of $1,000 is grounds for immediate eviction."

"This cannot be happening to me! This cannot be happening to me!"

"I'm afraid it is. You have until the end of next week to vacate the premises and return all keys. Your security deposit will not be returned."

"But why I am being evicted when I have been paying my share of the rent? Can't she move out?"

"I'm sorry, but in situations such as this, both tenants must leave. It's viewed as a liability to let either of you continue renting from us since we don't know who is responsible for the overdue balance because it's your word against hers."

"The proof is in the form of payment. I always paid with checks."

"Ms. Haddad, I see that there are checks for the entire amount as well as partial, and I will assume that the full payments are from instances where your roommate gave you her half in cash and you wrote the check. Is that correct?"

I start to cry.

"I'm sorry, Ms. Haddad; I know that this is very upsetting. I'm sure the situation will work itself out, but again, you have until the end of next week to vacate."

I hang up the telephone and sit on the edge of my bed sobbing as a rage brews inside. I am enraged at myself for moving in with Pia in the first place. I know that she is nothing more than a money-hungry, man-chasing, party girl. Immaturity and irresponsibility are Pia's trademarks; I should have known better, but I wanted to do her a favor, and I thought I could really help her get her life together. Again, why did I fool myself into believing something that was not real? I jump up and march to Pia's bedroom. There are designer clothes all over the bed and shoes scattered across the floor. She has been here, gotten dressed and is off on another one of her fabulous escapades. I grab her telephone, but there is no dial tone, and there is nothing else I can do but rip it from the wall and throw it at the dresser mirror, which breaks into jagged pieces that shatter all over the floor. I go to the living room and dial Pia's cell phone number. Pia picks up after the fourth ring.

"Cutie speaking, state your business."

Mahzi Kane   Tea Leaves

"We are getting evicted, how cute is that?! Why Pia?! Why didn't you pay your rent? The one thing I needed you to do? Why, Pia, why?!"

"Evicted? They can't evict us for being behind. That's why they invented late fees."

"And you say I'm dumb? I just got off the phone with them, and yes, they can, Miss Know-It-All. The lease says that back rent over $1,000 is cause for immediate eviction. So now that the obvious is clear, why didn't you pay your rent?"

"What happened was Man-Man was supposed to pay my rent for the last three months, so I spent the money I had, but then Man-Man found out that I was seeing Jason, and then Man-Man said fuck my rent. I've been saving the money bit by bit, but you know me, I only have half."

"Yes, I do know you, don't I? The funny thing is, they don't want half, so that isn't doing us any good. As a matter of fact, they don't want any of it, and although I've taken care of my adult obligations, I still have to be out of here by the end of next week. Thank you, Pia, thank you for making this the official worst day of my life!"

"Toya, I'm sorry, I'll make it — "

I hang up. I don't have time to listen to her hustle me into thinking that this is not her fault. This can't be how my life is supposed to be. Where is my peace? I feel like I need to sleep and never wake up, too weighted down by the things that I can't change. I can't think beyond right now because there are too many questions: Where will I live? How will I move my stuff? And what about Lamont? Too much has happened, and I can't find the strength to deal. I lie down on the sofa and pull myself into a tight ball. I hug myself, rocking back and forth, until I drift off to sleep … one riddled with demons, dragons and despair.

Mahzi Kane   Tea Leaves

Chapter Six

t rYnA Live : c L A r K e

I WISH THAT THIS GUY WOULD get up and go home. I almost never date overweight men, but Dean's cranberry Jaguar changed that. He's been begging to get with me since I met him a month back, and the diamond tennis bracelet convinced me that he was worthy. I let him sweat himself tired on top of me for five minutes, and then he rolled off like a beached whale. Anal sex followed, he went first. His eyes bulged out of his head, and he adamantly rejected any suggestion of me putting a dildo in his ass. We decided that a carrot would do just fine. He was hesitant, but the sashay of my sequined G-string allowed the idea to grow on him, and now he's sleeping like a fucking baby, slobber running down his jaw and all. I must say, I can turn a choirboy into a super freak. It's almost 8:30, and I have a doctor's appointment at 11:00. I think there is a possibility that I'm pregnant. If there is one truth about me, it is that I am way too selfish to be a parent. I don't even like kids. Rashida's son is as cute as a button, but after five minutes I'm ready to put him in a trash bag. I don't ever want kids, and I wish I could get my tubes tied now. I lack patience and surely couldn't deal with any of those hideous stretch marks; I'd die first. For all of those reasons and more, birth control has been my best friend since my mom found out that I lost my virginity when I was 12. A teenage pregnancy scandal was not an option for her, so she put me on the pill immediately. I've taken it every morning for the last 12 years, but even still, there have been slip-ups. Nonetheless, I am not having any babies, and I don't feel guilty about my choice. This is America; we're allowed to make mistakes and forget. What I can't forget is the jive-ass memories that I have of my childhood, and my parents' behavior is no model for good rearing. Yes, my parents are well-to-do; some might even consider them rich, but I can count the number of times I speak to them on one hand, and the occasions that I see them are far less. I understand that I'm not mother material, and I accept it because that's who I am. It's the truth I was born into, the truth that I can't discredit because doing so would make me a monster, and I'm too fly for that shit. Besides, I don't exactly know who'd be the father.

Over the last couple of months, I've been with Rahmel and Manny. Rahmel was led to believe that he was my steady since we'd been kicking it strong for a month and a half, but then he got a job promotion and relocated. I let him know in no uncertain terms that long-distance relationships were not my cup of tea and we should break things off, but if he ever came to Philly, for him to look me up. He agreed, and we made plans for one final tryst days before he was leaving. Well, when I went to his place the night of our goodbye banging, that's when I met his best friend, Manny. Fine as hell best friend Manny. Made my mouth almost drop to my knees best friend Manny. By the way he tried not to stare at my spandex tank top, I knew that he was interested. I pretended to need something from the trunk of my car as Manny was leaving, and once in the parking lot we exchanged numbers. The night that Rahmel left, Manny fucked me stupid all over my apartment. We didn't use anything because I'm on the pill and I don't

Mahzi Kane   Tea Leaves

fuck dirty people. There have been a couple of occasions after my wild nights and even wilder mornings when I have forgotten to take my pill, so here I am, on my way to take a pregnancy test.

Enough already, Dean has to go. The only reason that I'm not shaking his fat ass awake is because I want him to be well rested when I convince him to let me take him home and then drop his car off to him later. I can cruise around the city pushing something almost as fly as I am and pick up a cutie or two. After my doctor's visit, I'll swing pass Iris'. Ever since she started planning this wedding, I hardly speak to her, which I so don't get since she hired a coordinator. But she's busy all of the time doing all of the work. I wanted to be the maid of honor, and I'm still pissed that she's not having a traditional ceremony. Who wouldn't want a huge bridal party, especially one with plenty of potential sponsors for their fabulous girlfriends, especially when they look like I do? But that's neither here nor there since Iris is having an unwedding as she puts it. Sometimes she can be such a weirdo.

Just as I suspect, I'm knocked up. Nothing left to do except to find a clinic, and my girl Peanut will surely help me out because she probably has a frequent flyer card. My usual benefactor, Solomon, is still salty after seeing Darien coming out of my building a while back, so I am sure he won't be sympathetic. I told him that he had no rights to any parts of me, no matter how much money he spent. When will they learn that this pussy belongs to me and it's not for sale.

*

I ring Iris' bell like five times before she finally comes to open the damn door. I haven't decided if I should tell her that I'm pregnant. I don't feel like hearing one of her sermons, nor do I want to be judged by Ms. Perfect. In her world, we all do the right thing all the time. She better join us in reality where people fuck up every day, sometimes by mistake but often by choice.

"Were you resting? What took you so long to get the door?"

"I was working. Come in."

"Wassup, lady? Long time, no see. Is the wedding keeping you that busy?"

"No busier than usual. I've been finishing up other projects and spending time with Malcolm. He's going through some real shit at work."

"Word, like what?"

Is there finally a gray cloud over sunshine USA? It's not that I don't want Iris to be happy, but nobody is this happy all of the time, and I wish she would just show it.

"Dennis has been using his expense account for personal needs, and Malcolm fired him."

"Why he fire him for that? Everybody does it."

"Let's see … he fired him because Dennis was supposed to be his fucking friend, because it's one thing to have an expensive dinner on the boss here and there, but to take advantage and run hog-wild with money that's not yours is stealing. Malcolm should have and could have fired his punk ass many times, but he didn't, and I don't care who does it. Dennis should have fucking known better, and if you think you gonna walk up in here and justify that shit, you can roll out just as easily as you rolled in."

"Why you getting like that with me? I didn't take shit."

"First of all, you show up unannounced, and then you come off like Malcolm is wrong for putting the success of his business over a nigga that clearly isn't really his friend."

I can tell that I've struck a nerve because Iris rarely uses the word "nigga." I'm not in the mood for this. I came to see what was up in her, but this is too much and I have important problems of my own to deal with so I'm leaving.

"Well, my bad. I see that you're busy and in a bitchy mood, I might add, so I'll holla at you later."

Iris says nothing and closes the door in my face. Well, that turned out to be no fun at all, and I have nothing else to do. Peanut is working, and I don't hang out with Iris' crew alone. Rashida is cool, and I could see myself hanging out with her, but she has too many responsibilities that can ruin a good time. Toya is silly as hell, plus her cheap shoes clash with every fashion law I believe in, and her clothes are always loud, like she ain't big enough. Sage is not bad, but she has a tendency to be way too loose with the wrong type of men — the broke kind. I don't like that bitch Ila, and she don't like me, so we fake it for Iris. I go home to see if one of my hoes has called, and as I turn onto my block, there is a tiny crew of people forming in front of my apartment building. I park the Jaguar in the middle of the block and walk back toward the corner, and then I see what's getting all of the attention. "Catch AIDS, you Trifling Bitch!" is scratched on the hood of my car. The tires are slashed and the windows busted out.

"What the fuck happened?!"

"Damn, sis, is this your whip? It's fuuuuucked up."

"Thanks for the news flash, but I can see that! Did anybody see anything?"

Nobody in the crowd says a thing. I see three women from my building snickering. "Hating-ass bitches," I mumble to myself. "I look better than them and can have the man they'd die for if I wanted, and they know it." Carmen looks on with sheer delight, and when our eyes lock, she mouths "karma" and walks back into the building.

Carmen is one of the first people to the scene and enjoys every second. She thinks Clarke is an arrogant, self-absorbed bitch who makes all women look bad, and Carmen wished it had been her who vandalized the car.

I roll my eyes and wonder if Carmen is responsible for the damage, but that would be pretty stupid to live in the same building and destroy my property. Then again, Carmen does hate my guts, and you can't put anything past a scorned woman. We had a heated exchange once, and of course it was because of a man. I went out on one date with Stan, a very dull car salesman who talked of nothing but his savvy skills of convincing people to buy overpriced cars. Four months after the date from hell, I found myself on a three-way call with Stan and Carmen. Turned out, Carmen was Stan's ex-girlfriend, and during one of their many breakups, the date with me took place. Carmen was convinced that more than dinner had happened, especially when she heard gossip about me from the other women in the building. I laughed hard and loud at the insinuation that I would ever consider doing anything more than using Stan, and Carmen didn't appreciate that because she classified him as a sweet guy who was husband material, just a little too absorbed in his career. I hung up in the middle of her futile questioning, and from then on, she gives me her stank face grimace, as if I care.

I pace back and forth looking at my precious baby. Some fucker has destroyed the one thing besides me that I own, and I want to cry and scream and yell and let my pain stream out at the highest octave, but there is no way that I will show these people that anybody can get the best of me. Nope, not in a million fucking lifetimes would I allow that to happen.

Chapter Seven

n oboDY S eeS : i r i S

CLARKE SHOWING UP
UNANNOUNCED LIKE THAT and her
nonchalant attitude about Dennis' shady behavior
was all that I could take. Malcolm is right; she is
not a good friend. Everybody says that she isn't shit
and that I am a much better friend to her than she
is to me, but I constantly make excuses for her,
though I can't ignore that she is shallow,
backstabbing and self-serving. But enough about
her, I'm on my way to meet with Sasha to give her
my manuscript and then meet with Heaven for
wedding planning. Sasha and I are having lunch at
Kingdom of Vegetarians so that I can finally give
her the manuscript of my third poetry book, which
seemed harder to write and took way too long to
complete. *Look Into My World* is exactly that — an
in-depth exploration of my environment, my
thoughts, my experiences, my family — everything.
It's me, undiluted and pure, spread across the pages
in a bold statement of self-expression. My first
book, *They Shall Be Fulfilled,* was about revolution
and learning from history to build our future. It did
well, considering that I was virtually unknown. I
sold a couple thousand copies and didn't make
much money, but I did gain globs of experience.
My second book, *Everything Changes,* was all about
love — the thrills, the hurts and the mysteries. My

fan base embraced that book like it was the resurrection. I went on book tours with other new writers from Philly, D.C. and New York, held readings and book signings, and was the featured poet at local hot spots. I made the money back that I spent to publish both books, plus a respectable profit. I'm keeping my fingers crossed that the third time is a charm, and willfully it will propel me to national stardom, the best-sellers list or both.

"Peace and power, Iris."

"Sasha, you look great. Look at your tan."

"I know. I went with my sister, Carol, to the shore over the weekend, and I look like I've been to the islands. You look tired, honey. Are you all right? Don't run yourself ragged trying to do too much. How's the wedding going?"

"Let's sit down and catch up."

We take our seats in the back of the restaurant, and order our main courses along with several appetizers for us to share.

"Well, Sasha, first things first. Here it is: *Look Into My World.*"

"I can't wait to read it, Iris. If it's as good as you say it is, then I know it's 10 times better because you are your own worst critic. I've witnessed the growth between your first and second books of poetry, and I'm excited to peek into the world of a conscious, engaged, beautiful, introspective, young black woman on the verge of ultimate success. Yes, I love it, and I haven't read one word!"

"You make me sound important, Sasha. All I do is write what I feel."

"That's the most important thing there is. How many people do you know who actually say what they feel, let alone write it down for the entire world to see?"

"You've got a point there."

"I know I do, that's why I'm the editor. Now why do you look so beat? Is Malcolm keeping you up late?"

"No, nothing like that. It's like I don't have enough energy to last me through the day. I think I'm going to get a new multivitamin to help me keep up with all that I am doing. Getting that book done, planning the unwedding and making Malcolm happy is work … happy work, but work. "

We laugh and the server arrives to refill our glasses and remove empty appetizer plates. The café rumbles with the bustle of the lunch crowd, and we have to lean in closer to hear.

"It was pretty hard for Malcolm to fire Dennis, and Dennis didn't make it easy either. He accused Malcolm of being a sellout house nigger."

"No, he didn't!"

"Yes, he did. The fight almost got physical."

"Wow, that's sad and very unfortunate. Good people are hard to come by, and it's bad when people can't own their stuff."

"I can tell Malcolm is hurt. I'm giving him the space he needs to work it out, but at the same time, I'm here when he needs me."

"That's all that you can do."

"The unwedding is a different animal altogether. Everyone is trying to make me feel guilty for not having the wedding that they want. Grandma Rue is upset that my dad won't be giving me away how she sees fit. My sister-friends are mad that I'm not having bridesmaids. My mother is mad that I'm having a vegetarian menu. Everyone seems to be forgetting that this day isn't about what they want. This is a celebration of Malcolm and I. If I feed into the bullshit, I'll call the whole thing off, and we'll elope in the Caribbean. I'm serious."

"Family means well, but they can push pieces of their vision into your day and end up being a pain in the ass. They'll drive a sober man to drinking, I'll tell ya."

"I love them, but I can't deny who I am."

"No, you can't. Are you wearing white?"

"Nope. I'm not perpetuating that White Roman Male ideology. I'm wearing ivory."

"That sounds pretty. Where is the ceremony slash celebration going to take place?"

"Longwood Gardens in Brandywine Valley."

"That is going to be spectacular. How did you get that?"

"I have no idea. Malcolm pulled it off. I've always pictured our day outside surrounded by nature. He suggested a garden celebration and three weeks later came home with a brochure for Longwood Gardens and asked what I thought. I told him it was magnificent, and he said that was where we would hold the celebration. I asked him how, and he put a finger to my lips and told me to bask in the delight of the moment instead of asking questions, and that's what I did."

"Did they break the mold on him or what? That man is a knight in shining armor, but all I keep getting are the court jesters."

"I pinch myself several times a day to make sure this is real. I know how lucky I am."

Mahzi Kane   Tea Leaves

"Well, honey, I will have this done in roughly three weeks, and then we'll meet to discuss the usual — font, print, paper, foreword, etc."

"Sounds good to me. It's out of my hands."

Sasha and I enjoy a delicious meal over delightful conversation, say our goodbyes, and then I am back on the road for my meeting with Heaven, who I met through a friend of my mom's. She's stylishly Afrocentric, willing to go against the grain and is funny as hell. I admit, she's expensive, and she freaks me out a little by always talking about the ancestors, but she gets the job done and earns every penny of her fee. Clarke says that I'm doing too much work; that my coordinator gets paid to do it all. Wrong as usual. She has never planned the opening of a paper bag, let alone a wedding, so I have no idea when she became an expert on how I should do my shit. I think she should stick to what she does best.

I arrive at Heaven's right on time. She owns her business, Heaven Here on Earth, and operates it from her home, situated in Lansdowne. My favorite part of her rancher is the small pond located just outside the back deck. Not that the greenhouse, herb garden, pool, Jacuzzi and gazebo aren't beautiful, but the rainbow fish dipping their heads in and out of the tranquil waters make me want to stare at them for days. I park in her two-car driveway and ring the bell. Heaven answers in a brightly colored afghan, wearing her usual radiant glow and no shoes. Her immaculate French-manicured toes smile back at me. I hate to see a woman parade around with hard, crusty feet, forgetting that the special care we take to make our

Mahzi Kane   Tea Leaves

outsides beautiful is a part of what makes us women. Sage has horrible feet. I told her that she makes enough money to budget in a pedicure every week, and if shit gets tight, a ton of grease and socks on at bedtime does wonders.

"Ashe, Queen Iris. Welcome to my home."

Heaven hugs me, touching cheek to cheek, and leads me into her living room. My love for black art is futile in comparison to her collection.

"Heaven, where did you find this painting? I love it."

It is a colossal, black man with his woman on his back, she with their child on hers, and they walk into rays of the sun — a magnificent display of the unified black family.

"A client gave it to me."

"It's captivating. I would look at it all day and not get a bit of work done."

"Thank you, I'll give you her card before you leave. Would you like tea?"

"Yes, please."

"Country Peach Passion, correct?"

"Correct."

Heaven disappears into the kitchen, and I take a seat at her massive dining room table made of solid marble. She said it took three months to deliver because it had to come in six different pieces.

"So what have we decided on, Iris? The ancestors tell me that you've come to some finalizations."

The ancestors freak me out.

"Yes, I have. Ivory is my color with honeydew green accents."

"That's lovely. I know where we can have your bouquet done."

"Excellent. I've decided on a dress."

"Well, knock me over and call me Fred. Finally, the pickiest woman alive has decided on a dress and only six months before the celebration."

"I took forever, but this gown was made for me, Heaven. It's a one-piece corset princess gown with delicate floral tulle lace accentuated with bulge beads and crystals."

I was nervous about finding the perfect dress in time until Malcolm said we'd push the date back until I found it, if necessary. I slide the book toward the opposite end of the table for her to see when Heaven comes out of the kitchen holding a tray of tea and Danish. She sits it between the two of us and eagerly reaches for the magazine. A beam sets across her face, and I can tell that she is pleased.

"Iris, this is fabulous."

"I'm glad you think so too. When I saw it, I knew it was me."

"Goodness, yes! How about a kente or mud cloth for your sash and headdress? You need something that'll shake things up a bit — not too much to take away from the delicacy of the lace, but a sensible display of ethnic pride."

"I love that idea."

"I have swatches in the backroom. I'll go and get them."

Heaven disappears and just as quickly returns with a book of fabric swatches. Over the next several hours, I pick out my material of choice, programs, make phone calls to finalize the guest list, which tops out at 163, and Heaven provides me with a book of table settings and favors to look over for our next meeting.

"Has the groom decided on his attire?"

"Malcolm will be wearing an ivory suit, a Chinese collar shirt and alligator sandals."

"He will look quite dapper. What are your plans for the honeymoon, just out of curiosity?"

"Malcolm booked a trip to the Fiji Islands."

"The ancestors have sent you a fine man to marry indeed. Rest safely in the blessings that life brings you. Whenever things seem out of sync, look inside yourself, and the ancestors will come to you."

I play with the corner of my napkin as a way to try to hide the awkwardness I feel inside. I don't do well with mystery and feeding into the belief that things other than me control my destiny. Mystery always makes me uncomfortable. It's too intangible and unreasoning, too much like blind faith, which confused me even as a child. Something in me has always been fine with knowing divinity runs through every living thing and when I tap into that, that's my life's purpose, my intent and there will be stuff that seems to make no sense at all. And for that stuff, the best reason that I can come up with is that it simply is.

*

Tonight, Malcolm and I have tickets to see a play on the life of Sojourner Truth at the Merriam Theater. Subtle ass-kissing on the part of a potential client of Malcolm's. There is so much to Sojourner Truth's story. She was fearless - a true warrior. She was a black feminist long before it was fashionable, a fiery abolitionist in the mid-19th century, riveting preacher, powerful singer and a mother of five. Who said there is no such thing as Superwoman?

The play certainly did Sojourner's story justice. It told of her birth into enslavement and that of her children. The actors exemplified the fear, grief, anger and hope that all black people must have felt every moment in those times. The play ended with a speech by Sojourner. I can still hear it ringing in my ears, the heavy voice that seemed to speak from the grave through the young actress:

"Everybody's talking about black men gettin' their rights, but not a word about the black woman. I am a woman's right. I have as much muscle as any man and can do as much work as any man. I have plowed and reaped and husked and chopped and mowed. Can any man do more than that? I can carry as much as any man and eat as much too. I am as strong as any man. I have the right to have just as much as a man. If black men get their rights and not black women theirs, the black man will be masters over their women, and it will be just as bad as it was before. Black women are coming up, and a few black men are coming with them …" Who could object to that?

b reAK F ree : r A S h i D A

I AM SICK OF DRIVING THIS bus. What's even worse is that I come to this shitty job every damn day, and I still only got two nickels to rub together. After I pay my Ma her rent, pay Jaden's daycare fees, pay my telephone bill, buy food and pay for my cell phone, I am left with about $100. Erik's lousy $20 a week pays for milk. The best thing about my job is the benefits. I contemplate stripping, but having to give out lap dances, swing on poles and potentially have beer bottles stuck up my twat is hardly what I consider easy money. I went to family court last week and filed for child support again to end my struggling. Erik has to share the responsibility for taking care of our son all of the time, not just when he decides to be nice to me, and besides the money, I need him to spend time with our son. Jaden deserves a nonstop male influence, and not from that bastard Mr. Jenkins or Tommy's trifling ass, but from his father. I know what it's like to grow up without a dad. Mine is in jail for life with no chance of parole. Don't I deserve a break to keep my head from popping clear off my shoulders and rolling down the aisle of this bus or out into the middle of Turner Street? Sometimes I feel trapped inside a world of ain't gots: money, support, or a good education. The bags under my eyes tell of many sleepless nights when the ghost of bad choices refused to let me rest. Erik tells me that I should quit bitching about not having money and get back with him so we can put our family together and buy a house. He lives with his pretty-boy cousin, and together they

Mahzi Kane   Tea Leaves

operate broke-nigga enterprises where they specialize in playing women and dodging bills. Not exactly the kind of man I'm trying to get a mortgage with, and I know I should have thought about all of this before I laid down with the muthafucka. I can't change that mistake, but I can prevent myself from making any more.

"Hello."

"Hello, Sadot. Is Erik in?"

"Hold on, and let me see. How's Iris doing?"

"Still engaged."

"Tell her I said anytime she's up for an affair, just hit a nigga up."

"I don't think she'll be taking you up on that invitation."

"Never say never. Let me get my nigga for you."

Sadot has had his eye on Iris since day one and is on a serious mission to get her —in bed. Sadot settles down for one thing: pussy. And as soon as he gets it, he's out. Birds of a feather flock together, but some way, somehow, I still managed to give Erik my phone number that day we all met at the Odunde festival in South Philly while Iris and I were at a fabric stand. Sadot walked up to Iris, batted his gray eyes and asked her what she was mixed with because she was too pretty to be "just black." Iris spun around, told him that he was an ignorant asshole and for him to try reading a book if he ever hoped to come close to being the type of Blackman it took to be *her* Blackman. The vendor and I laughed so hard in his face, and Sadot saw that he was no match for Iris, but he's been stuck on her ever since.

"Yo, yo, wassup?"

"Hello, Erik."

"No, I don't have any money, and yes, I have plans this weekend."

"Each hoe gotta get her turn, eh?"

"Don't hate. I'd give'em all up for you. I know my name is still written on that 'cause those scrubs you roll wit' now don't have shit on me. What nut-ass nigga you seeing?"

"None of your business."

"Why not? You betta not be having my son all up 'round your new dudes, trying to have them play daddy and shit."

"I leave that type shit to you. Jaden has one father, and he knows that. The question is, do you? I have the receipts that you said you needed. Are you gonna give me your half or what?"

"A nigga is broke. You should have called me yesterday."

"Funny how Jaden always misses his stop on your money train. Do you miraculously forget about your responsibility when you get the money in your hands or what? 'Cause when I get paid, I got a list of things to take care of, one of which is our son. But it's cool 'cause I'll see your ass in court."

"Again with this court shit? You ain't learned yet. I got the judicial system beat when it comes to child support. How many ways do I have to tell you: I-am-out-of-work! And as far your list of shit to get for Jaden, first off, you spoil his ass too much. Second, if you would get back with a nigga, I would pay for everything."

"Who the fuck are you to tell me how much I should do for OUR son? You got a whole lotta nerve. You so busy screwing anything with a hole that I gotta be his father and mother. Fuck you, Erik, and not the way you'd like. Pigs will fly before you even smell this again, bitch. I'll see you in court, if your punk ass decides to show up."

How can the person I used to love so much be the same one that I loathe? Hate is a powerful word that I don't like to throw around without just cause. I would get Tommy to fuck him up, but he ain't even worth it, and it still won't solve the problem. In fact, it'll only make the circumstances worse. My cell phone is ringing, and I know it's Erik calling back to leave a childish-ass message.

"Rashida, you are yesterday's news. Been there, done that, every which way you liked it, actually loved it! I still can hear you screaming my name and crying over me. You ain't forget either. You got your school thing going on so you think you betta than a nigga now, like you too good. You still hood, and if you only knew how much cash a nigga is getting, you'd be all on my dick and not just for old times' sake, but forever, new and improved, yahmean? But I'll see you in court 'cause I ain't got nuthin' to lose. Enjoy your route."

He's so dumb that he doesn't even realize this is evidence. I'll be sure to save it and play it for the judge. He thinks that he's hurting me by not playing his part. I can't lie, he is making it harder for me because I have to make up for his shortcomings, but in the end, Jaden will see that he ain't shit. I think I changed my mind. I do still hate his ass. I need a glass of water to settle my nerves. I'm just glad that I didn't wake up Jaden.

"That's what your fast ass get for opening up your legs."

"Ma, what are you talking about?"

"I heard you on the phone arguing with Erik again. When you gonna see that he ain't shit, just like your daddy ain't shit?"

"And I guess Mr. Jenkins is the cat's meow?"

It's 10 in the morning, and already he has a beer in one hand, and the other down his pants.

Mahzi Kane   Tea Leaves

His dry-ass Jheri curl is hanging down over his eyes like a shaggy dog. He halfway stays here and shacks up with another old broad that lives on Carlisle Street, but he gives up the dollars, and that's all my Ma cares about.

"Don't be smart, bitch. Mr. Jenkins pays his way up in here, which is more that I can say for you. Where's my rent money?"

"Can I even brush my teeth, get the sleep out of my eyes or get a glass of water before you start hounding me for money? I got your money."

"You might got it, but when am I gonna get it?"

I go get her money to avoid a dumb argument over $200. It's ridiculous that my own Ma charges me to stay in one room with my son. I buy my own food and have my own phone line. Still, she's amazed that I can't save any money to move out. Meanwhile my brother Tommy don't pay shit mostly because he's in and out of jail. Where's my pass, where's my break, where is the sympathy for my struggle? Not here. In here I am overcome with a horrid feeling, like I'm going to fucking kill somebody today.

"Here."

"Bitch, don't be throwing money at me like I'm a damn stripper."

Mr. Jenkins then says, "Tell Jaden to stay out of the room, he was in my Old Spice."

I reply, "Go home, and you wouldn't have to worry about it."

Ma says, "Bitch, your name isn't on any bills 'round here. Who are you to be putting somebody out?"

"That's right, Ma, take his side, like you always do. He's always blaming Jaden for everything! He has him pegged as the first gunman on the grassy knoll, and the boy just started walking!"

Mahzi Kane   Tea Leaves

"I ain't taking sides; I'm only letting you know that you ain't in the position to be telling my old man to leave."

"I can't wait to get out of here."

"Me either. Let me know the date so I can book the band and I'll throw a fucking parade."

I have to get out of here if I hope to hold onto one shred of sanity. I can't have my son growing up in the dysfunctional bullshit. I love my Ma, but I don't like her, not one bit. The one thing she teaches me is how not to be. I would die first before I treat Jaden the way she treats me.

A nice, hot shower while Jaden is still asleep might help the knot tightening in my neck. Then I have to dress him, pack his bag, take him to Iris' since she's watching him while I go take my placement test, and then pick him up afterward. Iris is taking Jaden to the Please Touch Museum. I am thankful to have her as my best friend. She does so much that sometimes she's like his father. My Ma won't baby sit anymore unless she's getting paid. What grandmother won't watch her only grandson unless money is involved? That's Josephine. Unknown to her, I'm about to start giving her $100 less than usual. I have to save any way that I can and she can throw me out if she don't like it because at this point, a shelter is a step up compared to this shit. I drop Jaden off at Iris', and he is overjoyed to see his godmother. She makes me promise to take my time coming back so that they can stop for water ice. We get into her car and she comments on how much he looks like Erik, and it's the gospel truth. He has Erik's pretty, chocolate complexion, thick eyebrows and his bright smile. Sometimes it makes me sick to my stomach.

I arrive to the testing center 15 minutes early.

"You seem deep in thought."

I look up to see whose mouth this voice that moved my insides like an old Negro spiritual is coming from, and boy, do I like what I see. Standing before me is a man whose presence screamed sex – his toasted-almond skin, clean-shaven head and an inviting smirk that seemed to hum my name. He smells like sunshine. Test-taking centers are hardly a place for a love connection, but maybe God is answering my prayers. Since Erik and I split, there have been no men to follow. I wasn't ready to trust again or to feel anything except suspicion toward men and assume that they'd all break my heart. Mr. Jenkins made the insinuation that I turned gay, once again showing that he is such a douche bag. I don't want to punish the new guy for what another jerk did before he got here. Bitter is not attractive, so I have worked to mend my broken heart, and now I think I'm ready — not for love, but for companionship. I still have little trust issues, but I am mature enough to know that all men are not alike — some are dogs and some are kings. Maybe I can find out which category fits Mr. Toasted Almond.

"I like to zone out before a test."

"I can tell. I thought to myself, anyone that focused is destined for success, so I had to say something to you. I'll let you get back in your zone."

Before he could walk away, I pulled out the chair next to mine.

"No, it's OK. I think I'm focused enough for one test. What are you here for?"

"Court Reporter. How about you?"

"Paralegal."

"You must really care about people"

"I do. More importantly I need a job that offers stability. As long as there are laws, there will

Mahzi Kane   Tea Leaves

be people to break them. And as long as people break them, there has to be people to prove it."

"Interesting point. I'd love to probe that mind of yours and find out what other interesting points you have floating around in there. Would it be all right if I called you? Maybe we could grab a bite to eat once in a while?"

For so long I was used to giving guys the brush-off. I barely made eye contact with them because I didn't want to give off the false impression that I was interested or available. Though I knew Erik was a cheat, I never let him bring me to his level. It feels like ages since I gave a man my phone number. And even though there is no more Erik, I still feel like I'm doing the forbidden dance by flirting with this guy.

"What is your name?"

"Pardon my rudeness. I see a pretty face and lose my manners."

Handsome and charming makes for a good package. He extends his hand and takes mine. His hands are soft like he gets manicures.

"My name is Frank. You are?"

"Rashida. Very nice to meet you, Frank. Yes, you can call me. I'd love to see what's behind that smirk."

I retrieve a pen and a piece of paper from my pocketbook and give Frank my cell phone number.

"A brother can't get the house number yet, huh?"

"Nope, not yet. I gotta make sure you ain't crazy and deranged."

"I understand. Well, let me get to my testing room. You will be hearing from me real soon, I promise you that. Good luck and have a beautiful day."

It's refreshing to meet an attractive man who knows how to address me as a lady. No 'Yo, baby' or 'Hey, shorty'. It's not that hard to talk to a woman like she's a person.

I finish my test and I think I passed, even though I battled images of Frank in my mind. I kept hearing our conversation, listening to what I said and replaying it to make sure I didn't sound like a fool. I hope I didn't come off as desperate. I did pull that chair out kind of fast. He must have still liked me or he wouldn't have taken my number. I'll see what vibe he's on when he calls. I collect my things and make my way to the front exit in a throng of students. As I come down the side ramp, I see the object of my daydreaming get into a black Escort. A smile pulls at the corners of my mouth until I see him lean over and plant a passionate kiss on some girl, and by the way he tongues her down, there is no mistaking the nature of their relationship.

"Now I know his category."

I wait for the bus in utter disgust. I cannot wait until that dog Frank calls so I can cuss his ass out. It seems impossible to rebuild my faith in men. I have a better chance of getting struck by lightning than meeting a man who does not play games. Maybe Iris got the last real man. On second thought, that's not true because Justice is a good man. Ila just takes him for granted. He's not a challenge for her, she says. I had all the challenge I ever needed and much more than I bargained for with Erik. No, thanks. Give me a man who respects me, admires my independence and one that knows the true meaning of partnership. Erik's whole view on men and women is that a woman is supposed to follow a man's lead. Period, point blank, no discussion involved. If he goes gallivanting off to the pits of hell, she better follow him in gasoline panties if he asks. On the flip, a woman is supposed to take care of her man, in any situation. If he gets down on his luck, then it's acceptable for his woman to take care of him for a while. Erik is such a hypocrite. Glad I saw the light and dropped that zero. I decide to walk to Iris' from the testing center to milk the clock. As I approach her building, she is parking her car.

"Hey, Jaden! How's Mommy's special guy?"

I love the way his eyes light up whenever he sees me. It makes me feel complete. His joy confirms that my struggles to be a good mom are not in vain.

"I hope that he behaved himself. Did you have to wrestle him to the ground to get him out of the museum?"

"He was a prince. I did have to bribe him with a sticker, but we made out just fine. And as you can see by his shirt, he enjoyed the water ice too."

"I see. What a lovely painting."

By this time, Jaden has taken interest in a colony of ants.

"How do you think you did on the test?"

"Fine. Did I tell you that I go back to court on Tuesday for child support?"

"No, you didn't, but it's about time. Don't let up on that jackass."

"I called him this morning to tell him I had the receipts he asked for, so where was my money, he talking about I should have called him yesterday because he's broke. I swear, I'd get his ass slumped if I could get away with it."

"You're crazy, Rashida. Stay positive and you never know, it might come out in your favor."

"I'm trying but Erik knows what buttons to push to get me riled up."

"Stop letting him push those buttons then. I know it's easier said than done, but he wants you to get pissed, say forget it, and then nothing will change."

"After we argued, this asshole left a message talking about how much money he's getting and how he's not afraid to be at court because he's untouchable. He gave me all that I need to prove he has money. He had the nerve to tell me that I spoil Jaden too much, therefore it's my fault that I'm always broke."

"Erik is something special. If I didn't know better, I'd think he was slow. Make sure you take that message with you and play it for your lawyer."

"Without a doubt. Let me tell you 'bout the snake that's trying to play me like I'm slow."

"What are you talking about?"

"Girl, this fine-ass dude macked me at the testing center. How 'bout I walked out after the test and saw him tonguing down some chick. And you should have heard how charming and gentleman-like he sounded. That fast, he had me fooled into thinking he was a good one. I am so through with rotten apples."

"Some men can be a trip if you fall for it. That's why it's important for you to stay on your shit. Do you have to work tomorrow?"

"You know it. I had to use a personal day to take the placement test."

"Who's watching Jaden while you work?"

"Tommy. He'll do it for free. No money until payday."

"Tommy? So he can have my godson on the corner with him, Snoock and Knuckles? I don't think so. Let's go to your house and get Jaden's pajamas and things. He can spend the night here."

"Are you sure, Iris? I don't want to inconvenience you and Malcolm."

"Of course I'm sure, or I wouldn't have offered. I didn't realize how much I've missed Jaden until today. Let's go."

See why I love Iris? She's my guardian angel.

We go back to my house, I pack Jaden's bag, kiss my baby goodbye, and they are gone. Iris says that she is going to visit Mamie Ruth tomorrow and she'll bring Jaden back then. Free time on a Saturday afternoon, and I have no idea what to do. I'm sure as hell not staying in this house of ill repute. I'll call Sage and see what's up with her. I love all my girls, even Clarke, but Ila tends to bring out the not-so-good side of Sage. Whenever Ila and Sage are together, the conversation is always men and dick. I think Ila tries to make Sage into her protégé. I've known Sage for almost as long as I've known Iris. Sage's mother is Mrs. Queen's girlfriend, and Sage would come over to play. When we became teenagers, we all hung out, went to the mall and stuff like that. Sage was always boy-crazy, but around Ila it seems like she tries to be something she's not, and that is not the Sage that I know.

"Oasis, Katrina speaking."

"Hi, can I speak to Sage?"

"Sage isn't in. Can I take a message?"

"No thanks. Bye."

I wonder why Sage isn't in her shop on a Saturday afternoon. Only one way to find out.

"Hi, Sage, what are you doing?"

"Nada, holmes. Wassup with you, stranger?"

"Same shit, different day. Why aren't you in the shop on a Saturday afternoon?"

"I had to go lend my mother 50 bucks to pay her phone bill. At least that's what she said it was for, but who knows? Then I stopped to get something to eat. I'm not going back, the girls can handle it without me for the rest of the day. I finished all my clients anyhow. I'm surprised that you aren't at work."

"You are lending your ma money?"

"I know. I feel like I'm on a permanent payment plan to try to make things right between us."

"You can't buy a relationship with your ma. Either you have one or you don't."

"She's the only family I have. I need her even if it's just to be used. Enough about me and my mother, why aren't you at work?"

"I took a personal day to go take my placement test. Jaden's sleeping over at Iris', so I was seeing if we could hook up today."

"That's a plan. I'll be at your house in about 20 minutes. We'll go to the mall."

"Now you know a sister is broke."

"Think of what's left in your budget until I get there. Holla."

I shower and change because a day out with Sage always turns into an adventure. She is the party queen, and that's what I dig most about her: She's carefree, loves to have a good time, and when you go out with her you will have something to talk about the next day. The most unforgettable stunt she ever pulled was at a hotel party. All night this guy was up in her face, and she was right back up in his. Toward the end of the night, I was ready to leave, and I searched for Sage, but she was nowhere to be found. I started getting worried, hoping that guy didn't pull a funny move. Call it women's intuition, but something told me to check out on the balcony. I slid the door back and saw Sage taking it doggy-style on the 20th floor balcony in the middle of January with the same guy from earlier. The funniest part was that when she looked up and saw it was me, she said, "The party don't stop, but it get buck wild." Now to some people, she might sound like a whore, but you have to know Sage. Yes, she is a freak, but if you were to meet her on the street or walk into her shop, you would never know. It's not always what you do, but how you do it. I get out of the shower, and Sage is waiting for me in my bedroom.

"That Mr. Jenkins is a fucking pervert. He was all staring at my ass."

"You don't have to tell me, but that's Ma's money machine. Cha-ching at all costs."

"Um, Rashida, who is Frank?"

"What?"

"You heard me. Who is Frank? Don't be holding out on me, girl. You finally getting some?"

"No, no, no. It's not even that deep. How do you know about Frank anyway? The only person that I told was Iris."

"Your cell phone rang, and I answered. Girl, he got a voice to make a prudish woman's nipple stand up! When you meet him?"

"Today, while I was taking my test. He look good as hell, I can't front."

"And he called already! He must be on you something fierce."

"Yeah, well, I'ma cuss his ass out. After he got my number, I saw him kissing some girl. I have no time for games."

"Don't curse him out until you get something out of it — movies, dinner, dick, something. Ain't like you couldn't use some."

"You sound like Ila. That's not my thing."

"You betta make it your thing. I'm not telling you to do him dirty. All I'm saying is flip the script. Put it on him, and then don't call *him* back. Sometimes you gotta mack these so-called players and let'em know who running shit."

Mahzi Kane   Tea Leaves

Sage did have a point, as much as I hate to admit. Why do women always have to be the ones with egg on our faces, left in total disbelief when we find out the story was all bullshit and the person he claimed to be was all a scam? You never hear about men needing to "exhale." They get a new bitch and move on like it never happened and leave us in the dust. Stupefied.

"Let me think about it."

"His number is locked in your phone. I'm telling you, call him back. What do you have to lose?"

"I said I will think about it."

"What did you come up with for us to do?"

"We can go to the mall. Jaden could use new shorts for the summer."

"You are always spending your money on him. When do you splurge on yourself?"

"Girl, "splurge" is not in my vocabulary."

"Well, today I'ma treat you to anything you want. You go ahead and do your mommy thing. I'ma do my sister thing."

"Iris keeps Jaden, now you buying me stuff; this has got to be my lucky day."

"Luck doesn't have anything to do with it. You deserve it all. Wait, is this my baby Bo calling? Yup, it is. Let me see what he wants."

I wonder who Bo is. Last I heard, it was Jesus. I hope she uses condoms because I would hate for her to catch some shit. Nowadays the least of your worries is a baby. One night of fun can put you in a casket. I put on my denim skirt with the split up the front, a red tee, and red and white Top Tens. Red is my signature color. It looks nice with my honey-brown skin. I bumped the ends of my hair and by that time, Sage is finished with her telephone call.

"Who is Bo, and what happened to Jesus?"

Mahzi Kane   Tea Leaves

"Jesus wanted way too much head. Bo is my sweetheart. He's a young little something that I met after a basketball game. Wait until you meet him."

"How young is young?"

"He's 17."

"If a 20-something woman shows up at my door for my 17-year-old Jaden, I'ma slam the door in her face and dare her to come back. I'd lay her ass out with a right hook."

"Here we go. If you or his mother could see what he does or even hear how articulate and intelligent he is, you would know and understand that age is merely a record of how long we've been alive."

"I'm not hearing any of that. Find somebody closer to your own age to be articulate and intelligent with. What could you two possibly have in common?"

"Basketball, sex, movies, sex, life. The same shit that you have in common with any other person on the planet that you might meet. Don't catch feelings just because you have a son."

"Even if I didn't have a son, I wouldn't agree. I think you should find a grown man, not a growing man."

"Where? Please point me in that direction 'cause I keep running into cats straight out of Loserville. That is until I met Bo. Don't get your panties all up in a bunch. He's going to college or the NBA, so it's not like he's my husband. Plus I've been falling back. He's getting a bit attached."

"I wonder why. I'd be attached to a grown woman who fucked me cross-eyed too."

"He ain't no slouch in the fucking category either. But don't worry. I can handle this, and so can he. We just kicking it."

"If you say so, and remember you did say so."

Mahzi Kane   Tea Leaves

Sage and I make our way through Plymouth Meeting Mall, and she fills me in on her sexual romps with Bo and the gossip around the shop. I tell her about my court date and my plans to move. Sage buys me a pink and gray shorts set with a pair of pink sneakers as well as a black, slinky dress because she says every woman has to have a showstopper in her closet. I buy Jaden three pair of denim shorts, two pair of cargo shorts with matching bucket hats, and Sage buys him an outfit. We make our way to the food court to grab a snack to eat on the ride home. Walking toward us is Erik and Sadot. Talk about when good times go bad.

"For somebody who always crying broke, looks like you on a nice shopping spree, sis."

"For your information, Sadot, Sage bought this stuff."

"You hear that, Erik, her girlfriend copped her three bags full of shit."

"Rashida, why you try to play me?"

"Erik, you do a fine job of playing yourself."

"I'ma remember this when we go to court on Tuesday."

"You do that."

"Rashida, for real, you betta go 'head with all of that."

"Why she need to go head Erik? You ain't gone do shit to my girl."

"Sage, mind your business, that's between them. Let me holla at you for a minute?"

"It is my business, Sadot, especially if he tries to go Ike Turner out here. And no, you can't holla at me. You should know by now that you ain't ready for all this. Besides, girls talk and that little bit of dick you working with is a waste of good pussy and time."

"I don't want your ran-through pussy anyway."

Mahzi Kane   Tea Leaves

"Ran through or not, it don't want you either!"

"Come on, Sage, we ain't got time for these clowns."

"Clowns? Rashida, you know what's under my big top, so stop actin' brand new, girl."

"Erik you just have my money on Tuesday."

He always manages to piss in my bowl of cereal! So much for how broke he claimed to be this morning. There's no telling what he is up to, shady is what he does best. I've taken too much bullshit, believed too many lies and accepted too many sorrys. Too many games, men play too many fucking games, and I'm tired of losing. Time for me to start winning and see what that's like.

"Who are you calling?"

"Frank."

"That's right, girl, we don't love these hoes!"

*

I talk to Frank and set it up for us to hook up at 9. Sage lends me her car. We agree that I will come back to her house and crash there, and then she'll drop me off home before she goes to the shop. I put on the sexy, black number that we purchased earlier, Sage does my hair up into a bun, and I am out of the door at 9. I want to be late and make him wait and run to the window at the sound of every car door shutting to see if it's me and wonder if I stood him up when he realizes that it's not. You know, man shit. When we spoke, I made sure not to let on about seeing him with that girl. He still had his panty wetter voice on, but it wasn't cute at all. In fact, it was like a fly buzzing around my glass of freshly squeezed lemonade. I pull up to his door, and nervous butterflies take over my stomach. I check my face and hair in the compact mirror in Sage's glove compartment and make sure nothing is stuck in my teeth. "I can do this. He deserves it for trying to play me, just like Erik. Put on your game face, Ra-Ra, and go get yours." I step out of the car, dial his number, and he answers on the first ring.

"Hello."

"Hi, it's Rashida. I'm outside."

"There is a God. I'll be right down."

Like Flash Gordon, Frank is down the steps, in the vestibule and opening the door in one motion. It makes me feel good to have a man this fine want me this much, even if he is a two-timing dog.

"Wow, you look … refreshing. Like a breath of air I've been dying to inhale all of my life. Please, come in."

I can't help that I blush. He says all the right things in all the right ways. He looks relaxed, sexy even, in lounge pants and bare chest. I follow him up the stairs to his apartment on the third floor. As he climbs the steps, I watch his ass glide in sync with the rest of his powerfully built body. I imagine my hands groping every inch and I feel my knees get weak. I enter his apartment, and it's a typical man dwelling: futon, big screen television and entertainment center in the living room, no dining room, only a cozy kitchen and a mural-sized poster of Bob Marley swallows up a wall.

"Would you like a cold beverage?"

"Sure, what do you have?"

"Champagne, water, cranberry juice and beer."

"Champagne, please."

"Coming right up. Make yourself comfortable. Have a seat, and put on some music if you'd like. I got the bomb collection."

"Thanks, I'll check it out."

I go to his collection of CDs, and he has eclectic taste. There is everything from Marvin Gaye and the Stylistics to Nirvana to Public Enemy to Nas. I want to set the mood, to let him know that I'm here to get it on — no love, no romance, just sweat out my hair fucking. I place the disk into the player, and soon the sexy voices of Jodeci join us in his apartment. Just as I take a seat on the futon, Frank returns with two glasses, a bottle of Asti Spumante, and a plate of strawberries and whipped cream. I see this dude is really taking this Darius Lovehall shit to heart.

"How nice. Thank you."

"Tonight, your every wish is my command. Ask, and I will give you whatever you like and however you want it."

"That definitely has my imagination going."

"I really mean it, Rashida. I haven't been able to stop thinking about you since I had the pleasure of seeing you. You give off a vibe that I can't quite explain, but it's alluring."

I'm a fool for being in a strange man's apartment that I met only a few hours ago, but my adrenaline is on a crazy rush. I am high.

"Are you really gonna be my toasted-almond genie and grant all of my requests?"

"Like I said, your wish is my command."

He takes my hand in his and massages my fingers as suggestive lyrics over sensual beats thump deeply in my lady parts and make me wanna be freaky. With my free hand, I reach for my glass of champagne, empty it and position it in front of his face to refill.

"I see you like the champagne."

"I do. How about some head to go along with it? I like that even more."

"How pleasant to meet a woman who's not afraid to ask for what she wants."

I stand up while he holds my glass, slowly unzip the back of my dress and let it fall to my feet. Underneath, I am wearing no bra and a black thong. I can see his tongue fail at an attempt to catch the drool before it falls from his mouth. I undo my bun, and let my hair cascade down and eventually settle past my shoulders. I'm gonna make this Negro love me, I chant to myself as I move closer to him and gyrate my body to the rhythm of the music, all the while not taking my eyes off of him. I take the glass from him, drink until there is only a sip left and then drizzle the remainder down my cleavage. I caress my breasts, stopping at my nipples to make sure that he sees that they are happy. I take off my thong and lay spread eagle on his living room floor. He almost knocks over the champagne bottle as he reaches for the plate of strawberries and whipped cream. He smears the whipped cream on each nipple. His tongue is eager, savoring the feel of my flesh in his mouth, and leaves traces of the way he whispers my name with each lick. He makes a trail of sweetness between my legs and I realize it's been too long since I've felt the soft warmth of a man's tongue down there. Frank buries his face between my thighs until he finds my slit and sucks it like a nursing baby. My legs stiffen and my body is not too proud to shudder and then shake. He moves faster, and I feel my body detonate from the inside out. I grab his head, throw his neck back and demand to fuck him now.

"Lay back."

Mahzi Kane   Tea Leaves

I pull a condom from my purse and put it on him. I straddle Frank and let his manhood glide into me, taking my time so I feel every inch. He lets out a loud moan full with pleasure, and I smile. At a snail's pace, moving him around inside of me, touching every crevice of my special place, I dig my knees into the carpet so he can go as far down as there is to go. He digs his nails into my skin as he pushes himself farther and farther until it seems as if he is in my stomach. "You like this pussy, don't you?" He whimpers a "yes".

Quick and smooth as ceiling fan blades in 100-degree weather, I move circles around him until he screams my name at a thousand octaves. I grind until he is ready again, make him cum and then he blesses me with the best orgasm invented. We lay gasping for air, listening to Jodeci whine that they'd love you for life. That's what they all say, I think to myself. Frank stares at me in disbelief, like I am a pretty stranger, and no longer the woman he escorted up the stairs hours ago. I am ready for more so I replace the used condom with a fresh one and place his hands between my legs. He plays there, going in and out. We switch positions, and he takes me from behind. We exchange strokes and he holds on tight. I reach behind and wrap my hands around his neck to pull him closer.

"Fuck me, Frank. Fuck me right. Make me cum, nigga."

He shakes as he pounds away at me until we can contain ourselves no longer and it is the best thing since sliced bread.

"Rashida, you are too much."

Mahzi Kane   Tea Leaves

"You haven't seen it all, baby. I'm just getting started. Bang, bang."

He raises his eyebrows and shakes his head in amazement.

"Can I take a shower?"

"You can take whatever you want, baby doll. I would show you where it is, but I can't move my legs."

"That's OK. I'll find it while you get yourself together."

I stroll to the bathroom like the hottest thing since fire, get a towel and washcloth from the linen closet and stare at myself in the mirror. In the reflection, I see a happy face, a face that I haven't seen on me in what seems like forever. I put it on him and more than that I enjoyed myself to all ends. I take my time washing, cleaning every part of me, and then I wash my hair. I emerge from the shower, towel off and wrap another towel around my head. Just as I suspect, he is laid out on the living room floor. I tiptoe back to his bedroom and find the nightstand. After I flip on the light, I look for the piece of paper that I had written my phone number on. It is lying on his dresser, with a bunch of other numbers, right next to a picture of the girl I saw him kissing, along with his wallet. He's way full of himself, so I help myself to the contents of his wallet. Since he thinks he is a pimp, let me teach him what it is like to be treated like a hoe.

I look around for the telephone and see the base on the other nightstand minus the phone. I go back through the living room into the kitchen, and it is resting on the countertop. In the bathroom I look through the numbers on the caller ID until I find mine, and once I do, I delete it. He doesn't have a cell phone because he said there is no need to get in touch with anyone that badly, and anyone who wants him can leave a message on his machine. In other words, he doesn't want his girl being able to track his cheating ass down. I go back into the living room, slide into my dress and put on my shoes. I take the lipstick out of my pocketbook and scrawl across the television screen, "NIGGA, I SAW U!" I let myself out of his apartment, tiptoe down the stairs and hurry to the car. Once inside, I laugh. Finally, I've had a man my way. And it felt damn good.

Having slept like a log last night, when I wake up, Sage is grinning like the Cheshire cat from *Alice in Wonderland*. She keeps saying that I am glowing and I am a boss bitch after what I did to Frank. I guess she thinks that I am going to be the third member to her and Ila's player club, but I squash those ideas from the door. I explain that last night was just that — last night. I can't go around screwing whomever I want and leaving lipstick messages on expensive televisions as I dash off into the night. I have a son that I have to set an example of what a lady is, and I can't do things that may harm that. Sage understands and we move on from that topic, but first I make it clear that I don't want her blabbing my business to Ila or anyone else. It's mine to tell when I see fit. Sage drops me off around 10:00 so I can be to work by noon. As soon as I get in the house, my telephone rings.

"Where's Jaden?"

"Don't call my phone like that. Say "hello," "good morning" or something that gives the illusion that you are at least human, if not civilized."

"Helloooooooo, where's Jaden?"

"Not here."

"Where is he at this early in the morning?"

"He stayed over Iris', why?"

"I was gonna come scoop him up today, that's why. You got a problem with me seeing my son?"

"Not at all. I don't know when she's bringing him back, but you can have her number to call and find out."

"Why can't you call her?"

"Because I just got in and I need to get ready for work, that's why. You can call her if you wanna see your son so bad."

"Just getting in? Where the fuck have you been all night?"

"Where you been all night?"

"Don't answer my question with a question. I want to know where you were at that you had to ship my son off. What were you doing that you couldn't have him with you?"

"Erik, please. I was where I was. Jaden is fine, and you know it. All you worried about is me."

"Cause my son is supposed to be with his mother."

"He's supposed to be with his father too, but you ain't got no problems bending that rule."

"You full of jokes this morning. I'm only gonna ask you one more time where you were, and then I'm really going to be mad."

"Dogs get mad, people get angry. If you really want to know, I was out fucking the shit out of a no-good nigga who thought he would play me like

Mahzi Kane   Tea Leaves

you did. Now that you know that bit of information, have a nice fucking day, Erik. I will."

I turn my ringer off and get ready for work. Before I leave, I shake my head at every one of the 28 messages that Erik left on my voicemail. As long as he continues to worry about who I'm screwing, he will never be the best father that he can be for our son.

*

On the bench at family court, Jaden and I wait for our court-appointed lawyer, Leah Sotherling, a smart, vibrant sister who don't take no stuff, especially from deadbeats. With all my paperwork and the messages, Ms. Sotherling and I go over the strategy when she arrives. She is extremely confident that Erik will not slither through, and I pray that she is right. Erik comes strolling into court in a black suit and sunglasses looking like a wanna be gangster. He's a damn fool for coming to court looking sharp as a tack when he claims that he's out of work. It seems like the longer I know him, the dumber he gets. It takes 30 minutes for the judge to rule after being presented with the history of our case and the new documents. Erik said that the work force wasn't offering the type of pay that he should make, which is the reason that he has such a difficult time finding a job. The judge said that either he lower his standards or start picking up cans from the side of the road because children don't stop growing or living because he can't find a job that suits his salary requirements. She also told him that parenthood is not convenient and that if he is not equipped to make the necessary sacrifices, he

Mahzi Kane   Tea Leaves

should have remained a virgin. When the judge suggested that we seek counseling, Erik shook his head no, but I wouldn't mind going to at least try to learn to be cordial parents. I am awarded $2,713.13 in back support. He has to continue paying child support, document his job search and come get Jaden every other weekend and every other holiday. He finally has to be the man he so desperately claims to be. As we leave the courtroom, he comes over to say goodbye to Jaden and tells him that he'll see him on the weekend. He tries not to look at me, but can't help himself. I smile as Jaden, Ms. Sotherling and I walk out. Game over.

Tonight is Iris' performance at Spotlight, a club known for spoken word. She's the featured poet, and I'm thrilled to see her put on a show. Iris on stage is like studying a flower about to bloom as she reveals layer after layer of herself through prose in front of strangers and friends. The sincerity in her voice and the realism of her words let you know that she's not a passing fad: Iris is the truth. Tonight, I need her words to soothe and move me away from the life that I planned for and into the scary but undeniable life that is waiting. The club opens at 9, but Iris doesn't go on until 10, so we're all hooking up at 9:30 to make sure we get good seats. I pay my mom one last time to watch Jaden. Tomorrow I hunt for our very own apartment. I am busting at the seams with happiness and a slight twinge of anxiety because I have never lived alone or come home to an empty house a day in my life. The only room that I am responsible for keeping up is my own, and now I'm going to be the head of a household. Regardless of any fears that I have, I can't wait to have my own. It's the first step in a long line of great things waiting to happen.

We're finally going to meet the infamous Piccolo tonight. Sage offers to pick me up because she doesn't want to ride alone. Jokingly, I ask why she didn't bring Bo, knowing he's way too young to get into the club. She arrives and by the pitiful look on her face, I can see that drama has unfolded.

"Wassup, Sage? What's with the face?"

"I am getting sick of men and their bullshit. Whether young or old, they all have some mess with them, I swear."

"Trouble in candy land?"

"Now is so not the time for jokes."

"What happened?"

"I let Bo drive my car last night to run to the store, and he got a $300 ticket! He had the nerve to act like it wasn't a big deal. He got as much as the whole in a doughnut so it don't take a genius to figure out who's going to foot the bill. I don't care how well he's fucking me; it's not worth this."

"Why did he get a ticket?"

"For only having a permit."

"Did you know that?"

"Yea, I knew."

"And you let him drive your car anyway. Pay the price for being lazy. You're lucky the cops didn't take your shit."

"I'm not trying to hear that. It's his fault, not mine. I told him to make sure he drove safely and to put on his seatbelt so that he wouldn't draw attention to himself. Knowing Bo, he probably had the music blasting, leaning out the window, profiling like he got fans."

Mahzi Kane   Tea Leaves

"Once again, that's on you. If you thought he was going to act like that, then you shouldn't have let him hold your car. Period."

Sage turns up the radio to quiet my good advice because she knows that I'm right, which is the reason why she's annoyed. She passes me the joint and blows the smoke out slow and hard. I hate it when she tries to push her bad choices off on something or somebody else. She can't see how she causes this stuff to happen and then complains when it does.

"If you're gonna be a sourpuss, you should have stayed the hell home."

"I'm not a sourpuss, and I don't care how many tickets Bo would have gotten, none of that will make me miss the chance to meet Piccolo."

"I know that's right, he got Ila's nose wide open. This is the first time that I have ever seen her act like she needs a man."

"The whole thing has me tripping. They haven't even had sex yet."

"Now I most certainly have to meet him."

We pull up at 9:30 and circle the block for another 10 minutes to find parking. Sage refuses to pay for parking because she says it's her right as a citizen to park without a monetary obligation. She says it's just another way for The Man to get you — No Parking signs posted on every other street, making the only option one of the many and oh-so convenient parking lots. We park four blocks away, but it's free, and that is Sage's bottom line. After we pay our cover charge, we head inside to see if the rest of our group has arrived. Clarke spots us from the bar and eases off her stool like she knows a man in a far-off corner is watching. That chick always has dick on the brain. I look around for Toya because none of us have spoken to her in weeks. I left a message earlier, and Sage says that nobody has been answering her telephone.

"Hey, ladies, how y'all doing?"

"Cool. How 'bout you, Clarke?"

"Fine. Keeping busy by checking out the men up in here. I see a couple of potentials. I gotta find me a new sponsor."

"Sponsor? You a alcoholic?"

"Rashida, a sponsor is a reliable friend, a special one you can call on to pull you out of any jam. I need to get my car fixed. I got an estimate for $2,000, and you know I don't plan to pay it. Of course the number one game plan is to mack the mechanic, but I gotta have a backup man."

"What happened to your car?"

"Sage the better question is who happened to my car. The windows are busted out, tires slashed, and the hood is all scratched up. It would be worth the two grand if we could catch the bitch that did it."

"We? Sounds like you need to stop fucking somebody's man."

"It could be one of many that's hating on me, so don't assume it's over a man. My beauty intimidates insecure women and makes them jealous for no good reason. They automatically don't like me without getting to know a thing about who I am. I'm not even tripping though. My shit will be fixed in a matter of weeks, trust me."

"If you say so. Have you seen Iris?"

"She's backstage. Let me go work the bar until her set starts. I'll be back."

Nothing seems to faze Clarke. Having somebody destroy the one thing I owned would be enough to make me get extremely introspective and analyze my ways and actions. As Clarke takes her seat at the bar, Toya ambles into the club. Her usually seductive eyes are red and puffy, and we know what that means. She has been crying over Lamont.

"Long time, no see. Give me love."

"Sage and I stand up and give Toya hugs. We take our seats, order a drink, and that's when I have to ask.

"What the hell is wrong with you? You look like shit. I hope you ain't been boo-hooing over that Lamont 'cause he ain't shit. I'm not trying to hurt your feelings; I'm just being real. He's not leaving his wife, and even if he did, is that the kind of man you want? Do yourself a favor and cut your losses, sweetie."

"I have not been crying over Lamont. I have been crying because I don't have a place to live!"

And with that confession, Toya breaks down like a house of playing cards caught in gusty winds.

"Aww, boo. I'm sorry. Here, wipe your face."

"Toya, why don't you have a place to live?"

"Because my reckless cousin didn't pay her half of the rent for the last couple of months, and instead of telling me, Pia was too busy trying to trick up the money. One of her men found out about the other and left her high and dry, but by then she had spent the money she had saved. Our lease has a clause about back rent that says we have to leave."

"When did this happen?"

"Two weeks ago, Sage."

Mahzi Kane   Tea Leaves

"Why is the phone still on and where have you been staying?"

"I'm too embarrassed to get it cut off. I don't want people to think I'm broke and can't pay my bills, neither of which is true. I've been staying at my mom's."

"Back with Gwen, Danielle and Granny Marion? I know you are sick about that shit. Where is Pia staying, not there I hope?"

"Heck no. The trifling whore tried to get my mom to let her stay there, but my mom wasn't having it, and Danielle went off at the fact that Pia even asked. Say what you want about her, but Dani don't like anybody messing with her big sister. I don't exactly know, and I don't care, but I think Pia's shacking up with some dude. More than being furious at her, I'm pissed at myself. Eventually I'll forgive her, but I wanted to crack her upside her fucking head. Excuse my language, but I'm hot behind this whole situation. She had the nerve to bring me a Dooney & Bourke pocketbook, like that would make me forget that I am homeless. I would rather have the four-fifty somebody paid for the bag, because I know it wasn't her. I've been on a crazy search for a new place, I mean going to three apartments a day. I don't know what I'm going to do. There is way too much estrogen colliding in my mom's house as it is. I have to get out of there and soon."

"You can stay with me until you find something. I would love to have you. It'll be an extended slumber party, you know, somebody to keep me company on lonely nights."

"Are you sure, Sage? I would really appreciate it, but I don't want to be a burden."

"Of course I'm sure. We can go get your stuff tonight if you want."

"No, it can wait until the morning. Thank you, thank you lots!"

Toya leans over to give Sage a tight hug. I know what it's like living at home, and I wouldn't wish that on my worst enemy. I'm sure having already lived on your own makes it more difficult to go back.

"Looks like we can apartment-hunt together."

"You're moving?!"

"Don't say it with that much shock in your voice, Toya. We are celebrating tonight. Erik and I went to court today. I was awarded back child support. He has to pay $450 a month once he gets a job and get Jaden every other weekend."

We slap hands and stomp our feet as we relish in my victory and order a bottle of wine. Clarke comes back to the table, and just then, Ila and Piccolo swagger in, and Ila feverishly waves her hand to get our attention as they make their way over to us. All conversation ceases, all thoughts are lost, all eyes are on Piccolo, and it is quite evident what all the fuss is about. This man is an Adonis. Ila wears the biggest grin, like she is holding the winning ticket to a million-dollar jackpot. She never looked this way with Justice.

"Wassup, divas?"

"Heeeyyyyyy."

It is the only response that any of us can drum up, and it rolls together to form one monotonous sound. Ila leans in closer to Piccolo as she sees the starved look in Clarke's eye, sizing Piccolo up from head to toe. It is obvious that all of us are taken aback by his presence, but Clarke is a bit too noticeable, like she is forgetting that Piccolo is off limits.

"Everybody, this is Piccolo."

"Good evening. How is everyone tonight? I hope you're having a good time."

"Piccolo, I'd like you to meet my sisters. This is Rashida, that's Toya, here's Sage, and oh, that's just Clarke. Has anyone seen Iris?"

"I saw her earlier backstage. Her set should be starting any minute now."

As Clarke says the words, her sights never leave Piccolo.

"Pardon me for staring, but you look familiar."

"Really, Clarke? I can't imagine how you might know Piccolo. He's a teacher, and that's not really your corner or your salary range, now is it?"

Ila's icy glare backs Clarke down, but I sense that Clarke is enjoying the discomfort that she is bringing to the moment.

"I get that all the time. I guess I have one of those familiar faces people talk about."

Piccolo chuckles to try to lighten up the tension, but to no avail. He pulls out Ila's chair, and they take their seats. Ila tries her best not to let her irritation show, but each time Clarke speaks Ila rolls her eyes or changes the subject. The lights go down, and the master of ceremonies takes to the stage.

"Good evening, brothers and sisters. I trust you all are enjoying the music, the ambiance and the drinks. It's time to give you all something special. She's been here many times before and other venues here in Philly as well as D.C. and New York. She's a published author and a close friend. Put your hands together, and show some love for Iris."

It is pitch black, and all you can hear is the thump of a deep bass drum. Suddenly you hear Iris' voice.

"Fear and loathing has her holding onto what really isn't hers. Disturbed nerve endings sending synaptic signals to surrender the totality of herself to a fragment of another woman's husband and father of two children building multi-million-dollar mansions on sandbox foundations."

The bass beat drops, and the spotlight flashes on Iris, who sits on a stool wearing a sparkling white dress, a white headwrap and black designer sunglasses.

"Shit is bound to collapse! Chasing nickel-plated dreams that taunt her, dead babies haunt her, selfish abortion is their official cause of death his sentence reverberates: 'Don't be stupid.' She slept with dogs came up with fleas itching to erase his neglect, like the time he put her out of his automobile, and still she accepted his apologies and explanations, and oh yeah, could he come over tonight 'cause his bite is equal to his bark mangling the center of her being into believing they'll have the white picket fence and good Christian church on Sundays. Maybe one day she'll get the gist, that he's not hers since he's not even his."

The stage goes dark and the crowd erupts in a storm of applause and finger snaps. Toya's head hangs low, and her shoulders sway from side to side because the effect of Iris' message is fierce. We all know that Toya is the inspiration for Iris' piece. The truth hurts, but it also heals, especially when eloquently spoken. I reach over to hold Toya's hand as she brushes away the tears that begin to fall. I begin to cry with her, knowing what it's like to be with someone that you know you have to leave, but you can't seem to figure out how, so you stay. The more you stay, the more your soul aches. Finally you have to pull yourself up and move on because not doing so would mean death. You realize that love is no guarantee that someone won't break your heart.

Chapter Nine

r eDemption t ime : i L A

ALL I CAN THINK ABOUT IS that Clarke looking at Piccolo like she wanted to slop him up in gravy and toss him down her throat. Clarke is the type of woman that you can't trust around your man because she has no loyalty. Then she tried to throw in that, "You look familiar," bullshit as a smoke screen, like I don't know her methods of operation. When she went to the ladies' room, I trailed right behind to let her know that she can look but the thought of touching had better not enter her brain or I would beat the dog shit out of her. "That's just me, it's hard to turn it off," were her exact words. After a nervous laugh she told me that Piccolo honestly did remind her of someone. She tried to assure me that it was innocent and that teachers don't make enough to finance her lifestyle. I heard the words but I'm watching that bitch nonetheless.

"Hey, sugar, what are you thinking about?"

"Clarke and how she was throwing herself at you."

"Don't even trip. I left with you."

"I never did trust Clarke, and now she's giving me a reason not to. If you can't trust your supposed girl around your man, who can you trust?"

"Me. It doesn't really matter who's throwing what at me. You are who I want."

I swear I love him. He makes me feel secure, something more than simply liking a man and his company, but how I feel when I'm with my daddy.

Mahzi Kane   Tea Leaves

I feel like could be his wife. Technically, he has not asked me to be his lady, but I've assumed the role. We spend the majority of our free time together, I leave my things at his house, and they're always in the exact spot that I left them in when I return. When we walk down the street, he doesn't notice the mobs of women staring in his face. It baffles me the most that this whirlwind of emotions has happened without us having sex. I've had more than my fair share of men, most of which never waited longer than a week to be intimate. It's been a month, and we haven't done anything other than kiss. My resistance is growing weak, especially with him looking so scrumptious tonight.

"Are you going to do me the honor of spending the night, Ila?"

"What do you mean?"

"I was hoping that I could make love to you until there is none left to make, until you're drained of all of your energy … and bodily fluids. I want you until I can't do anything but fall into a child-like sleep. I want you to ride me until – just until."

I run my tongue over my teeth and nod my head in agreement as I part my legs a bit to let the heat escape. Good thing I wore my just-in-case lacy bra and panty set. We arrive to his house, and Piccolo flips on the light switch set at dimmer, and as usual his home is immaculate. The smell of Somali Rose tickles my nose as he reaches for my hand and holds it in his while staring into my eyes.

"I have always loved your cat eyes."

"Thank you."

It's not hard at all to make a man want you, if you're a real woman, that is. All you have to do is be the girl he likes and be like no other one he has ever had. I step closer to him and he steps back. He bites his bottom lip slightly, tilts his head and says,

Mahzi Kane   Tea Leaves

"You are so beautiful. Almost too pretty to unwrap."

He leads me upstairs past the master bedroom and down the hall. The hardwood floors are covered with pink and purple petals. I don't know what flower they are from, but it looks like a masterpiece. To my surprise, we stop at the bathroom.

"You have to go?"

He slides the door open with one arm. The trail of petals continues into the bathroom and mushroom into a lavish bath with bubbles so big they look like they'll swallow me whole. He pulls a lighter from his pocket to light the five candles perched along the mounted sconces. He sits me on the stool and stands before me as he strips away every piece of his clothing. Time had done his body good, damn good. He is methodically chiseled, like someone has truly molded him from clay, intent on making the perfect male specimen. This man is beyond fine, beyond the bomb, simply beyond. He motions for me to stand up. I do and with tender care he moves his face close to my neck, takes a deep breath and inhales. I'm ready to skip the bath and put it on him. He must hear my thoughts because he whispers, "I want this to last forever. Be patient with me. I've been waiting for this for a very long time."

I get inside the bathtub and Piccolo washes me, letting the suds run down my back, between my breasts and then reunite with the others to engulf my entire body. He massages my feet and runs his index finger up and down my thighs. He leans forward to French kiss my nipples with expert precision, making my eyes snap shut, as my nipples seem to melt into his mouth. Piccolo joins me in the bathtub. He sits me on top of him and I move my body against his, feeling him expand by

Mahzi Kane   Tea Leaves

the second. He sticks his fingers inside of me, pulls them out, licks them and then I lick them too.

We exit the bathtub. He reaches for a towel and dries my body inch by inch. I take the towel from him and I dry the massive chest, embracing arms and powerful back that I'd admired in passing – when he reached for the salt, the way a particular t-shirt fit or when he walked around in his boxers looking for something to wear. I dab at his stallion thighs, pausing at his manhood. He gets the Big Dick award hands down. I kneel down and touch him, ready to give what I vowed I'd never do. I back Piccolo up against the wall and take him in my mouth until it reaches the back of my throat. His knees kinda buckle, signaling I'm doing the shit pretty well. I go slow and then fast, and when I take it out and flick the tip of it with my ring, the crowd goes wild. So I do it again and again. I kiss, lick and suck until it glistens like the ground after a summer's rain, all the while letting the thought of his stiffness overwhelm me with excitement. I hold it in my hands and ask:

"Do you like it?"

"Hell yeah, why did you stop?"

"I wanna make sure you like it, I mean *realllllyyyy* like it."

"I really fucking like it, I mean REALLY. Keep going and I might love this shit."

I put my hand in the wetness between my thighs and place it close to his mouth. He tastes each finger - a delightful image to watch. I go back to pleasing him, and soon he cums all over my chest. It's not that bad after all. He sits me on the edge of the sink and licks where I like to be licked. He kisses my middle soft and slow. My neck rolls from side to side as all of the muscles in my body relax. I pull Piccolo up and start doing the things

Mahzi Kane   Tea Leaves

I've been holding back for too long. Trying different things wasn't really Justice's strong point. He found his master position, him on top, and saw no reason to try to reinvent the wheel. If it was a special occasion, I'd get on top, but that was it. Don't get me wrong, it was very satisfying just nothing like this. Piccolo stands, and I wrap my legs around him as we bump our bodies into one another with ferocious passion. He leads, my skin meets the cool dampness of the bathroom wall, and he puts one of my legs on his shoulder, the other still around his waist. We hump as if our lives depend on making sure we do this right. I pop and bounce until his body jumps and he screams out in an orgasmic delight of wanton desire, and collapses under the power of my lovemaking.

The next morning is perfect. The sun is shining bright, dancing on the leaves of crab apple and oak trees. Blue fescue grass shimmers with a light morning dew. A girl could get used to waking up every morning after nights like the one we shared. When I look over and see Piccolo asleep, I feel closer to him than I could have imagined and I want to give him my all to make sure our love is strong. I must confess that this shit is scary. It's like I'm high, strung out on his love drug, not wanting anybody else but him and willing to do whatever needed to have this man. He could be the one, the soul mate Iris is always musing about. It turns me on that he gives no more than what I can take and takes what I can give without trying to force or remake me into something that I am not or don't want to be.

"Good morning, sugar."

"Good morning. How are you?"

"Happy."

"I must say that was the best fucking I've had in my life. Thank you for making me feel special.

Mahzi Kane   Tea Leaves

The only other man that makes me feel this loved and cherished and protected is my father. He used to say that he gives his little girl whatever she wants so she'll never have to need a man. That taught me not to settle for less than that. I finally feel like I'm not settling."

"You shouldn't have to. Besides, you're not a little girl anymore, you are a grown woman with grown-woman needs. I can attest to that fo' sure."

"Yes, my body is sore - signs of a job well done. Kudos to you. I'm glad we're a part of one another's lives again. I've missed you."

"I've missed you too."

"Well, I have to get up. I have errands to run, and later on I'm going to a party with Sage. What's up with you for the day?"

"Not too much really. I might hook up with Black. I don't really know yet. Maybe I'll call you later on and possibly come spend the night with you."

"Maybe you should."

I smile and get out of bed to take my shower and dress. When I finish, there is a message from Sage on my two-way. All it says is, "I don't want no more drama!" What the hell does that mean? The last thing I need is Sage bringing me down with her drama-queen bullshit. But that is my best friend, and it comes with the territory. Sage and I are different but the same. We clicked from the moment Iris introduced us at one of her jam sessions. I met Iris at a Conflict Management Skills for Women seminar about four years ago. I was sent there by my job after getting into a verbal confrontation with one of the children's parent. She repeatedly sent her 10-month-old baby to the center without giving him a bath. The poor child's neck had that sour milk stench, and there was a line

Mahzi Kane   Tea Leaves

of dirt behind both his ears. I made it a part of my daily routine to give little Justin a bath, but after a week or so, I felt it was my duty as a responsible childcare provider to address the issue. Well, his mother got snippy, like I was the one with the dirty baby, and soon other teachers, parents and students were peeking out of classrooms to see what all the commotion was about. The center's director, Meagan, suspended me for one day and sent me to the seminar. She said that while I had a valid point, my methods were uncalled for and unprofessional. At the seminar, Iris, who was there doing research, was seated next to me and we struck up a causal conversation that turned into bighearted sisterhood.

Everyone thinks that Sage follows what I do as far as men are concerned, but that's not it at all. Sage wants a man so bad that I think being around a person such as myself makes her appreciate the freedom of being single. Sage is carefree and enjoys life to the fullest. I love her sense of humor and the way her smile lights up any room. And that girl will do anything she can to help somebody out of a jam. Growing up, I didn't really have close female relationships because my mother passed away when I was 3, so I grew up in the company of men and found it easier to connect with the guys instead of the girls. Of course there were Dad's many girlfriends who tried to play stand-in mom, but I wasn't buying the shit they attempted to sell. I have slight memories of my mother: I know she was beautiful, spunky and smart, with the prettiest laugh ever. It came from way down inside of her, and it made others laugh too. Whenever I feel really sad, like I'm missing her to death, I pull out a keepsake box that holds nothing but pictures of her, and it makes us feel closer. My dad tries to make up for my mother not being around, but there's no substitution. All of my life I've felt left out, like I stick out like the weird one because I didn't get the chance to do all the mother-daughter stuff that other girls do. Soon I eliminated the two girlfriends I managed to have and kept only guy friends because it didn't cause the pain of knowing that I am different. I am missing the most important part of my existence — the woman who brought me here. I talk to her every day in my mind, and I try to explain not being as good of a woman as I know she would have raised me to be. She would not approve of all the men that I've been with or how I treat them, especially Justice. They say I'm mean but that's because I'm honest. I knew that soon Justice would have popped the question, and that level of closeness and the obligation to be with him would be too much stability and no adventure. No thank you. My dad has given me stability all of my life: the best schools, curfews, attention, chores, activities and vacations so I don't need a man to teach me that. My father taught me to go for what I want in life and never be afraid to be the best and have the best since we are kings and queens by nature. We had plenty of fun, and I can admit that I was spoiled, but he also drummed the importance of taking care of business into my head on a daily basis.

I have no desire to go through the same thing over and over again, living one continuous day. I like experiencing the sparks that happen when the unexpected sneaks up to interrupt what's safe and sound, and it be OK because we've done the work to establish a base. Piccolo gives me all of this and I'm sure my mother would approve of any man that can effectively handle being mine. I leave Piccolo after some early morning loving to swing by Sage's, but first I stop home to check my messages. Only my dad called to say he loves me. Sage answers the door looking a hot mess. All that I can do is laugh because I know it's over more dumb shit.

"You look real stupid."

"Thanks for the comforting words, Ila."

"What's the deal?"

"Come in."

I walk into Sage's apartment still amazed that she did her entire apartment in a Chinese theme. It looks like a sushi bar exploded in here. It's cute, just a bit too much for my taste, but then again, that's why this is her apartment and not mine.

"OK, spill it."

"That fucking Bo had the balls to come into my place of business, into my shop and start acting a fool, girl!"

"Word! When, what did he do?"

"Like an hour ago. I'm so upset I left. I gave my clients to Katrina and Kelly, and I've been here trying to calm down."

"I can see that whatever happened got you stressing and puffing on that joint like a smoker. What did boy wonder do?"

"He got a ticket for driving my car without a license, and I told him that he has to pay for it, and he blew the fuck up like I'm asking him to give up his first-born. This was on the phone, and I was like, "You know what, Bo, fuck you and this young-boah drama. If you can't take responsibility for the ticket that you got, then I don't want no parts of you." He was fuming. He started screaming and yelling about how I think I'm gonna throw him to the curb over a dumb-ass parking ticket when he knows that I have the money. He went on and on about how it has to be somebody else because I would never let money come between us. I told him that I would, and it has. I told him not to call me anymore and I hung up the phone. Ten minutes later he came busting in my shop, grabbed me by the arm and drug me outside."

"Talk about that Jerry Springer shit! Was it crowded in Oasis?"

"Hell yes! I am mortified. How am I gonna be able to go in there and get respect from my employees when I got drug outside by a 17-year-old boy like he my fucking daddy?!"

"Calm down. Them chicks up in there go through worst and stop worrying about what other people think."

"I don't care what other people think; I care about running my business in peace."

"What happened when y'all got outside?"

"I told him to take his fucking hands off me. He did and then he apologized for acting crazy, but said he couldn't lose me. I told him that it was too late; I couldn't take his disrespectful attitude and now this tirade. He pushed me up against the glass, and that's when Katrina came out with a hot curling iron in her hand and told him that he better leave or she would call the cops."

"Did he let you go?"

"Of course. Bo is young and stupid, but he ain't trying to do a bid. He kept saying, "I love you, girl. I was gonna take you all the way to the top with me, but you fucked up, girl. We was gonna change the game, but you fucked up, girl." Man, whatever. He can take that drawing shit elsewhere, no matter how good the dick is."

"You keep picking the wrong men."

"No shit."

"If you spent less time looking for a man to sweep you off your feet and more time loving yourself, the right man would be drawn to you. Desperation gives off a bad smell, and sister-girl you are funky as a skunk."

"I'm not desperate. There is nothing wrong with wanting a man, Ila."

"Yes there is if you want a man more than you want what's best for yourself."

"I have a place to rest my head, a car, and I own and operate my own shop. How is that not the best for me?"

"Are you happy? And remember, you were settling for a teenager, trying to convince us that he was mature enough to handle it, and look where you are now."

Sage opens her mouth to respond but decides to say nothing.

"I don't know."

"You don't know if you're happy or not?"

"I'm happy to be alive and well, I'm happy to have you and the rest of the squad, I'm happy with my success. I'm not happy that I don't have a man to share it all with. I'm not happy that I can't talk to my mother. I'm not happy that I go from one jive-ass relationship to the next and I feel empty after every one of them. Do I seem happy to you?"

"What it looks like and what it is are often two separate things. It's not for me to say if you're happy or not. You know the answer, and if you don't, you'll figure it out 'cause sooner or later life will see to that shit, please believe me."

I persuade Sage to go back to her shop and finish out the rest of her day. No best friend of mine will let a youngster run her away from her own shit. We decide to hook up later for a party at Bash, a new nightclub that opened up on Delaware Avenue. I try my best to cheer her up before I leave because even though she can prevent her drama, I still don't like to see her hurting. I decide not to tell her about my night with Piccolo. I check my phone, and there is a message from Justice of all people saying, "Thinking of you, of us. No need to return my call. I still love you. Justice." There hasn't been enough time for me to miss him. I haven't had a second without Piccolo, either with him in the flesh or having him constantly in my thoughts. I don't know what I'd say to Justice. It's not as if I can tell him about the new man in my life, and what else is there to discuss? Our breakup? Who wants to go back there?

I pick Sage up at 10:00 PM. We go to the club, and I must say, it is on and popping. It is jam-packed by 11, and celebrities are sprinkled throughout the VIP section. Sage and I sweat to each hot track on the dance floor and break down all of those who thought they could fuck with us. When the DJ got to his house mix, we sit at the bar and order two shots of tequila, our personal drink. Once she went to New Mexico for a hair convention and bought back an authentic bottle with a worm at the bottom. The legend goes that the person who eats the worm will be the drunkest because the worm absorbs all the alcohol. Neither of us ate the worm, but we were both pretty wasted. After we finish our drinks, we walk to the ladies' room to freshen up, and that's when I decide to drop the bomb about Piccolo.

"Piccolo and I had sex last night and this morning!"

"Well, it's about time! Was it worth the wait is what I want to know? He looks like he can knock it out the box."

"A word hasn't been invented to properly describe this shit, Sage. It felt like a million firecrackers were going off inside of me all at once. He was a total gentleman; he gave me a bubble bath and washed my feet like a romantic movie scene. Ohhh, girl, I felt like a princess! Then we got good and nasty; doing it every which way there was to do it, freaky to the core with it, and I even did … you know what."

"I know what?"

"You know what."

"YOU SUCKED HIS DICK?!"

"Say it a little louder next time, I don't think the people in the parking lot heard you."

"How was it? Did you like it? Did he like it?"

"He liked it by the way he was going off, grabbing my hair and shit. I thought he was going to yank out one of my braids. I stopped in the middle and asked him, and he said "yeah." I don't think that he would lie."

"Jesus once told me that even bad head is good head, but he was an addict."

"I don't know why his mama named him Jesus, he don't know shit. Anyway, it wasn't what I thought it would be but I don't know if I exactly liked it, if that makes sense. It turned me on, you know, how much I was able to turn him on. It was empowering. I had him right where I wanted him."

"Do you think that you'll do it again?"

"To him, yeah. He might be the one."

"The one what?"

"The one: the man that I marry and spend the rest of eternity with, my soul mate."

"I ain't never, ever heard you talk about being with anybody forever, not even Justice. You really love Piccolo, don't you?"

"Yes, and it's really scaring the hell out of me. I'm vulnerable as shit but so comfortable around him that I feel safe."

"Is he seeing anyone else?"

"All the signs say 'no.'"

Mahzi Kane   Tea Leaves

"Why don't you ask him?"

"That's not my approach. I want him to want me. He gotta be the one to profess his love first, and then I know that I got him, feel me? Speaking of which, did you see how Clarke was opening her legs to him and telling him to help himself?"

"We all did. That one there is a trip. I never had beef with her, but that was wrong. We are squad. Yes, Piccolo is finer than fine, but he is yours. We were afraid that you were gonna reach across the table and slap the shit out of Clarke."

"It took everything that I had not to fuck her up, but I let her know in the bathroom that she better not even think about it or I'm going to beat the dog shit out of her."

"You said it just like that?"

"Just like that. I wanted to make my message plain so there's no misunderstandings about what I meant."

"I don't think that Clarke would cross that line."

"You can't put anything past a whore, friend or not."

We leave the ladies' room and run into a mutual friend, For Real. He got the nickname because after everything somebody says, he replies, "For real?" He's real cool people, like a big-brother type. We used to hang out on campus, get high, all that kind of stuff. He tells us about an after-hours spot that he and his crew are heading to and asks us to come. We walk out to the limousine he rented to do it up big for his birthday. Sage and I get in and say "hello" to all of the occupants while For Real goes back into the club to round up the rest of his crew.

"I don't know why Travis keeps piling people up in the freaking limo. God! This is not a hoop ride from the 'hood."

A chick with a big mouth. One of her wiser friends tries to get her to simmer down. She'd be wise to listen because either she's stupid or pissy drunk, and that makes her an ass-whipping waiting to happen.

"Travis keeps bringing all these bitches in the limo. Not too many of us can fit back here comfortably. I don't want any of those bitches smashing my fur. God!"

"Listen Barbie, I think it is, we all were asked to come along, so relax and be easy. The other spot isn't far."

"That's not the point, whatever your name is."

"Ila."

"Excuse me?"

"My name. It's Ila."

"Whatever. My fur is going to be ruined because Travis keeps piling bitches into the limo."

"For Real can do whatever he wants, it is his birthday."

"Who is For Real?"

"Travis."

"Oh, how cute, your little hood names, that is. All I know is that not one more bitch is getting into this limo, or I'm going home."

"Go the fuck home then! Don't nobody feel like hearing your snotty, high-and-mighty ass complain for the rest of the night anyway. Whining over a fur coat. Who the fuck wears a fur in June any damn way! I don't know about the other females up in here, but I'm not gonna be too many more bitches."

"What are you gonna do? Put me out? You BITCHES — "

Mahzi Kane   Tea Leaves

That is it. I've had all that I will take. I grip Barbie up by the back of her head and slam her down, face first, into the limousine floor. I flip her over and she starts clawing at my braids so I punch her in the face until she realizes how helpless she really is and I'm the boss. Her legs flail, her arms windmill a mile a minute and she screams bloody murder like a fool.

"Now, who's the bitch?" I punch her in the stomach and grip her by the neck. Next thing I know, For Real is pulling me off of her.

"I bet you'll think twice before you start coming out your mouth wrong to people you don't know."

"I'm pressing charges! You are going to jail! I can't believe this is happening to me! Travis, you better do something right now. Call the police!"

"Fall back, Barbie."

"But Travis, she fucking attacked me! I've been assaulted!"

"Shut the fuck up, Barbie, damn!"

For Real turns to me after putting his little friend in her place to make sure I am calm. I tell him to watch the company he keeps because somebody will hurt that girl one day and ask him has he learned nothing from O.J. and Kobe. Sage and I decide not to roll with them after all. I'm getting too old for this fighting bullshit, but I refuse to be disrespected and besides, Barbie had that shit coming.

reADY.AvAiLAbLe.WAiting: t o YA

THEY SAY YOU NEVER KNOW a person until you live with them and that is the God's honest truth. Before now, I rarely paid attention to how steadfast Sage is about her business and about doing hair in general. She has stacks of books to keep up on all of the latest styles and trends. Her bathroom looks like a beauty supply store. All I use is TCB hair grease and holding spray. She said that she's going to have me going natural in no time. I think my hair is too nappy to go without a perm, but Sage said that once it's healthy, I'll be surprised at the real hair I've been hiding. Staying with Sage is giving me the chance to see a different side of her, not just the mack. Don't get it twisted, Sage does have a lot of male friends, ex-boyfriends and those that fall somewhere in the middle. The first night I got here, her ex-young boyfriend, whatever he is or was, called her nonstop for four hours begging her to take him back. When we stopped answering the phone, he left messages ranging from depressing to explosive. I was biting my fingernails thinking that he would show up at her apartment and continue the drama. Sage assured me that he was all talk and I guess she's right because he never did show up. I notice that Sage has something missing that surfaces whenever we talk about our moms. I can tell that it is a sensitive subject so I'm leaving it alone. My mom's feelings are hurt because I am here. She said that my soul will rot with the devil if I start being fast like Sage. Her gossiping church friends have convinced my mom that Ila and Sage are loose jezebels. I tell my mom not to believe everything people tell her, in case she hears anything about Danielle or about me sleeping with Lamont.

Currently, there is no me and Lamont. I have not spoken to him and not because I don't want to, but because he has not contacted me. The phone at my old place is disconnected, which is no excuse because I have a cell phone that he convinced me to get. A part of me wants to call him, but the other part of me is terrified of what he will say. Danielle says he is the last person I should be worried about. She says: "That's what you get. So busy with your head up Lamont's ass that you weren't paying attention to Pia. Now you ain't got a place to live or a man to keep you warm at night. Well, you never had that, but now you don't even have the sneaky leftovers that you swore was the bomb. I am glad he hasn't called and you should be too. What you need is a new man so you can forget Lamont."

Danielle set me up on a blind date, which I despise, but maybe she has a point. I need to feel like I'm moving toward something, even if I'm not sure if it is over between Lamont and I. The guy that I'm meeting is named Circus. I don't know what to expect. Dani describes him as stocky with freckles, reddish-brown hair and a connected beard, like Malcolm X after his hajj to Mecca. I like a full beard on a man. He's picking me up tonight to go to a movie. I've been nervous since she set it up, and it feels awkward talking to him on the phone, like I'm totally hopeless and cannot find my own dates. When Sage found out that I was going out with a man other than Lamont, she did a cartwheel in the middle of the living room. She's happy that I'm doing anything other than waiting for Lamont to call. She says you never put all of your eggs in one basket; you never know how many might be rotten. God must be smiling down on me. I missed a call from Lamont. My stomach trembles, and my shaky hand cannot hold the telephone steady. I take three cleansing breaths and dial the number to Auto World.

"Lamont speaking, how can I help you today?"

"For starters, you can explain why I have not heard from you in close to a month?"

"You would not believe the hectic schedule that I've been having, sweetness."

"Don't call me "sweetness," and I guess your schedule would be busy, preparing for a new baby and all."

Lamont is quiet. The knots in my stomach get tighter, and I feel like I will throw up.

"Is it true? Are you and Felicia having another baby?"

"Where did you hear that?"

"Is it true?"

"Let me explain."

"There is nothing to explain! All this time you've had me under the impression that we were going to be together. How is that possible if you and your wife are having another baby?"

"What does that have to do with me and you? My children and my family shouldn't stop our love, not true love anyway. I need you in my life, Toya. I didn't want this to happen, but it has, and I have to deal with it."

"But I don't."

"Are you trying to tell me that you still don't want me? C'mon, be real. I know you do, sweetness, I can hear it in your voice."

"Why is our love always the reason to make me do the wrong thing? Why isn't it true enough to make you do the right thing?"

"Look, I don't need this extra stress; I have a wife and kids at home, which you knew from the gate. This is about the real thing, not the right thing. I can't leave them; I won't leave them, and I don't want to. But I still want you, and I know you want me."

"I want happiness, and this doesn't make me happy anymore. Felicia called me at my job, at my JOB — this is serious, Lamont. I don't know what she's capable of doing and I can't jeopardize that."

"I'll handle her."

"Like you've been handling her? How does she know where I work, where I lived? She even knows my mama's name! Explain that."

"I don't have to explain shit, you're not my wife. Look, if you wanna go, then go. I got plenty more waiting to take your place. It's up to you."

What could I say? The man that I love, the one that I broke all my rules for is telling me that I can go. Like it's as simple as deciding what to order at a restaurant. I put my morals on the back burner for the promise of being with him, and his bottom line is that I'm replaceable.

"Let me tell you something: Neither you nor your dick is that good for you to talk to me like this. How can you treat me this way, Lamont? You said you loved me, but I guess it was what you had to say so you could have the best of both worlds. Get whoever you want, have as many babies with your wife as you like. I'm done being your fool."

I am in tears by the time the receiver hits the base. Everybody was right, and I didn't listen. Why am I so stupid? If he really wants to leave his wife, he would have already left. My dad sure as hell left my mom; I don't even know him. I thought that I was good enough. I could give him a home. I could give him babies, so why shouldn't he leave his wife

Mahzi Kane   Tea Leaves

for me? I didn't get it. He doesn't want to, and that is something that I would never have accepted until it came straight from his mouth. I am glad that Sage is at work. I don't want anyone seeing me like this.

After three hours of crying and throwing out every picture or item that Lamont ever gave me, I wolf down two giant-sized bags of cheese curls and a liter of diet soda. Comfort food is a crock of bull because I still feel like nothing. I get up from the spot that I was stuck in and look in the mirror.

"Get it together, Toya. Getting fatter is not the solution. He is not worth it, and I'm worth more. Move on. I can do it, and if I can't, I'll die trying."

I go to the guestroom that's temporarily mine and look for an outfit to wear for my date with Circus. I contemplate calling him to cancel, but for what? To sit here and eat my way into depression? It is sad to say, but I'm not the first nor will I be the last to have my heart broken. What's even sadder is that I'll take Lamont back in a flash if he'd be true to his word. I slip into my pink jeans and matching shirt. Clarke hates this outfit. She said that I look like a bag of cotton candy. Clarke has lots to say about the way I dress, but I try not to let it affect me. It just makes me wonder why she's so concerned with the way that I look. After I curl my hair, I put on my white sneakers and wait for Circus to arrive. When the bell rings, I almost don't answer it, but on the third ring, I run to the intercom and say "hello."

"Is Toya here?"

"Hi, Circus?"

"I was starting to think that you stood me up. Are you ready?"

"Yes. I'll be down in a second."

Mahzi Kane   Tea Leaves

I check myself in the mirror, and I must admit, I look good for someone that was dumped by her married boyfriend. I go downstairs, and Circus doesn't look half bad. He's no Lamont, but he's not ugly. He hands me a bouquet of flowers, earning major cool points. He opens the door of his car for me and closes it after I get inside. I don't know what kind of car this is, but it's really nice. He is blasting a rap song, which I can't stand, so I ask him to turn it down.

"Sorry about that."

"That's OK. I like gospel music."

"Oh, I'm not into that. I guess you're a churchgoer, then?"

"I haven't been lately, but I am very religious. I'm surprised that Dani hasn't told you that we've been born and raised in the church."

"Danielle doesn't really talk about church much."

"I can only imagine what she does talk about."

We laugh and proceed to the theater, the whole time finding out different things about one another that were not covered in our phone conversations. I find out that Circus was recently fired from his job. He tried to switch a display from his store with that from another store in the mall so that when the salesperson went to look for the item, it wouldn't be there and it'd be a big, funny prank. The problem is, he got caught trying to steal the other display. Why am I not surprised that this guy is a clown? The rest of our date is nothing more than a chronicle of immature stories. I can't enjoy the movie because he falls out laughing at anything with a hint of funny. The popcorn and Raisinets lodged between his teeth halt any considerations of a goodnight kiss. When he drops me off, he leans in, but all he gets is cheek. Circus is out of cool points. Dani owes me big time for this one.

The next day, I use my breaks to check out the guys in the office. I come up with two people whom I think I'd like to date and whom I think would be interested in me. One guy is Levi; he's a manager for another region. The other is David, who recently came out of the new employee training class. I call Sage to ask her what I should do, and she advises that I make small talk. I ask how do I decide which guy to approach, and she says both; it's too soon for me to make a choice. I'm giving her way a try since my way hasn't gotten me far at all. I spot David at the vending machine and rack my brain for something brilliant to say.

"Nice shirt."

"Thank you. There's nothing like getting a compliment from a pretty woman."

"Thank you. There's nothing like having a handsome man call me pretty. Hi, I'm Toya."

"Nice to meet you, Toya. I'm David."

"You just started, right?"

"Yeah. This is my third week."

"How do you like it thus far at CTI?"

"It's good. It'll be a steady paycheck, so I can't complain. How long have you been here?"

"Almost three years."

"I guess you more than like your job then?"

"Yes. I'm looking to go for a Patient's Services position as soon as one comes up on the board."

"Drive and ambition. I like those qualities in a woman."

"Maybe you can take me out and see if there are any other qualities that I have that you may like."

Did I say that? I have never been able to be this forward. I think I could get used to it though.

Mahzi Kane   Tea Leaves

Granting a man's every whim has left a nasty taste in my mouth and a dent in my heart.

"I'd like that, I'd like that a lot. How about I come by your desk later and we can exchange numbers? I don't carry pens. Wouldn't want to be considered a player, you know."

"Sure thing. I'll be waiting. Bye, David."

He seems nice. I didn't even think to ask if he has a girlfriend or wife before extending an invitation for a date. Will I ever learn? For the rest of the day, I check and recheck my hair and breath while peeking over my cubicle to see if David is coming. Just when I am about to give up hope, he arrives.

"Sorry that I took long. I wanted to make my quota before I got up from my desk. Here's my number."

"That's OK, I was busy myself. Before I take your number, are you single? It totally slipped my mind to ask."

"Yes. I would have told you then if I was seeing somebody. I'm not the player type, remember?"

"Good. Here's my number."

"I was thinking, if you're not busy tonight, maybe I could come over and watch a movie. I like casual things, so we can talk some more."

"I'd like that. Here's my address. Give me a call around 6."

"Talk to you then, Toya."

I call Sage to make sure she doesn't have plans. I don't want to step on her toes, overstay my welcome or get too comfortable. She keeps telling me that I don't have to rush to find my own place, but I don't want to lose sight of my goal. She said that she'll be at the shop late and I'll have the apartment to myself. The end of the day comes and

I see David on the elevator so I tell him to come over at 7. Once at home, I shower, change, straighten up a bit and order hoagies. I pull out my favorite movies for him to decide which one we will watch first. At 7:00 on the dot, the doorbell rings. I buzz him in and wait. When he enters, he looks nice and neat. David is my height and about my weight with brown skin like a cuddly teddy bear. He has a clean, baby face and adoring eyes. He has an earring in his nose, which doesn't quite go with the clean-cut, boy-next-door appearance, but like they say, everything isn't as it seems. I offer him a seat on the couch.

"I didn't notice the nose ring at work."

"I don't wear it at work; it's not business-like."

"So that would mean that you're here for pleasure?"

"Certainly."

The next thing I know, we are on the living room floor ripping each other's clothes off. This is good, really good, and on the first night! I am such a slut. If my mama could see me, she'd keel over from shame. I didn't think anyone except Lamont could make me feel like this. Boy, was I stupid. David tosses me back and forth around the living room like I weigh 98 pounds. He smacks it, flips it and almost rips it out. It is one hell of an adrenaline rush. Unlike Lamont, David lasts a long time, and afterward, he does not push me away. We cuddle and it fills me with contentment, something that was a distant hope when I was with Lamont.

"Toya, I apologize for not controlling myself. I've wanted to do this since the first time I saw you, since you spoke the first word to me. I will understand if you want me to leave."

"David, we didn't do anything that I didn't want to do. You have been nothing but a gentleman since I met you. I hope that you don't think this is how I get down because it's not. Having sex on the first date is new for me. Please don't think I am loose."

"I would never think that about you, Toya. You're hard-working, beautiful, and from what I can tell, a decent young lady."

"Thanks for saying that. I feel better."

"Good. Now what do you have for me to eat? I've worked up a serious appetite."

*

Since David came over, we're getting closer as the days go by. We talk to each other on the phone about three times a week. Conversations with Lamont felt one-sided, like I was the one always answering his questions or prying to get his opinion on a subject. David and I share a love for reading, and we spend hours talking about books that we've read and loved, and also the ones we hated or didn't get. We eat lunch together, and he comes to my desk in the morning and in the afternoon. In our time spent together, we divulge so much and learn our common areas. I am happy that he too was raised in the church. His parents married last year after being separated for seven years, proving that if it's meant to be, it will. When you really love a person, you do what has to be done to be with them, or not be with them. He has a knack for making me laugh and not about stupid things like Circus. I feel like I'm 16 when I'm with him, so young and giddy. I remind myself to take it slow because there's no rush especially since I still love Lamont. I know that's not good, but I can't just turn it off. I try hating him; I try pretending like it never happened, but none of it works. The only thing that I haven't tried yet is talking about how I feel to my girls.

Today in the bathroom, Kima and Agnes make snide comments about David, saying he is my new boyfriend. I tell them that David and I are friends. Kima says that she hears differently, and I tell her to stop believing everything that she hears. As I leave, I hear Agnes say that she doesn't care what I said, she knows that I'm fucking him. David and I are more than friends, but it is nobody's business but our own. Working in an office environment is a major hassle. Everybody is always watching. Somebody comes to your desk three times in a row, and by the end of the day, the rumor mill has y'all married with children and on the brink of divorce. I don't even talk to any of the girls anymore. I tried to make real friends when I first started, but I learned the hard way that the people here want to get in your business and tell it to someone else for it to be thrown back up in your face later. I don't need that, and besides, I have enough girlfriends.

On my way to the fax machine, I bump into Amir, or I should say he bumps into me. Amir has a cute thing going on, but he knows it. Every other female at this job has been throwing her panties at him at one time or another, except me. Amir is like Lamont: cocky, arrogant and self-absorbed. The last thing I need is another Lamont.

"Hey, Toya, my bad. You know a brother is in a rush."

"Don't run me over trying to get to wherever it is that you're going."

"Where I was going don't matter because I'm here with you. Wassup?"

"The sky and the ceiling. What's up with you?"

"The real question is what is up with us? I'm saying, Toya, I've been checking you out, making eye contact with you and all, but you still ain't showing interest in a brother. Wassup with that?"

"Every girl in here wants you, Amir. Why are you worried about me?"

"For that reason."

"You're not my type."

"And what is your type?"

Amir asks the question as he leans his body into mine, letting the smell of his musk cologne tickle my nose. My eyes flutter, and for a minute I forget that we are at work.

"The type that doesn't pin me up against copy machines."

"You know you like it, don't front. I've dealt with your type of chick before: goes to church, some nigga done broke your heart, and all you looking for is a man to be the one. Well, baby, I'm that real nigga for you, just give me a chance. Let me teach you a few things."

"I'm not in the market for any lessons. I have somebody who's putting in work just fine, thank you."

"You mean choirboy David?"

I try to hide the shock and surprise, but I think it's shining through. Amir is the last person that I want to know about David. I like David and he's cool to hang out with, but there is something about Amir that brings out my bad girl. And he is right; I do like it.

"Yea, I heard that he be at your desk and y'all eat lunch together and all that. That's cute, but eating at your desk is not my idea of fun."

"What is your idea of fun then?"

"Eating you on my desk."

My mouth drops wide open. How can he be this raunchy? And yet I'm still here. Amir is not the kind of man that is good for me, and I know it, but I know that I want him with everything that I am. I want him to do all the nasty things that lurk in those arousing eyes. Amir licked his lips, flashes his "I got you" grin and props his chin on his hand while he waits for me to respond.

"Looks like I got you speechless. Think about it and come by my office when you think of an answer."

He walks away with his chest sticking out like the chicken hawk. I, on the other hand, stand there like a deer caught in a set of headlights. Suddenly I feel a pair of arms wrap around my waist. I spin around and it is David smiling at me with an angel's halo.

"Not here, David. People will talk."

"They already talk. I missed you."

"I love being missed, but David we have to be smart. The company discourages relationships at the workplace. You know I'm trying to get a promotion soon. Help me out."

"Sorry, didn't mean to risk your job advancement. I was only trying to show you how I feel. Let me go back to my desk and give you some space. Wouldn't want people to talk."

"David, wait, David — "

He is gone. Hurting his feelings is the last thing I intend to do, but having another person ask me about David is something that I am trying to avoid by all means. My heart is being torn into three parts. I still love Lamont, which sickens me to even admit; I like David, and he is the type of man to consider starting a real relationship with; and then there's Amir, and all I want from him is hot, butt-naked sex. Something has got to be wrong with me.

When I get back to my desk, there is an email announcing impromptu overtime for today and tomorrow. I jump on it and email my supervisor to let him know I would be staying an extra two hours both days. Then I email David and let him know that I'd have to take a rain check on our dinner date tonight. His response read, "Fine." See, this is the mess that I don't need. I can't walk around on eggshells trying not to damage a man's emotions or his pride. Who's walking on eggshells for me?

Five other people stay for overtime, including Amir. I can't keep my mind off of him and his invite to come to his office. It's like there's an angel on one shoulder and the devil on the other, each trying to persuade me to see things their way. The devil is winning. Nervously and having no idea of what I'm going to say or do, I walk to Amir's office around the corner and at the back of the hallway. As I approach I can see that his door is closed. For a minute, I contemplate if this is a door that I truly want to enter because once I go in, there is no turning back. I tap lightly on the door and bite my bottom lip as I wait for Amir to answer. He opens the door and without saying a word, he grabs me by the arm, closes the door and backs me against the wall. He is all over me, and all I can do is blush like an inexperienced schoolgirl. Amir is in total control. He whispers freaky things in my ear while he fondles every part of my body. After he rips my panties off, he hurls me up on his desk and fulfills his racy promise. He flips me over and takes me from behind like no other man has ever done. I am so loud, I have to stuff my underwear in my mouth to muffle the pleasure-filled incantations that pour from me. When we are done, Amir looks at me like the pussycat that ate the canary.

"I knew you'd come. And I know that you'll be back. If you don't mind, we both have work to finish. Come see me tomorrow, chocolate thunder."

I smile, kiss him and leave. As I walk back to my desk, my thighs ache with a feeling that I haven't felt since I lost my virginity. Back at my desk, it feels as if Amir is still inside of me. My back shudders and tingles run throughout me as I replay the event over and over in my head. He has my nose open and I can't wait until tomorrow.

*

I walk in the door, and Sage sits on the couch watching music videos. Her dream is to snag an entertainer and fill her days with shopping and being the perfect Hollywood wife. Somehow I doubt that any one of these guys in the video will find her in a Philly natural hair salon.

"Wassup, Sage?"

"Nada, holmes. Wassup with you?"

"Same old, same old. They have overtime, so I had to take advantage. Did anyone call for me?"

"Yup, David called you like three times."

"I wonder why he didn't call me at work."

"I asked him. He said because he wanted to speak to you when you came home."

"Oh OK. Guess what? Oh, you'll never guess! I just had an out-of-body experience. It defies description; it was like heaven right here on earth."

"What happened? Did you get a raise, the promotion you wanted? Did you win the lottery, what?"

"Girl, no. Me and Amir had the best sex of my entire life in his office!"

"Oh my God, Toya, I can't believe you! How did this happen? Miss Lady, you learning the ropes quickly I see."

"It all sorta happened on its own. Amir bumped into me at the copy machine. He started talking that talk, and then one thing led to the next. It was great, Sage. I think I'm whipped. I can't stop smiling."

"I can see that. Settle down, you have to keep your head. First off, never let a man know that you're open after the first time. If you do, soon he'll be dogging you out, calling you at 3 in the morning for ass. Second of all, there's David, and you can't slip up on your pimp game. Always keep your options open. Third of all, Amir is a hoe, and remember, we got no love for them."

"I don't love him, but I sure do like how he put that thang down."

"Listen at you! You are too much. Take a puff of this sticky icky to calm your ass down."

"You know I don't smoke."

"I thought you didn't fuck at your job either, but you never can tell. Take a puff. God put this here for you and me."

We fall out laughing. What the hell, it can't hurt me. I take a pull off the joint and don't feel a thing, so I take another one. Soon I am grooving and the room spins, but not in a scary way. The phone rings and Sage grabs it.

"It's David."

"Hey, David, wassup?"

"Nothing. What's wrong with you?"

"Nothing. Why do you ask?"

"You sound different."

"Just tired. I heard you called me a few times. What's your deal?"

"Do you know Lamont?'

"Huh?"

I sit straight up and am sober as all heck. Sage sees the look of urgency on my face and mutes the television.

Mahzi Kane Tea Leaves

"I said, do you know Lamont?"

"Why are you asking me about Lamont? I thought you said that you had no interest in knowing about my past relationships?"

"That was before I found out that you are the whore that's been fucking my sister's husband."

"Felicia?"

"How could you, Toya? The sanctity of marriage is sacred and you almost ruined that for my sister and over what? The promise that Lamont would leave her and my nieces and come to be with your fat, trifling ass?"

"Wait one minute, jerk-off. It wasn't all that when you were up in my fat, trifling behind, now was it?'

"Toya, you are a fucking liar!"

"How did I lie?"

"Because I showed you a picture of Felicia in my wallet, and you could have said something — no, you *should* have said something."

"What would I say? Oh, I've been madly in love with her husband and playing the fool waiting for him to love me back? For what?"

"To be an adult and own up to what you did."

"Look, David, I'm sorry that I didn't say anything, but I really don't see what that would have accomplished. I don't have to explain how I feel about Lamont because it's none of your business. If you still want to get to know me, you can. If not, I understand, and that's your right."

"I guess you are the slut you desperately tried to convince me that you weren't. Don't say shit to me because I'm not saying one word to you. You won't even catch me looking in your direction. Goddamn you, adulterer."

"What was that about?"

"Only in my life could something like this happen! Turns out that David is Felicia's brother. Lamont's wife Felicia. Only I could manage to run off a nice, intellectual and all around nice guy."

"Her brother! Six degrees of separation like a muthafucka."

"What does that mean?"

"Six degrees of separation is a theory that every sixth person I know is somebody that you know and vice versa. In that way, we are all connected."

"I feel like the scum of the earth."

"For what? Yes, you made a huge mistake with the Lamont situation. But who is David to judge you? I'm sure he's done some not-so-nice things before. I don't buy that clean choirboy, I-always-do-the-right-thing act. Believe me, we all have skeletons in our closets. Your biggest bone just popped out. Why feel bad about it? That's life, fuck it, and move on."

"But David is really upset with me. He said things that only a hurt and disappointed person would say and you know what, he's right. I am a slut. I had sex with David on the first night, with Amir after one conversation, and on top of that, I have been sleeping with another's woman husband. I deserve everything I get."

"Quit the pity party, for goodness' sake! None of what you describe makes you a villain. Don't make what other people think about you alter what you think about you. Public opinion does not decide your fate. If it did, I'd be stoned in the town square for the things that I have done and will continue to do. We have one life to live, and I say live it to the fullest. Life has enough rules on its own without letting other's impose their moral standard just because you decide to throw caution

Mahzi Kane   Tea Leaves

to the wind and do what feels good in the moment. As long as you can live with the outcome, there is nothing wrong with having a good time. Some may say that's not responsible, but shit, we only get to do this once, so I say make the journey un-fucking-forgettable 'cause it'd be a huge waste not to. My way isn't the best way, but it's all I've got."

"I hear you, but I still can't help but to feel like a failure. Nothing is the way it should be. None of this is what I ever planned on, and it's not making me happy. I'm miserable, if I have to tell the God's honest truth. I don't know who I am right now. I have no idea what I want anymore because everything I had planned was all tied to Lamont. I need to be alone. Later, Sage."

I lay in my bed reading my favorite Bible verses, trying to gain the understanding that I know is lurking behind my pain. I turn to where is says Jesus turned water to wine. The message that I draw from it is that with the right state of mind, we can make the best of the worst situation and you can pass any test put before you. There was a time when all my family had to eat was canned tuna, but my mama made it taste like roasted turkey with mashed potatoes and gravy. And she made it stretch to feed all of us and sustain our bodies. Our everyday miracle.

"Toya, pick up the phone."

"Hello, this is Toya."

"Hello, sweetness, I'm missing you."

"Who is this? Lamont?'

"Damn, it's like that? You have to ask who it is?"

"What do you want?'

"You. I need you and some of that sweet loving. How about we meet at our special place in an hour, you know, for old times' sake?"

"Since your wife's brother called me a no-good adulterer for trying to break up y'all marriage, I think I'm going to have to pass on that. You're not worth ruining my reputation any more than I already have."

"Why are you always letting outside shit affect what me and you got?"

"We don't have ANYTHING, Lamont! That is what I haven't been getting all of this time. It was sneaky sex, that's all, and I can get that from a man who doesn't have a wife. We are both selfish people, only after what we wanted for ourselves this whole time. And after the way you spoke to me, you expect me to creep out of my bed and slink into a hotel with you? I can't go that low for you anymore. Go get one of the many replacements you threw up in my face. Lamont, let me be. Toya is no longer easy and convenient coochie for you."

I hang up and bawl like a baby. Not because my feelings ache, which they do, but because I've mishandled people by being selfish. I cry because while I can't be with Lamont, I still love him. I weep the dread of admitting that I did look at myself as less than, which allowed me to settle for mistress instead of misses. I wipe away the blues of knowing that all of this time I have been a hypocrite. And finally, I wail for myself, because I don't know who I am or how to find out.

Chapter Twelve

D rAmA Q ueen : S Ag e

TOYA IS GOING THROUGH ROUGH
TIMES. I wish I had plenty of advice for her or
words of wisdom to try to make it all make sense,
but I don't. I barely know what the hell I'm doing
with my own love life. After that Bo fiasco, I have
little faith in my ability to make good decisions
when choosing men. So there's nothing else for me
to do except work and party. Katrina and I are
going for drinks after work.

Katrina's been at Oasis since its origin, and is
someone that I can trust. She's a talented flower
child: curly, bushy hair, peace sign medallions, and
that girl wears the oddest things. But it's all her, and
I appreciate that. Katrina is a free spirit and an
optimist. Her glass is always half full. I'm the only
one at the shop who knows that she is gay but of
course everyone suspects it. I can hang out with
Katrina because she's not one of those angry
lesbians that man-bash. She's outgoing with guys,
and we always have a ball. Gay or not, she's cool as
hell.

It has been almost two and a half weeks since
I had sex, and I'm about to pull my hair out at the
roots in huge, frustrated clumps. My sex drive is off
the meter. I love sex and I'm not afraid or ashamed
to admit it. Many men have called me a nympho-
maniac, but I don't believe that at all. Sex is my
natural high. I like feeling good, and there's nothing

like the intimacy to be had when you engage in sex. Ever since I lost my virginity, I've been hooked. It took me a while to have sex. I had heard horror stories from girls at school and my older cousins about the pain of getting your cherry popped. I was determined to keep mine intact until I met Malik. Sex is the one thing I know for sure that I'm good at — it's almost like a call to greatness to share this highly coveted and appreciated talent. It's the notes from Jimi's guitar mixed with the power coils of picked-out Afros marching in unison; sex is my independence, it's where I can fly and soar and twirl and be all of who I am, unadulterated, unfiltered, wild and jungle-like; sex is my playground, my carnival, land of make believe, and every other magical place where we expect to be entertained and mesmerized.

After work, Katrina and I go to Cool Currents for happy hour. Half-way through our bottle of white wine, I have a nice buzz going on as Katrina vents about the ongoing troubles that she's been having with her girlfriend. I can't fathom going through the bullshit that I endure from men with somebody that bleeds once a month just like I do. That's way too much for me, but hey, she's free to live her life just like I am free to live mines. She don't need my permission.

The music is hot tonight. They are playing the oldies and the goodies. Katrina and I sing along to our favorite songs. I spot Gordon and Slick, two guys from the party scene. Gordon is a drummer in a band. He's damn good and looks even better. He is tall, dark and handsome with nice hands. Hands that look like they are made for holding ass. Slick was born with the gift of gab. He can sell anything to anybody whether business or pleasure. Slick is one of those salesmen for top-of-the line children's toys. You have to be a special individual to walk up to a complete stranger on the street, go into a pitch and come out with a sale. Slick is not drop-dead gorgeous, but he has this sexy thing going on, plus the grapevine says he lays his pipe something fierce. I wave them over to buy the next round of tequila shots.

"Hey, ladies."

"Hey, fellas, what's the deal?"

"A stone-cold groove."

"Gordon and Slick, this is my girl Katrina from the shop."

"Hey, guys."

"Nice to meet you," Gordon and Slick chime in unison. We throw back shots like sailors at port and before any of us know it, we are 100% shit-faced. Both Slick and Gordon try to get us back to their places until Katrina blurts out that she is gay.

"I'm saying Sage, what are you trying to get into tonight?"

"Depends on what you have in mind, Slick."

"It's a full moon, ripe for some extra freaky shit. I know my man Gordon is down."

"Without question. So you tell us what you in the mood for, Sage."

"A true ménage à trois scene, huh? What a sexy proposition."

"You said it, we didn't."

"I need to use the bathroom. C'mon, girl, let's go."

Katrina and I stumble to the ladies' room, where we erupt into drunken laughter.

"I can't believe they are trying to get me in a threesome."

"Are you gonna do it?"

"I don't know. Do you think I should?"

"If it was two chicks, I know I would, but you're not me. Do you know them like that?"

"I know them enough to know that they won't try any dirty shit. And I am about due for some good sex. Fuck it, why not?"

"Go 'head with your bad ass. I'm outta here. Have fun and I will see you at work."

Back at my place, my two joy boys and myself creep into my bedroom so that we don't wake Toya. We roll up a joint to really get the party going. Slick pops a couple pills and Gordon downs yet another 40 ounce, and then it is on. I must say that they do not disappoint. They do things to me that I've only seen in movies. I am the focus, the center of worship, the star lighting up the darkness – my chance to be the consummate alpha female who directs and leads our fun. It is exhilarating like a roller coaster, and not the rinky-dink kind, I'm talking splash waterfalls. They tinker with my erogenous zones and open up all my favorite spots. Them in my middle, me in the middle of them, imaginations in flight, taking us to another world. Multiple sensations all over, a million untamed kisses all at once, four hands doing what I allow them to do. Their lips fight for position between my legs. One is a master manipulator of the clit, while the other prefers holes. My eyes roll back so much that I think they'll be stuck. Crazy moans mix with dirty words and screams for air. I compliment their performances, knowing how men love to please and they eagerly try unique moves to take me to the outer limits of desire. I am a freak me song riff directing two men who want to please me. They write lust notes with super sensual finger and tongue combinations that work my body for hours. Our energies play well together in a free-fall of spirited fucking. Stroke, suck, switch. Once the rhythm of double penetration is right, the adventure reaches new heights. We take turns watching the slither of mangled limbs, both of them attached to me, submitting to pleasures of the flesh from every angle. I alternate rides as if I am some kind of weightless wonder until the crevices of my thighs scream for an intermission. I cum for them and they cum for me. By the time we pass out, everything is numb.

Morning finds me up singing about how it feels to be a natural woman. Toya looks at me with a suspecting eye, but doesn't inquire and I don't offer. Sharing this type of stuff can be a dangerous thing. This is Ila-only information.

*

Lately I've been missing my mother. The distance between us would make you think we live miles away from one another. My mother has never been a mother to me. Trying to talk to her is like trying to scale a 50-foot wall in stilettos. She has fed and clothed me, put a roof over my head and made sure I received a good education, but she never shows a genuine interest in me as a person. I get little to no support, encouragement or enthusiasm from her. As a child, I felt alone, isolated and afraid. I saw my father abuse her from the time I can remember anything. I remember his yelling and ranting, broken dishes, lamps and furniture. I remember her crying and her bruises and the hatred I saw when she looked at him, and that I'd eventually see when she looked at me the more and more she blamed me for the beatings that didn't start until I was born. It's ironic, funny even, how she holds me liable for something that I had no control over, yet I don't fault her for something she had total control over. She could have left and taken us both away from that hell. She could have saved me from the insanity that took place in that house. How they would fight, and in hours I'd hear the creaking of their bed and her moans. They sounded so different from the cries. She sounded happy when the bed was creaking. Other than that, misery and sadness were her makeup. She could have given me a real childhood instead of the façade that I had to keep up so that no one grew suspicious of what was really going on behind our closed doors. I don't blame her. How can I? She was mentally, emotionally, spiritually and physically beat down and ripped apart. I wish she could have been strong enough to flee his madness, but she wasn't. We both endured the same nightmare, and I feel her pain. I just can't understand why she can't feel mine.

I've been thinking about relocating for a year or so. Someplace like Arizona or Atlanta. A part of me wants to see the landscapes of Arizona with their sandy-brown and burnt-orange hues for myself. I read in a magazine article that Atlanta is one of the top cities for black folk, and both spots are excellent for black-owned businesses. It's not that I don't like Philly; I guess I have grown tired of this big city with a small town attitude. Same kind of dress, same type of talk, same style of music. It can get sickening, lost in a land of make believe where they all seem hell bent on recreating the same music video look. I need people who embrace individuality as a rule.

Today is my day off. Toya went to work, and the only thing on my to-do list is nothing. I'm going to sit on the sofa and watch television. Maybe I'll tackle a couple of chapters from a book or listen to my favorite soulful classics and relax, and even that ain't etched in stone. The one absolute of the day is no men. A break is due. I prop myself up on the oversized pillows that almost jump off my sofa with a bowl of cereal in hand and flip on the tube with the other. By noon, I have seen DNA testing, trashy teen makeovers and a couple about to split up because the husband kept screwing the babysitters. There is no way in hell that I could sit and watch this junk day after day. Thank goodness I have a job.

I return to my spot on the sofa after fixing myself a Caesar salad. Just as I settle in, Toya bursts into the apartment. She startles me, I jump, and the salad flips into the air and lands on the floor. We scream and Toya slips on the rug behind the door and falls. Her pocketbook flies across the room and lands in one of the potted plants. I help Toya up off the floor, and then we clean up the mess in between laughs. Once calm, we sit and I can tell she is bothered by something bigger than a taking a spill.

"What is going on with you?"

"I got fired!"

"How the hell did you get fired?"

"I was reckless and sneaky, just too disgusting to even think about! I was fired for being me."

"You're not making any sense."

"None of what I have done makes sense! Where do I begin?"

"At the beginning."

"Since the first time that Amir and I had sex in his office, we have kinda started using overtime as a way to see one another."

"And by see one another, you mean fuck?"

"Yes."

"Let me guess, the big secret got out and you got fired?"

"Exactly. It was probably Kima. That girl has never liked me! She was talking trash about David being at my desk. She is too interested in me and what I do!"

"Who told doesn't matter. If you weren't doing it there, it wouldn't have been anything to tell. You cannot mix business with pleasure. It's one thing to have a one-time fling at the job, but y'all make that the spot. Girl, I don't know what to say about this one."

"You got your nerve! You had two guys at the same time. Yeah, I heard y'all, so don't try to preach to me about what's right. You don't have to say a word because I know that I made the dumbest mistake of my life. I wanted to advance in the company and get a real title behind my name. All of that is out of the window. I have to go start all over, and at what? What is wrong with me?!"

"First off, what I do in my own house is really no concern of yours. Secondly, remember that you are a guest, and it's quite unappreciative to throw shit in your hostess's face that you are only privy to 'cause I was nice enough to let you stay here. Thirdly, you are the dumbass that lost a job over sex. You and Amir should be guests on one of the crazy talk shows I saw this morning."

"Sage, that isn't funny. Do you realize that I don't have the house I rented anymore and now I'm out of a job? I love you, but I'm not trying to be here forever!"

"I love you too, and you won't! I'd give you a gig as a shampoo girl before I see that happen."

"The best part is Amir didn't get fired. They transferred him to another department."

"Wow that's fair. Corporate bullshit is what drove me to work for myself, but I have to say it, sweetie. You brought this on yourself."

"Like I don't know that, SAGE! Way to point out the obvious, oh wise one!"

Mahzi Kane   Tea Leaves

"Don't get snippy with me. We crew and you know how we roll. I got your back always, but don't get it fucked up, I will let you know when you are out of line. You can take it how you want to take it or not at all."

"I'm going for a walk. The air up in here is stale. Later."

I'm glad she left with that funky attitude. It's hard to be a player and not get played. I forgot that she lacks the common sense needed to maneuver man-and-woman relationships. I know, people in glass houses shouldn't throw stones, but I am well-aware of my problems concerning the opposite sex. I look for love in the wrong men, but I don't know that they are the wrong men until after it's too late. One thing for sure, I'll never lose my salon because of a man or sex no matter how great it may be to have them in my life. Of course the ultimate goal is to have a decent man and a good career, and that's the dream we all chase. I'm striving to stop searching for true love and let it find me instead. I hope I can stick to this new motto.

As soon as I get to work, Katrina probes to find out what happened with Gordon and Slick. Without affirming or denying, I manage to get her out of my face because my schedule is full, and the last thing I feel like doing is droning on about my sexual exploits. I don't need to keep talking about it - I was there. It's hectic as hell in the shop, and by the middle of the day I need a 15-minute break. Rosa, Marisol and Jamie all seem to be friendlier than usual with Katrina, and every time I turn around, one of them is at her station. I'm not jealous; it just strikes me as odd because they normally wouldn't touch Katrina with a 10-foot pole since they swear her secret mission is to turn them out. I decide to pull her card on it while we are in the back on break. She is smoking a cigarette as I puff on my clove stick.

"What's the deal with your new friends?'

"I was trying to figure out the same thing. I seem to be the shit up in here."

"You know? I peeped the swarm around your station, and it had me tripping. Watch them, girl, 'cause they stay caught up in he-said/she-said shit."

"Good looking out. I'll keep that in mind."

Leaving Katrina to finish her cigarette, I stop off at the ladies' room before my next client arrives. While inside the stall, two voices interrupt my quiet.

"Yessssss, Ana, she fucked both of them at the same time."

"That is nasty. I would have never thought!"

"Please, where have you been? If it's one thing she's known for, it's keeping her legs open. That's why I never bring my man up in here because I'll cut a bitch if they look wrong at what's mine even if she do pay me."

"Please, don't nobody want Tyrone but you, Marisol. Back to the gossip — where did she meet them?"

"Katrina said they were two guys that she already knew. They hooked up at the bar."

"So she did know them. That's not too bad. I've always been curious about having two guys at once."

"I ain't into all that. Even if she did know them, Sage needs to watch herself. That young dude was just up in here a month ago showing out, and now she's screwing two new dudes. She better slow down before she catches the HIV."

"Um, um, um. Juicy, juicy, juicy! Let's get back to our stations."

Mahzi Kane   Tea Leaves

In the confines of the stall, I stand mortified. Here I am listening to my employees talk about my personal business like it is front-page news. How could Katrina come back and run with the same snakes that have bitten her back out so many times before? I thought she was my friend. I burst from the stall, flinging the door back and knocking pictures from the wall. Everyone jumps and all eyes are on me as I emerge from the ladies' room. Katrina is at her station with Marisol, no doubt laughing at my expense.

"I need to talk to you out back, Katrina.

I point and make my way to the break area. I don't even wait for her to respond.

"Wassup, girl, you OK?"

"Fuck no. I thought we were cool, thought you were my dawg. Shit, I've told you things that only my extremely close friends know. I thought you were worthy of that information, but I see that you like the other bitches up in here. Can't wait to run your mouth!"

"What are you talking about, Sage? We are cool. You've been nothing but nice to me since I started here. Why you coming at me like this?"

"Cut the innocent act. Did you really think that the broads in here would keep a secret? I heard Marisol and Ana in the bathroom talking about how you told them that I fucked two guys that I picked up at the bar. Explain that shit, Judas."

Katrina's face says it all. I tap my foot with one hand on my hip while she bites at the corner of her mouth trying to come up with something to say.

"What can you say? There is nothing to be said to make this better. You came up in my shop telling my business like they aren't my employees! I hear them call you dyke day-in and day-out, and I stick up for you. You're foul, REAL foul. I got the right mind to fire your ass, but that wouldn't make me any better than you. Business is business, and you're good at what you do, but please know you are a step away from the unemployment line. On a personal level, we are through."

"Sage, I didn't mean — "

"Don't touch me, don't say shit to me. Tell it to your new friends."

As I yank my arm out of Katrina's reach, someone yells for me to get the phone.

"Fuck you, Katrina."

I storm from the back, and all eyes are on me. By now I am sure that everyone has heard the news, and I am beyond pissed.

"Marisol and Ana, I want to talk to y'all in the back as soon as I'm finished with this call."

Marisol and Ana glance at one another not knowing what to anticipate. They look to Katrina, but she avoids their eye contact. Marisol starts nibbling at her nails, something she only does when she is caught in a lie.

"Oasis, Sage speaking."

"Ms. Warner, this is your doctor's office."

"Yes?"

"We're calling to schedule an appointment.'

"I was there last week."

"I know and your Pap smear came back abnormal. You have to come back in."

"What's wrong?"

"We're not at liberty to discuss that information with you. Your doctor will do that. When can you come in to the office?"

"Today. Tomorrow. Whenever."

"OK, we'll see you tomorrow at 9:30 a.m. Is that OK?"

"Yes, I'll be there. Thank you."

I sit in my chair paralyzed. Am I pregnant, do I have a disease, am I dying, what is going on? I take three deep, cleansing breaths and remove my face from my hands. Now is not the time or place to deal with a slew of maybes, and there is no way that I can leave early because I am booked solid. Nothing left to do except put bitches in their place and finish out the day. I rise from my chair and head to the back. I hear Marisol and Ana's voices, but can't make out what is being said. Once they see me, they shut the hell up.

"Look, I don't care who told who what, but this is where it stops. This is my business, and I sign the checks. Y'all can think what y'all wanna think about what I do in my private affairs. Just remember that judge not unless ye be judged 'cause Marisol I heard tales about Tyrone's ass, so you ain't better than nobody. And Ana you can't buy a man, so try not to be a hater all your life, OK? In here, I want nothing but respect and professionalism. Gossiping is cruel, and I think that there are better things to do with your time. Furthermore, y'all don't even like Katrina, but when it came time to get information, y'all were all up her ass. Check that shit at the door. If I hear my name pass either of your lips in a derogatory manner again, your services will no longer be needed here at Oasis, and you will not get a reference. Now get back to work."

*

The news hits me like a ton of bricks. More like the fight I had in sixth grade with Big Tammy as she tossed my ass around the schoolyard like a twig, leaving me with a ring around my right eye. Time seems to dawdle as the words come out in super-slow motion. G-e-n-i-t-a-l w-a-r-t-s. I have genital warts with no firm idea of when I got them, who I got them from or who I may have given

Mahzi Kane   Tea Leaves

them to. I have never even heard of genital warts! Dr. Graves schedules me for wart removal on Friday. The procedure freezes them, and then they fall off, but the HPV virus remains in my body, which means that the warts can come back at any time and are contagious. I feel dingy, like a $2 whore, and the shame is not worth a million orgasms. The way I use sex is supposed to be freeing and juicy like the feeling I get when I eat a pomegranate. It's how I connect and get to know a man, even if it's not going to get serious, even though I really want it to get serious and lead somewhere magical, I still get to visit that place where my fingers clench and my insides dance, and I fuck like I'm on top of the world. My sex is like cotton candy and firecrackers energized with desire and arousal and I never had a reason to think about giving it up. I mean I absolutely love my sex life, but now it weighs on me, and I have to question if my ways have been improper. I read that if you stop having sex for a long period of time, it tightens back up. I don't know about that, but I do know that I'd go crazy waiting until I find Mr. Sage to get my groove on. Plus husbands cheat all of the time and bring home diseases, babies and mistresses who don't want it to end, so it makes me wonder if anything is safe? Can anybody be trusted with my body, let alone my heart?

After speaking with Dr. Graves, celibacy is my new birth control. It's not as drastic as secondary virginity, but it will give me time to analyze my sexual practices. She also suggests counseling, but I don't need all that. I have warts, I'm not dying. Besides, I can't talk about this to anybody yet, and definitely not a complete stranger. Dr. Graves gives me a bag of condoms, just in case, along with the title of a book on celibacy and dating techniques. I

Mahzi Kane   Tea Leaves

drive to the bookstore and purchase my new literary ally in my fight to save myself from myself. I give too much all in the name of having a good time, and now my mental and physical health are in jeopardy. I can't go out like that.

At work, I am polite to my clients but barely speak to anyone else. I cut my eyes hard at Katrina. Today is not the day for some fake-ass reconciliation. I've reached my epiphany, my rock bottom, if you will. The people I employ are calling me a slut behind my back, I've contracted a venereal disease, the relationship that I have with my mother sucks, and on top of it all, I still don't have a man and am giving up the one thing I love more than my business. This is my turning point. The question is, which way do I go to find my joy?

Chapter Thirteen

m iSS u nDerStooD : c L A r K e

DEAN PAYS FOR MY ABORTION, AND
then I cut him loose. After one month, his fat ass is
running around telling his family and friends that
by the end of the year we'll be planning a wedding.
That's a fantastic world of "hell no" that he is living
in with that line of thinking. I have access to a vast
and prosperous land of portfolios and money, so
why on earth does he think he's the chosen one?
Getting married isn't even a doodle in the margin
of my five-year plan, let alone a legitimate goal. As
a matter of fact, it has no bearing on who I am or
how I want to be. Why settle down when I can ride
it until the good falls off of it and move on? Why
saddle myself with the burden of another person's
continuous happiness? Look, I keep it real, and as
much as I despise that saying, it fits me to the letter.
I like having the option of being by myself and not
having to consider somebody else's feelings before
I do anything all of the time. Like how Iris has to
think about Malcolm or let him know where she's
going to be or what she's doing all of the time. I'm
grown and I don't want to answer to any man if I
don't feel like it. There are too many options out in
the world to tie myself to a pain in the ass
masquerading as love. Love is overrated. Nobody
warns you about how much you have to give up in
order to be in it until it's too late. On a simplistic

level, I grow tired of men quickly. As soon as they start nagging about this or that personality quirk of mine that they've uncovered, it's time for them to go. I don't need any man to make me over and then complain and throw it up in my face that I'm not the same person. No, thank you.

Solomon pays for my car repairs, and now we're laying up for the weekend at our spot in New Jersey, trying to act as if we haven't stumbled into the friendship zone. After spending that kind of money, any other man would assume I owe him a good time, but Solomon likes me for the stubborn, spoiled woman that I can be, even if we're not fucking every time he foots the bill. He actually takes the time to get to know my other parts, not to mention he helps me out when I need it and no one else seems to give a damn. The rainy day confines us to watching movies in the room, but we brave the evening showers to get a bite to eat at the nearby shopping mall along with a new handbag and monogram bucket hat. It helps that Solomon's adage is that it's not tricking since he got it to spend. Though I'm no trick, I'll gladly take his disbursements. There's nothing wrong with showering lavish gifts to show appreciation for the female in your life, especially if she's feeding and fucking you right. There should be no problem with dropping a few hundred here and there, right? What can I say, I enjoy nice things, and love does not pay the bills or sparkle like a brand-new diamond. A woman has to use more than her heart to meet her needs. I'm not 16 anymore, and if a man won't or can't do for me, then why should I invest my time? But don't get it twisted, I'm the boss and I call my shots no matter how much he can afford because once a man feels like he has you in a particular position, once he thinks that you need him, he tends to show his entire ass.

Mahzi Kane   Tea Leaves

Boredom has set in, and it's time to reclaim my rank among the gainfully employed. After several interviews, nothing is tweaking my interests in the Philly fashion industry doing visual marketing or buying. At the end of the week I'm going to the Big Apple to check out the job market and submit resumes to department stores and boutiques. My career is the one constant in my life. A man is just a man, but my intellect, my talent and my credentials are valuable, and I refuse to let the hard work and dedication it took to get them fizzle into nothing. With all the crap that's been happening to me, my come up has got to be waiting around the corner.

Given that the last time Iris and I spoke it ended on a bad note, we haven't hung out, although we spoke briefly. But it was very strained, and I don't understand why. Marriage is changing her already. It can't be me. All I did was speak my mind, which is nothing out of the ordinary, and Iris normally appreciates my frankness. Besides Peanut, Iris is my only real friend, and I don't want to lose her over a difference of opinion. I sent a balloon-o-gram as a peace offering that she should get this afternoon. After Solomon drops me off, I'm playing the crib so that I won't miss her call. Like I said, Iris is my girl. Peanut is good peoples, but two words describe her: ghetto fabulous. The type who has three recycling bins full of empty 40 bottles outside her house by the middle of the week. She dates men with no jobs, living in their grandma's basement, but with a mouth full of gold teeth and a row of brand name sneakers way above their means. Every other word out of her mouth is "bitch" this or "my nigga" that. There's nothing wrong with using slang or profanity, but there is a time and place for it, and unfortunately Peanut hasn't figured that out yet, so she can't roll with me all of the time. After all, you are the company that you keep.

By 4, Iris calls and we subtly apologize for our behavior. She attributes her snippiness to wedding stress, and I tell her that I could have been more tactful when expressing my point of view. Once that is taken care of, it feels like a huge weight is lifted from my shoulders, so I prepare to hit the streets. Maintaining female relationships has always been a struggle for me. I developed early, which made me an instant hit with the boys and an instant enemy of all the girls. It began in middle school, gained momentum in high school, and by college it was in full speed. Throw in the fact that my parents have money, and I became the rich girl with the big boobs and thick thighs that nobody trusts and without good reason. Girls are cruel, and before you know it, rumors evolve into reputation and nobody bothers to find out the truth. But instead of bending over backward to prove them wrong, I became exactly what they all assumed I was: a woman to watch and fear. I mean who the hell did they think they were to prejudge me and not even take the time to get past how I look on the outside? Where is my fair chance?

Waiting at the red light and jigging to the radio, the sound of a horn beeping shakes me from my groove. Sitting in the car next to me is none other than Piccolo. I could drink that Negro, that's how much I want him inside of me. I turn down my music and get into mack mode. He's seeing Ila, and if she's taking care of business then I am no threat.

"Long time no see, Clarke."

"Um, Piccolo, right?"

"Yeah … remember I looked so familiar to you?"

"That's right; you're Ila's man, correct?"

"Depends on how you look at it."

"Interesting response."

"Very. Where you headed to, Miss Lady?"

"Nowhere in particular, just out and about with no destination in mind."

"You never know where you might end up."

The cars behind us blare their horns in agitation since our chat holds up traffic. Piccolo motions for me to pull over. He parks and emerges from his car in a pair of denim shorts, construction boots, and a yellow and blue polo shirt. His hair erupts into a knotty bush that perches off his head. His broad shoulders sway as he strolls over to my driver's side window. I hold my breath waiting to see what is going to happen next.

"This is what it's hitting for. You're just cruising, and I'm in no big rush to have another night with the fellas, so how about we kick it together? We can do whatever. Grab a bite to eat, see a movie, go back to my place, it's your call. Let me know what the deal is."

I sit here playing his game. I have every intention on having this man. Ila swears her man is upstanding and loyal. Dumb bitch, she just doesn't know that even the best man will be the worst dog for some good pussy. Piccolo flashes his sneaky smirk as I contemplate his proposition.

He tries to hide the fact that she's been on his mind since their introduction at Iris' show. His yearning is apparent, and she's making it obvious that she wants to get it on with the not-so-subtle way she uncrosses her legs to let him ogle her bush. Ila who?

Mahzi Kane   Tea Leaves

"Seems like you're ready, Clarke."

"Piccolo, let's go back to your place and do some of that whatever you mentioned. Are you ready?"

"I'll lead, you follow."

Chapter Fourteen

b eSt in S hoW : c L A r K e

MY SWEATY HANDS LOSE THEIR GRIP
as I try to keep up with Piccolo, who drives like a
bat out of hell, his excitement fueled by the parting
of my legs and the peek I saw him try not to notice
back at the traffic light. When we arrive to his
house, I get set to perform. I keep a get-your-freak-
on kit in my car containing flavored body oil, THC-
infused lubricant, handcuffs, whips, feathers,
blindfolds, candles, cock rings, vibrators and anal
beads. I pull one of my feminine refresh cloths
from the glove compartment and do away with any
unwanted moisture. I check my teeth, wipe off my
lipstick to apply a light gloss and then redo my bun.
I undo the top three buttons of my shirt.

He strolls up to the car and opens my door,
and I get out. He presses me up against the car, and
I can feel the bulge in his shorts as he runs his
hands up my thighs and under my skirt. He bites
the back of my neck and says, "I hope you can
handle this." He has no idea how much I can. I
turn and follow him up the steps to his house.
Once inside, Piccolo sits down on the couch next
to the stereo and uses his musical selection to set
the tone. Aaron Hall cautions, "Don't Be Afraid,"
while Piccolo and I lock gazes on a search for the
brazen soul to get this party started. As if sensing
my anticipation, he commands: "Take off your
clothes."

I stand in the middle of the living room and
wind my body to the erotic beat and peel away my

Mahzi Kane   Tea Leaves

clothes like a ripe banana. Once naked, I pull the flavored body oil from my bag of tricks and polish it onto my skin, hypnotized by the freaky lyrics. I glisten like a brand-new penny in the sun and station myself with my back to Piccolo, and once I am sure I have his attention, I do a full split and raise my cheeks in the air to give him a total view of where all his wishes will be met. I know that Ila can't freak it like this, and I plan to show Piccolo all that he is missing. I know I am the epitome of all of the nasty things he wants to be but that he can't with Ila.

"I knew you'd be into all types of kinky shit. I can't wait for you to use alllllll your nastiness on me. What else you got?"

I kneel in front of Piccolo to reveal the contents of my buck-wild bag. Once I dump everything out, I continue to show off my stripper moves. Piccolo stumbles toward the side table and grabs the tequila as he watches. The burn of the drink moves through him while he closes in and drizzles the Mexican liquor through my cleavage. I giggle like a young girl who's sneaking with her boyfriend when she should be on her way home. I take the bottle from him and sip while he lights six candles, one of which he uses to put a line of hot wax down my arm. I bite down on the side of my lip, turned on by the twinge of pain. I place his hand around my neck, and he applies more pressure. My airways constrict, taking my arousal up a notch, and my walls tighten. He breathes deeply, somewhat like a grunt — animalistic and primal — overtaken by the power of his fantasy-turned-real.

"Even your smell drives me crazy. Look how ready I am. I want to be in there."

"I want you in there. It'll make me feel so good to have you now."

Mahzi Kane   Tea Leaves

He pushes me on top of the sofa table. My back slaps into the cold surface of the wall, and he raises my legs until they hit his shoulders. We move like synchronized swimmers, propelling our bodies into the fluid shadows and flickers of deceit and delight. He holds my face, not letting go, and my eyes fix on his contorted expression, pleasure apparent in our slippery friction. He reduces the pace and then turns me around. I am excited by the feel of him slithering along my backside and am happy to receive more of his good time. His unhurried stroke makes me wetter, and I whisper for him to grab the beads. He slips them in one at a time, smacking my ass to make it shake. I whimper between inhales of air as he wraps me up in his wonder. He snatches the beads out and takes me higher, going to the places most people deny.

I enter my zone, free of inhibitions, able to explore what feels good, and he watches my fingers meander from my hole to my clit and back again, and I squirm from the self-satisfaction. He laps at the juices dripping from my manicured fingertips then crams my head down into his lap. My jaws and his hips work in tandem, and I slurp hard between "ahhhhhhhs" and "mmmmmmms." I tickle, kiss and suck as he puts everything except his thumb into my warm opening, and I moan with excitement from his twists and shoves. Ecstasy glides along my bottom lip and flushes over my cheeks, neck and shoulders until it feels like I am smothered in it and turns on sounds I can't quiet. I feel a rush of adrenaline as he fucks my face in fast and short spurts as his sighs turn low and coarse until he sputters like a stalling car engine. He leans me back, blowing softly and letting the light touch of his lips brush against my skin, sending my body into tremors. He nibbles at the creases of my thighs that twitch on command with each slip of his two fingers. In and out and out and in of me, who babbles in a nonexistent language, controlled by the sexual musings of another. His face is in my treasure, his hands on the small of my back digging in to get a good grip, and I am impressed. Then he tongues me, and I can't help but to lift my hips up in the air and welcome the tingling sensations as they expand inside my walls.

"You look so sexy when you do that."

"Show me what it makes you wanna do to me."

He flips me over and positions me on the couch with my face down, spreads my legs as far as they can go; and thrusts inside of me with the force of a thousand horses and a hope to reach my stomach in one swoop. I try to stifle the salacious confessions fighting to get out and float from my mystery places and land inside his ears.

"Let it out, I want to hear you. Don't hold it in."

He's all in it from angle to angle, making this shit deliciously rough and exciting. I let myself go, going more into the feeling, totally connected to my sexual power. Our breathing is shallow and swift; our bodies drenching with sweat; vision blurred. His effortless penetration is so focused that it makes my nipples tremble with passion and each toe go numb. Our grind builds until we lay sprawled somewhere between the couch and the floor, unable to speak. My throat feels dry, almost raw, trying to catch bits of breath. Once I do, I grab my handcuffs and hold his hands in place over his head so I can close the cold metal around his wrists, and then I blindfold him. I taste a decadent mix of salty and sweet, licking it in the cracks of his defined chest, juiced up by the carnal outline of his muscles, culminating in the perfect V shape. His skin begs for my attention. Kisses across his slender torso make his body jump and I smile hard.

"If I'm not careful, you'll end up as my permanent secret lover."

"Ooooohhhhh, I make you feel good, don't I?"

"I can't front, Clarke, you keeping it hot in here. I like it. Really like it."

"What can I say, I know how to have a good time."

"You know how to have a great time. I could spend days between your legs . . . make you my sex slave. You got me waiting for more."

"Come and get what you want."

"I can't see and my hands are bound. Why are you teasing me?"

"Come and get what you want, if you want it as badly as you claim."

Piccolo tries to scoot toward the sound of my voice. I stand over him and let my breasts dangle over his lips. He groans and moves from one to the other. He sucks long and hard on one and bites the other, sending a delightful bolt that causes them to grow bigger and fuller, and I let him feel them against his forehead and cheeks.

"Your nipples are delicious – a blend of strawberries and heaven."

I scrunch my eyes and open my mouth really wide to let out all that he's putting in, freeing the passion of it all, and letting the tip of his tongue and the amazing circles they create overwhelm all the parts that never want him to stop. I slide a cock ring in place and straddle Piccolo on the floor. I feel his outer layer push back my insides as I take him up and down, twirling magic wands of wetness around him until my shins bleed. I free him of the blindfold and cuffs and sit astride, with him pulsating inside, me ready to push out the truth.

"What are you trying to do to me?"

"Fuck you the way I know you wanted me to since the first time you saw me."

"Is that right?"

"Piccolo, after this you'll never look at pussy the same."

We are insatiable, almost in a sex trance led by nothing more than an inclination to fuck. This ain't no love thang connected to sumptuous imaginings that this pussy is his and he is king of our elaborate sex circus. Nope, not this. This unforgettable casual encounter is an invitation to thrill me, to go with me, to use different ways to turn me on because I am committed to satisfaction - orgasms guaranteed. And give me what I want with uncurbed enthusiasm. Sex is happiness taken out of the box. The place to play with it rather than keep it trapped while you waiting on love and a connection. This is deliberate satisfaction, sinful in its fulfillment yet triumphant and liberating like the people's revolution. Damn butterflies, good sex should give you earthquakes until you can't move, can't speak, can't think. Anything else is bullshit. Nigga welcome to the Clarke show.

I go to work on a full-fledged blowjob with no hands. When he is done I place my mouth onto his to share the nectar of his manhood. He looks at me like the fuck goddess that I am, and we can't help but to do it again. This time he props my thighs up with a pillow for ultimate penetration, and it feels so good to have him back inside of me, stroking left, right, up and down in a fury of bump and grind maneuvers. I grab his ass while he is on top of me, rocking my body back and forth until he is all up in it, pulling my hair while stroking the right points along my spine. He tilts his body farther into mine, anchoring me by the shoulders while knocking on my sweet spot.

I fly and fall, getting dizzy with each movement from the bursts of sexual aggression that propels me forward in violent jerks. I press my forehead onto his as we shove our hips together until time slows and everything fades to black.

I go clean up in the bathroom and place my gold bangle bracelet on the sink. I hadn't planned on making him a regular, but after this experience, his is a ride I'd revisit. When I return to the living room, Piccolo is sitting in a chair drinking bottled water.

"That was fantastic."

"It sure was, Clarke. We might have to do this again."

"Maybe we will. Except …"

"She's not my official girlfriend. I mean, what I'm trying to say is, I don't have an actual verbalized commitment to her … so."

"So what, this would be cool with her? Doubt that shit highly."

"No, I'm not saying that at all, but … look, I don't throw nothing up in her face, the others know their place, and I would never let her find traces of another woman."

"No heavy explanation required, Piccolo. Like I said, maybe we will."

With a wink and a smile, I leave without him having to ask. I speed off his block like a woman with a million bucks in her pocket. I don't know what the hell is wrong with Ila. How in the world can she let a man who lays it as well as Piccolo does out of her sight for one minute? I'd LoJack that Negro just in case an opportunist such as myself was prowling around for a stiff one. I never liked her and from what he just told me, she should have

Mahzi Kane   Tea Leaves

kept Justice's ass — at least he was loyal. If she spent more time taking care of her so-called man and less time being such a bitch, maybe I wouldn't have just fucked him cross-eyed. Oh well.

Chapter Fifteen

A h ArD p iLL : i r i S

CLARKE AND I SETTLE OUR DIFFERENCES today, once I decide to be the bigger woman and call after I receive the balloon-o-gram she has sent. We both somewhat apologize, and all is good. Malcolm gives me a cockeyed look as he eavesdrops in on my side of the dialogue. When I hang up, I find myself smothered in a 10-minute lecture about true friendship and hanging onto dead weight. I listen and do not respond. He can have his opinions, but Malcolm fails to realize that keeping female relationships is a test of tolerance. People are who they are, and it's up to us to accept or reject any feelings, habits or even beliefs that we see in them that are different from our own. I don't like everything about Clarke, but no one is exempt from flaws, and that's not an excuse, it's reality.

I'm teaching myself to appreciate the crust and the cream of a person, for example, Malcolm. He is a kaleidoscope of temperaments — outwardly driven to do well in business with the right touch of thug, a dash of arrogance, an ounce of revolutionary and a twist of intellectual wit. He can be stubborn, judgmental and inflexible, allowing little to no gray area when it comes to the actions of others toward their loved ones. He scrutinizes free will, calculating a running tab of positives and negatives that measure one's propensity toward common sense or stupidity, and once his Spidey senses tell him that an individual is of a particular nature, one that doesn't mirror his expectations, nothing said or done can alter his assessment of that person. You're either for him or against him. I remind Malcolm that everything is not about him, but after the scandal with Dennis, he is even more skeptical of those who tout loyalty. To him, death is the equivalent of maintaining alliances with people we suspect don't have our best interests in mind. I admit to loving the conspiracy theorist in him, but it gets on my damn nerves.

Today we plan to visit the Philadelphia Museum of Art, which houses some of the greatest public collections of art in a half-million square feet of space. It displays European art, masterpieces from Asia, the Near East, Africa and virtually every major 20th century artist. Inside and out, its artistry inspires the creative thinker in me. The art museum area is filled with birch and bald cypress trees, lavender snapdragons and peach geraniums, handsome landscapes, eastern white pine hedges and beautifully kept lawns. The roof of the museum is covered by four acres of blue tile and guarded by bronze griffins. The Azalea garden down the hill beyond the Italian water fountain should be in full bloom, and I can't wait to experience the smell of flowers growing.

We sit on the Art Museum lawn sipping lemonade under the comfy shade of a red maple tree enjoying our day, and Toya calls. I can hear the lost hope in her voice as she asks if she and I can hook up because she needs to talk. We arrange to meet at my house at 4 p.m. Malcolm's furrowed brow lets me know that I am in for another unsolicited lecture once the call ends.

Mahzi Kane   Tea Leaves

"And the chronicle of the weak-minded continues."

"Malcolm, please. You ever hear that if you don't have anything nice to say, then don't say anything at all?"

"Did you ever hear that the truth hurts?"

"I don't come to you with the things that go on in my sisters' lives, yet and still, without a break, you have a comment. You are compelled to weigh in for some reason, and if you feel that adamant about their situations, give your sound advice to them and not me because the hurt and truth that you speak of does not belong to me."

"I'm sick of you, my wife-to-be, making your silly-ass sister-friends' problems your own. Can't they solve one issue without you? They are supposed to be grown-ass women."

"Everybody needs somebody to listen. I offer my guidance and a shoulder to cry on because I care about them. That's being a friend. Why does that bother you?"

I remind myself that Malcolm is no good at overlooking when people take little things for granted, like the time it takes to correct a bad decision. He seems to forget that the sad reality is that everyone isn't afforded the luxury of time to do so. His parents were killed in a car crash when he was a boy. I imagine a little Malcolm, isolated and alone and pissed off by the realization at too early of an age that the people you love can disappear. For the most part, Malcolm kept to himself, I guess trying to create a protective ball to keep out the possibility of feeling orphaned again. His Uncle Saul and Aunt Faye raised him until he relocated to Philadelphia to attend college and left

Mahzi Kane   Tea Leaves

the only relatives he knew. Uncle Saul passed away six years ago, so Malcolm visits Aunt Faye in Atlanta twice a year, and she never misses her monthly call to make sure we're doing OK. She once confided in me that she had worried for years, wondering if he would open up to love somebody, considering the loss that he carried in his heart. Malcolm was a playa to the letter — never letting a woman get too close or any sexual encounter get too serious. It's a tall order to be someone's first and last, and trump all that took place in between the two.

"And before you respond, how about we concentrate on the good stuff in our life and in this relationship, not the shit that my squad goes through? We are about to get married, got-damn it. That's reason to sing, shout and throw a fucking parade. Instead, we're going tit for tat about things that don't directly affect us. Malcolm, trust me when I say that I am truly learning to be a friend without being the burden-carrier."

"You're right. I respect you, and I love you. I respect and love the way you think, and so if you say that you have a hold on these friendships, then I'm backing off. What goes on is y'all business. Cool?"

"Cool."

"It's about us, right? So let's talk about us. Do you need me to help with any decisions about the unwedding?"

"Miraculously, it's finished. The final menu is approved, we chose the honeydew green and white ankh place settings, the favors are done, the photographer and videographer are confirmed, the Rolls-Royce is reserved, and yesterday I booked the room at the Marriott hotel for my last night as a single woman."

"Make sure that no sweaty men packing grotesquely sized johnsons crash that little shindig."

"Crash? They are invited. Seriously, it'll be me, my girls, good food, weed and drinks. It's gonna be off the hook."

"A couple of the guys from work have a thing planned for me. I'm not sure what it is."

"Yeah, right. You know it's some nasty broads ready to pop it, shake it and do whatever else for them dollars."

"Dollars? You mean checks. Seriously, it'll be me, my fellas, good food, weed and drinks. Oh yeah, and specials from the titty bar."

With that last response, I spring onto Malcolm, and we roll back and forth across the lawn laughing amidst a blitz of kisses and tickles. A tent caterpillar crawls over the oak trees in the midst of our merrymaking and reminds me that while our love is big, huge in our estimation and in comparison to other things in the world, it is but a section of a bigger universe filled with other things that also experience our thoughts and feelings, our highs and lows, our loves and our losses. Hand in hand, we walk home chattering about our pending nuptials, and upon our arrival, Toya is on our front stoop. Malcolm's eyes soften inch by inch as they absorb the sadness pervading her spirit. Her hair is a shabby mess, a perfect complement to a raggedy gray sweat suit. Puffy eyes connect with ours when she finally notices us while fiddling with her sleeve. Malcolm walks over and gives her a hug.

"Toya, you're gonna be OK, girlfriend."

He offers to run errands and give us time alone. Before I can even start thinking he's a jerk, he is already making up for it, and I love that shit. I kiss him and watch the man I adore disappear into the flow of the crowd. I put my arm around Toya's shoulder as we walk into my building. I quickly check messages, pull off my sandals and get the weed while she halfway notices the music videos she has turned on in the living room. I don't know where to start with her, or how to put things in a perspective that can help her get it together since I don't exactly know what has happened. I heard things, but Toya and I haven't had a girl talk in months. Judging by her obvious disorder, it's definitely past due. I know about the eviction, but there has got to be more to the story than that to push her to the edge. She looks like she is breaking. The blunt smoke fills the space between us, and Toya reaches for it, and I know for sure that she is losing her mind.

"You smoke weed? Since when?"

"Three words, girl: living with Sage."

"I have missed so much, I see. What about 'drugs being the gateway to the devil' and all that jazz?"

"Trying to cope changed my frame of reference."

"Really now? Let's have it, what's going on? You look like shit."

"Good. That's how I feel. That's how I act."

"Tell me what's up. Sorry for being unavailable in recent months. I have been running around looking and searching and — "

"Don't apologize. You can't be my crutch. I have to at least attempt to run my life. Independence is a major requirement to be considered an adult. I've been doing a horrible job. I thought I had it together, but I am a mess."

"What is your problem?"

"Trying to be who I am not and being me all at once."

"If you keep talking like that, I'm not going to pass you the blunt again. Clear and specific, please."

Mahzi Kane   Tea Leaves

"Felicia called me at my job. She knows about me and told me that Lamont is a serial cheater who never had any intention of leaving her for me and she's having another one of his babies."

"I knew he wasn't shit! Selfish bastard … I hope he catches some strange disease."

"Here I'm thinking we are working on a future, thinking I'm special because of this man, and excited because he genuinely loves and cares for me but is only stuck in a bad spot that would be temporary. Those excuses, all the mind tricks I played with myself to believe and justify why I chose to share something so devious and immoral with him, don't make any of this right … but I love him, Iris. Oh God!"

Toya looks away from me before she continues.

"I feel like a fool for loving him still, and at the same time I hate him. I hate Felicia. I hate myself for settling for another woman's husband when I know it is wrong, but I decided not to care so that I could have love. Now all I have is hatred. I guess that's a blessing because without it, I'd be empty."

"Don't waste time or energy hating anybody, especially yourself. Of course, you still love him, you can't fake like you don't, and nobody expects you to, but the last thing you want to do is make the mistake of covering love up with anger. If you think you got a raw deal, imagine how she feels? I know your emotions are all over and your heart is broken, but I have to tell you, you are not the victim. You messed around with a married man. You can't shake the rules of that game or count on luck or love to lessen the risks of playing it. That's the chance you took, and like many before you, you loss. But the best part to all this mess is an open spot for somebody new because you don't have to run back to his fake-ass love. That they are still married to each other says a lot; be grateful to be out of that dysfunction."

"To tell you the truth, dysfunction is my middle name these days. Pia and I got evicted because she wasn't paying the rent, and I was too busy worrying about Lamont to notice. As if that's not enough to deal with, I was lonely and wanted to shake off my Lamont blues, so I hooked up with a nice guy named David from work, who ended up proving just how much of a low-life home wrecker I am and then dumped me. He's Felicia's brother."

"What kind of soap opera shit is this?"

"I think I made it worse because I had the chance to tell him when he showed me a picture of them together."

"Ya think? Why didn't you tell him? It was only a matter of time before he found out, right?"

"I didn't know how to explain it without looking bad, and at the time, I didn't see how it would hurt not to say anything."

"That's bullshit and you know it, Toya. Nothing is better than the truth. Even if it means accepting yet another man's rejection and once again when it comes to Felicia."

Tears reel down Toya's cheeks as she pulls hard on the blunt.

"I am trying to have fun. Men do this all the time — no strings, just sex. Look at Sage, look at Ila! Why is it that when I do it, I end up getting fired when the big bosses find out about my harmless fling with the playboy manager?!"

"WHAT?!! This is all types of crazy! They shouldn't be able to fire y'all over a personal relationship."

"We were having sex in his office."

"Well, that is brilliant."

Mahzi Kane   Tea Leaves

"During overtime."

"I see why you're walking around looking like the living dead. Clearly, you've been doing a bunch of dumb shit like you don't have one bit of common sense."

"I've been praying and searching for an answer, looking for a light to help lead me out of this hole. I am doing so many things that just aren't me, and it's making me not like who I am becoming. I've lied and crawled around in secrecy with that man, and compromised so much of my own value. Why do I feel like I have to have a man's stamp of approval in order to feel whole? I love myself, I really do, but having a man's love vindicates me. Why doesn't anybody want me?"

"Do you want yourself? Or do you want a man to validate your womanhood? Well, they can't because that's your job. You have to decide what kind of woman you want to be before you get to the man part."

"How do I do that? By reading those 'Stop Being Dumped' books?"

"If that's what it takes. You need your own love before you can accept somebody else's. You are the one to fix whatever it is that is missing. The world is yours — focus on where and how you choose to step — in the back alleyways and gutters or in the bright sunlight out on the avenues and boulevards, where big dreams grow into real life. Think long and hard about the things that you've always wanted to do. Create your miracle. Start doing things that bring you pleasure, and get to the core of your true self."

"My true self?"

"The you that's not tied to your career, your appearance or your religion. The you that draws people in … your loving and giving nature. The you

Mahzi Kane   Tea Leaves

that smiles at life because you are clear and certain. The you that knows without question that your happiness is unshakeable."

"I always believed that any sane woman had to have a man and a secure relationship to be happy. God put man and woman here to be made into one flesh. Two loves is better than one."

"Not if one of those loves is half-ass and the other is mis-guided. Happiness has to be in your heart before an outside person can exist there. Misery may love company, but they're a sorry, festering bunch. Why should any man, or anybody for that matter, want to be with you if you don't even want to be with you? What do you like doing for yourself? By yourself?"

"Reading the bible comes to mind, actually reading in general."

"Then begin spending time at the library. Clarity doesn't come in a rush, it's a process of learning, discovering and sometimes rediscovering what is important to you. Be open to it. It's scary as hell, but you gotta go through it."

"My life has been nothing but Lamont and his stuff, and that was the only important thing. All my goals were tied to him, but it's time to put my big girl panties on and look for ways to restore and heal my broken heart. Maybe I'll meet a nice-looking fellow at the library."

I look at her like she's crazy, and she explodes in laughter. Toya and I smoke another blunt and philosophize on the what, how and why of relationships. Her chocolate skin turns colors from the emotional whiplash of her untold sadness, rage, and cynicism - far too deep to hide.

Chapter Sixteen

F AmiLY tiDeS

RASHIDA CALLS AT THE BUTT-CRACK OF dawn begging me to go to Atlantic City, saying she's feeling lucky. She's lucky that I am growing into a morning person. I agree since Malcolm will be in meetings all day and I am set to leave in the afternoon. Back in the day, we were good for sneaking off to college campuses for parties. The Reading and Lansdale shopping outlets could spot my car miles away, and nearly every shore on the eastern seaboard has felt the dips of our big toes. Road trips were our answer whether we were depressed about a dumb boyfriend, at a roadblock or just looking for a small adventure. We use this private time on the road to talk, and what feels scary and bothersome turns into a fresh perspective. We all need advice to figure out what to do when we don't know what the hell to do, and that strengthens our bond. I get recharged from my sister-friends and the soft space they provide to unwind. Needless to say, traveling is our special thing, and a trip to the casino is perfect timing.

Before any road trip kicks off, I have to see my Grandma Rue. It'd be wrong to be in the neighborhood and not stop. I could use a sit down with my grandma. Maybe she can warm my cold feet with her wisdom. Marriage is terrifying at times when I think about the things than can go wrong. I have a slice of strawberry shortcake from her favorite bakery, and I arrive to the sounds of her singing Al Green and the hard snap of green beans.

The only thing she loves more than family and strawberry shortcake is Al Green. I mean she has the man's picture in our family photo albums. It gets no deeper than that.

"How's my kitten doing?"

"Great, Grandma. Finished my book finally."

"That's great, baby. You make me prouder by the minute. Malcolm's getting a pearl, he truly is. How's the wedding comin' along?"

"Done. The months of shopping, looking, picking and reserving are finished. I don't want to talk to another wedding professional."

"August 22 can't get here soon enough. I get goose pimples just thinkin' about it. I know my kitten did it up right, even if you ain't having no meat."

"Grandma, pleeeeease."

"OK, OK, even though I ain't even said nothing yet. An old woman can't even talk in her own house. Imagine that."

"You too much, Grandma. Let me ask you this: Before you married Granddad, did you have doubts about the marriage lasting and if he was really the one that you were meant to be with for all eternity?"

"Gal, everybody gets nervous, it's normal. If you didn't know that Malcolm was the one, it woulda been called off. Don't be silly, you two will be fine. A happy marriage is the foundation to a happy family. It ain't all wine and roses, but I suppose you know that by now, with y'all living together and what not. Men have they good days and they bad days. Me myself, I'm convinced they gets a menstrual worse than us. The trick is to love them no matter what. Don't get me wrong, I'm not saying to put up with no foolishness. If he start acting simple, let'im know that you ain't about keeping no man that don't wanna be kept and that

Mahzi Kane   Tea Leaves

he can take his act down the road 'cause you ain't
amused or entertained by bullshit. A husband
always gotta respect his wife, always — and vice
versa. I must admit, it ain't nothin' like the security
of knowing that the man you love loves you back."

"How will I know that he won't leave, or that
I won't get bored or that I'm being a good wife?"

"Kitten, life has no guarantees and surely not
love. Doing your best is the only safety net. If you
spend all your time worrying about what could go
wrong and wondering what might happen, well,
that's a quick way to end up in divorce court. Being
a wife is part natural and part experience. You
won't know until you know."

I absorb the insight pouring from such an
aging frame. Her mind is infinite though, using the
next 40 minutes to spill tidbits that inspire me to
love with everything that I am. I leave her house
brimming with the confidence that Malcolm and I
have what it takes. I can't get this from just
anybody. She is my legacy and I am her
immortality. Her wisdom is limitless, the things she
told me when I was a little girl mean more now
than they did then, like good manners always
matter and don't cost nothing, people forget how
you look but will remember how you made them
feel, and family first.

I zoom to Turner Street to get Rashida,
anxious to hit the highway. Jaden is with his dad,
and she plans to enjoy her freedom to the max.
Babies, career, lovers, family, friends, household
obligations - we have so much to handle, we have
to make ourselves not feel guilty about structuring
time to make us a priority. Our aspirations are left
to rot in the attic of what could-have-been and if
we don't rediscover them, eventually we burn out.
Superwomen need breaks too, even if it's a

conversation in a circle of sister-friends. I saw on a talk show that it is this mechanism that helps to reduce high cholesterol, high blood pressure and heart disease because that is how we deal with stress. We heal our wounds by befriending other women.

"I love Jaden, but there is nothing like me time! Many of my anxieties have melted away since Erik is stepping up. I can see the pieces of my life coming together."

"Patience is the key. Since infants, we all want what we want when we want it. That's not how shit goes. We have to prepare for our time to shine, or not only would we not be able to appreciate it, but we would be under the misconception that the success made us, when really, we make it."

"True, very true. When are you and Malcolm gonna have a baby for you to school?"

"Children are not in the immediate forecast."

"You're telling me that you don't want a baby?"

"Of course I do, but I'm not pressed. When we are ready to be parents, nature will step in."

Rashida cranks up the system, and hip-hop overflows the speakers as we blaze a natural, aromatic leaf for a slow burn filled with White Widow on the way to America's favorite playground. The casino of choice is Bally's so we can gorge ourselves at the Chinese buffet. Bellies full, we hit the slots. I have $50 with me, and once that's gone, so am I. Under domed ceilings we slide our 20s into the machines and pull the levers, hoping for three lucky sevens to pop up. The nonstop clank, tinkle and beep of the machines, the hum of spinning wheels, broken dreams and cigarette smoke are almost stifling. Without warning, Rashida's slot machine goes wild spitting out quarters. We shriek to the top of our lungs like fools, excited to see that much silver, until the attendant comes to give Rashida her winnings: seven crisp $100 bills. Rashida has Lady Luck in her back pocket all night and cleans up, winning three hundred at blackjack and twenty-five hundred at the money wheel. I win back what I lose plus another hundred bucks. Not wanting to spit on our good graces, we jump in the car and speed down 95 with our winnings burning a hole in our pockets.

*

"Iris, somebody is at the fucking door. It's 4 in the morning. Who the hell is it, and what do they want?!"

"Be calm, Malcolm. I'm up here with you, so how should I know? It can't be good at this time of the morning. I am in no mood for drama!"

I wait at the top of the stairs while Malcolm answers the door. The sound of Rashida's voice sends me flying down the stairs.

"What is it? Is it Jaden, is it ya mom, what's going on?"

"I had to get us out of that house. I'm so sorry to be here at this time of the morning, but I can't keep my son there one more night, and I didn't know where else to go. Please, can we stay here tonight? Tomorrow we will be in a place of our own, believe that shit."

"Sit down and calm down! I'm taking Jaden upstairs."

"You look like you're about to kill somebody. What happened, Rashida?"

"Malcolm, I feel like I'm going to kill some fucking body. I need a damn drink!"

"Want a beer?"

"Hell yes, I need something to help me free my mind from this bullshit these people keep taking me through."

Malcolm walks in the kitchen and grabs a Heineken out of the fridge with no idea of what is going on, but it is obvious that no one is going back to bed anytime soon, so he gets the weed as well. There never is a dull moment with this bunch. When one crisis ends, here comes another one, but this is different. Rashida is the only one who is true to Iris, the only one who acts like she really cares and has her back. She matches Iris' ambition and is not about having a man grant her every wish or jump to satisfy every one of her silly whims like the others. She is his last belief in genuine friendship, the closest example of balance and reciprocity. A realist sees everything, and she is the realest one on the team. Malcolm hopes Iris sees it too.

When Iris returns from upstairs she joins us at the kitchenette.

"What is going on?"

"I wouldn't believe it unless I had seen it with my own eyes. When you dropped me off, I walked in the door and heard a strange noise, like maybe a mouse was messing around in the trash. I made my way to the kitchen, and there was Tommy with Sherice pinned to the floor with his face all up and in her box! Mind you, that sloppy bastard was supposed to be watching my son. What if Jaden would have gotten up? Anything could have happened! He could have fallen down the steps, or made it down the steps and walked in on his uncle going in on her coochie like Lardo from *Stand By Me*!"

Malcolm fights hard to hold back a chuckle.

"I tried to beat that bitch Sherice down! She had the nerve to say that I'm jealous because I ain't getting any on a regular, and that there was no way for them not to have heard Jaden if he would have gotten out of bed. I leaped over Tommy and tried to knock her fucking head off. Tommy grabbed me talking about I'm trippin', and by then, ma and Mr. Jenkins were down the steps cussing and making me out to be the asshole. I told them that I didn't have to explain shit and that I am sick and tired of them and that house. Talking shit about old stuff like when Jaden broke this and when I borrowed that. I threw a few things in a bag, got Jaden and was out."

"I should have known. You got that crazed-mother look."

"It may seem like a small thing but fuck that! There are certain things you expect not to walk in on, especially when your baby is there and the people that are supposed to protect him are on some bullshit!"

"You'll get no argument outta me. Only you know your limits, and my guess is this is it and you're ready for more. What is right for us has a way of putting an end to certain shit, giving us no other option but to face what is waiting on the other side of our choices. There is nothing like a made-up mind. On that note, the guest room is yours until you find a place for you and your boy. And I will leave y'all to the deep sister talk that I know is about to happen."

"Thanks, Malcolm, but I'm gonna have me a place in a nice neighborhood and with reasonable rent. I am no charity case. It took time, but I'm finally getting rid of the dead weight. I can't let nobody hold me back, even if that includes my family. They're so negative that it's like they expect the worst from me, almost pushing me to be, and that shit messes with my energy, and I need that to achieve my goals. I'm mad as all hell right now, but this is what I need. What we need."

Malcolm finds Rashida's ability to break out of the prison of emotionally painful familial ties commendable. That is a trait of a mentally strong person, one who can scrutinize people for who and what they are. If only Iris would follow suit when it comes to that sneaky-ass Clarke. There has always been this thing about her that as a man, Malcolm didn't like. It could be that arrogant air about her that brazenly assumes every man can be hers just because of how fly she thinks she is. Only a trick would up and quit a job and then depend on men to cover the cost of her immaturity. Mostly it is the depraved look in her eyes, acting as a public announcement that everything is her prey and Malcolm knows that she is not to be trusted.

Chapter Seventeen

p Art Y . n o b uLLShit .

THE SQUAD MEETS ME IN THE lobby of the Marriott Hotel in Center City, the hub of Philadelphia's business and historic districts. We cross Marquis Bedsitting Suite 1717's threshold, tip the bellhops and embark on a retreat of stylish comfort. Dazzling clusters of ivory roses sit in the brightness of the sun's beam while honeydew melon scented candles smell up the room something good. The hot tub, parlor, full bath, balcony and abundantly stocked bar speak to the celebratory spirit of the occasion. The master and two connecting bedrooms are consistent with the rich design of the establishment and its eye-catching attention to detail. The girls and I settle in and sit down to hash out our plans over a blunt.

"I say we go down to one of the hotel restaurants, have a four-star meal and tons of drinks, then we come back up to the room, finish getting twisted and chill in that hot-ass hot tub."

"I like that idea, Sage. Maybe I'll snag me a potential husband … NOT!"

"Clarke, you know you ain't even the marrying type."

"For the right amount of zeros, you never can tell."

Ila rolls her eyes at Clarke's comment to Sage, trying to rid herself of the aggravation and sheer insanity in tolerating the irking behavior of this gold-digging bitch on the strength of her being Iris' high school friend, and by Ila's standards, not a very good one at that.

"Look, let's order room service and do the damn thang for Iris up here — strictly girls night. This ain't about finding no man; this is about celebrating with our sister."

Toya stands near Ila, throws an arm around her shoulder and declares: "I agree. We should hold up in this room pajama party style for Iris."

Never thought I'd see Sage and Clarke side against Ila and Toya. Surely didn't plan on being the tiebreaker, either. You never can be sure when the bad attitude of a sore loser will show up and shit on all the fun.

"All I want is a decent meal. I say we let fate decide."

Puzzled faces look on as I reach into my pocket and pull out a shiny quarter.

"Call it in the air."

I throw the coin up and Clarke calls heads.

"To the restaurant we go."

Clarke and Sage slap hands while Ila sucks her teeth and Toya plops down on the bed. Ila thinks it's no long shot that Clarke won by way of head.

"Why you wanna be held up in this suite anyway? We got all night to talk shit and get high."

"Sage, I'm not in the mood for a bunch of strangers or random dudes."

"Nah, Piccolo got that ass on lock. Since he hit it, you haven't so much as looked at another dude. What — the — deal — Ila?"

"There is no deal, Sage. Let's just say that our thing is more than a fling."

Mahzi Kane   Tea Leaves

With a girlish grin, Ila saunters into the bathroom to freshen up and I feel like the cat that ate every canary in the pet store as I reapply my makeup. Besides being the only one in the room who knows that the shit with Ila and Piccolo isn't as deep as she presumes it to be, I arranged for some adult entertainment later on that night, which is the real reason I want to go to the restaurant so that Darkness, the Sex Instructor and Hot Rod can set up their stage show. Iris said that she didn't want a stripper, but what does she know? Somebody has to salvage an inkling of tradition so this thing isn't a total washout, and I decided I am the only one who can pull it off. Clarke to the rescue.

Refreshed and ready, my girls and I head down to the steakhouse. We hit the door like celebrities with eyes trailing our every move as we zigzag through tables following the hostess. We take our seats, and Clarke immediately flirts with the adjacent table of men. After the waiter takes our orders, the circle of admirers send over a bottle of Chablis. In true floozy mode, Clarke sends back a Thank You note that none of us see but can bet money that it's totally inappropriate. Over our meal, we whoop it up and revisit old events as if we're in our 70s and have seen so much of life pass by. The spectrum of our dialogue lightens each burden and helps to smooth out the uneasiness associated with the new changes on the horizon. At this table, with these women, is the power to regain optimism about our choices. Our feelings are heard. Here we can reflect on who we are and help one another cope with personal shortcomings, and this support prevents our bond from spoiling. Instead it thrives and helps us grow as individuals. By 9, we are borderline drunk, overfed and eager to return to the room. The liquor has us singing loudly off the elevator and down the hallway. Up in front, Clarke whispers into Sage's ear and then Toya lingers in the back with me. Clarke opens the door and the quarters have taken on a burlesque vibe of green and white feathers, a spinning silver strobe light, glitter balloons, a mini-stage with a chair in the center and a gaudy trunk full of black lace fans, sequin masquerade masks, colorful wigs, boas and a glitzy "bride" tiara on top.

One foot inside and they yell, "Surprise!" as the chorus of "Shake Whatcha Mama Gave Ya'" plays. My flushed cheeks tell my story — caught off guard but pleased that they did this for me, although I told them not to. Ila passes shots around until we all have two, Toya hands out props, Rashida readies the weed pipe, and Clarke places a stack of dollar bills in front of me as we look forward to an action-packed showcase of debauchery.

Hot Rod is a tanned man of 200 pounds of nothing but muscle that balloon through the slits of his tasseled vest. Bulging eyes, baldhead and a studded tongue approach, take my hand and lead me to my throne. I sit in my assigned seat and witness his bulky gyrations transform into a thousand contorted positions timed perfectly to the bass. With each pop and lock, he moves his body like magic, and his glistening chest muscles and bubble butt go bang-bang to the beat. Each grind is an aggressive and domineering reminder of his skill and intent to prove he has what it takes to put it on you in a big way. Clarke and Ila stuff his tan camouflage trunks with dollars while Sage and Toya hoot like construction workers on their lunch break. By the time his set is done, he is as sweaty as a pig and wearing nothing but his G-string pouch. We refill our glasses and pat the perspiration from ourselves, feeling like wanton women of the night.

"He is unbelievable. Toya, I never heard you holla like that, girl!"

"Ila, he has the athletic body of a God. I got to give it up for what the good Lord made!"

Darkness emerges, and his name describes him on all counts. He is as black as black can get; that motherland, Shaka Zulu black. His teeth are elephant-tusk white — his body lean and cut, accented by black suspenders and skin-tight, black booty shorts that make me wonder what is in his package. This man wears sex like a scent you can't help but notice. When the R&B classic "Pony" starts to play, I know it is about to get crazy. Gripping his black hard hat, his slow-wind style has a sensuous and methodical allure. He stands on the stage and slowly rubs his black do-rag over his face with one hand while he motions his other to mimic the backstroke movements of a tall, dark and handsome fantasy rider. He moves me to the stage, lip-syncing the chorus and rocking to the beat. Darkness flips me upside down and puts the front of his head between my legs, my face against the slickness of his stallion thighs, until he lays me out and slinks his body up, down and against mine. This black God stands over me, places his hat on his erected bulge, and makes it bounce up and down like he's dying to do something bad with it.

Mahzi Kane Tea Leaves

His upright position is one of controlled teasing, and his steady gaze of interest mesmerizes each set of eyes glued to this talented display. After an erotic tea-bagging, a steamy meat show, and wearing nothing but his beautiful black skin, Darkness exits to catcalls and a storm of dollar bills. We smoke and engage in another round of shots while we re-enact our favorite parts of the sex show so far.

"Clarke, he is an amazing piece of work — I mean he is ridiculously hot."

"I couldn't agree with you more, Rashida. He got sex appeal for days. The things I would do to that ass is criminal!"

I take my seat and wait on the finale like it's free money. The Sex Instructor is caramel-colored in a white sleeveless hoody, his shoulders slightly slumped, with long tattooed arms, and at least size 12s in his white leather boots. His eyes sing seduction, and his lips advertise pleasure, but it is his body that amazes us with nasty percolator moves. I can almost hear each raunchy tongue flick as he strokes himself and uses his imagination to perform a simulated masturbation, where he reveals way too many inches of manhood. One word: impressive. He grabs a glass and traces the rim of the glass with the rim of him. I stand up and clap, Toya holds her mouth in shock, Sage smacks his ass, and Clarke throws a bunch of $20 bills at his feet in out of this world objectification.

Sage yells, "You betta make this money, boy!!"

He sheds his breakaway, sequined thong and flings his body back and forth like the pit in the pendulum. He is used to being used, I see, if not directly from his line of work, certainly from his

Mahzi Kane   Tea Leaves

exploits as an accomplished lover. My internal film reel of freaky possibilities is interrupted by a handstand that confirms that the number one wonder of the world is a Blackman with a big dick.

The tour begins. The Sex Instructor moves to Toya, picks her up and jiggles her butt as she braces herself in his twirls of dirty dancing. He angles Rashida around in her chair, pushes her head down and pounds away at her to the rhythm of the drums, the heels of her shoes helplessly flapping mid-air. He greets Sage, his leg on her shoulder, and flings his stuff in her face like a flag in gale-force winds. With little effort, he anchors Ila by her waist, flips her around, upside down and slams his face is between her legs like a sex machine. Before he has the chance to do anything, Clarke jumps on him, wrapping her legs around him, and whips her hair back and forth while circling one hand around her head, looking like a full-fledged horn dog. Seemingly unimpressed, he puts Clarke down, and Hot Rod and Darkness join him as they approach me to deliver the most erotic lap dance invented. Between grinds, they violently jerk my chair and change its position as they each plaster me with lies, rubbing me lovingly as if caressing their most favorite thing in the world. I am on all fours with the Sex Instructor behind me and Darkness in front for a pretend threesome, one grinding my face to the grove of the bass line, the other with his shiny dome below, and before I know it all three of us roll from one side of the floor to the other, the newest version of stop, drop and roll, I suppose. The ladies shower us with loose dollars and lively cheers, under the influence of the same spell they just put on me.

The live entertainment departs, we get into our swimsuits and hop into the hot tub, where four pre-rolled blunts dipped in cognac and a bottle of Hennessy wait. In a hodgepodge of smells, crackled voices and giggles, we attempt to take the mood from excited to relaxed but we are still feeling it — feeling this moment that we won't be able to get back, except over future girl talks where we attempt to relive the sentiment.

"Iris, you impressed me tonight, girl! You actually let yourself have some real fun. Now that's the Iris I know and love. We haven't done it like this since our apartment days."

"Clarke, I will admit that I haven't enjoyed myself like that in a lonnnnng time."

"Those were really first-rate strippers. I have to give you your props, Clarke."

"Thanks, Sage. I told the service to only send those who could get an old granny wet. You know how I roll, only the best for my best friend."

I had to cut my eye at Clarke. Iris' best friend? Yeah, whatever. After all, I knew Iris the longest, and on a profound level. Our history is like no other woman in that room. Iris was in the delivery room for Jaden's birth when Erik was nowhere to be found. I was the first of the squad to know that she and Malcolm were engaged. Just because Clarke and Iris shared a stank apartment and made up some dance steps however long ago, she thinks that qualifies her as a best friend. I will let it slide because Clarke considering Iris to be her closest friend doesn't mean that it is reciprocated. It still bothers me though, because Clarke has the balls to say it in front of us all.

"OK, y'all. Let's take it back to our college days. Time for a game. It's called I've Got a Secret to Tell. Who wants to start?"

"I will, Iris."

"Toya has secrets? Let me clutch my pearls and say three Hail Marys."

"Clarke, be nice."

"I am being nice. I didn't think you did anything outside of falling in love with married men. But I do have to remember that you're a church girl, and you know what they say about ya'll."

"Then you'd fit right in. As I was saying, me and Lamont aren't seeing each other anymore."

"Well, it's about fucking time! There's no reason for you to be letting somebody who's already on lockdown put you on lockdown. Ain't no money in that."

"Clarke, that is so shallow. Toya, I'm happy you've finally stopped settling. If a man isn't making you his number one, you don't need him."

"That's what I meant, Ila."

"That's not what you said, Clarke."

"Can I finish? His wife called me at my job and told me that she always knew about me and that he was only in it for the sex. They're having another baby."

"He's a no-good son-of-a-bitch, and she's simple for putting up with his ass. The first man to cheat on me will be out the door."

"How can you be sure that a man has never cheated on you, Ila?"

Mahzi Kane   Tea Leaves

"The same way you can be so sure, Clarke."

Dead silence, and you can cut the tension in it with a butter knife, fry it up and pop it in your mouth as Ila and Clarke face off. Toya begins again, and the spotlight is off of the usual cat-fight.

"I'm dealing with it. I don't want to be with him, but I'm not going to lie, the love is still in my heart. I put so much into loving him that I can't stop caring overnight."

"I can't feel that. The last thing I have for Erik is love. I mean I don't want anything bad to happen to him because he's Jaden's father, but after he treated me the way he did, the love is most certainly lost and will not make a comeback!"

"I'm not that callous."

"Neither am I, Toya, but I can't tolerate dumb shit. Forgiving and still loving a man that broke my heart left me feeling like a fool, not once but twice, so no, it's no longer in me to ride with a man on the strength of love."

"I'm next."

"What you gotta say, Sage?"

"I'm celibate."

The entire hot tub bursts into laughter, and Ila knocks over her drink.

"You are what?! You love sex more than I do. How is this humanly possible?"

"Ila, I had an eye-opening experience that made me realize that I have to be careful with my body."

"What happened?"

"I got a sexually transmitted disease."

"Jesus in heaven!"

"Toya calm down, I'm not dying. I am embarrassed and ashamed, but I'm growing from it.

I haven't had sex in almost a month, and I feel good about my resolution not to. It has to be more to life than fucking men because they look good or have money. Why buy the cow if they can get the milk, eggs and cheese for free?"

"Sage, why didn't you tell me? We dawgs, roadies, closer than close, and you know I would have helped you through this - went with you to the doctor's, you know, supported you. I don't like to think of you feeling down on you, like you've dishonored yourself for doing what comes natural."

"Ila I know that but I had to handle it on my own. I was humiliated, and I felt like an idiot for not using a condom every time. It has nothing to do with you. You know me and you are ride or die, but at the end of the day, I am responsible for my actions, and I had to deal with it my way."

Sage reaches for Ila's hand to show her that nothing between them has changed.

"I had oral sex with Piccolo."

"Now this I can't believe — you must truly love that man!"

"Iris, I don't know what I feel. I went from thinking about it to doing it, and I don't know why, but I want to give him so much of me, you know? I haven't felt this way about a man before, and I've never had any other's thang in my mouth, and on that alone, this has to be something deep."

"Did you like it?"

"Do you like it, Clarke?"

"Why are you so hostile toward me, Ila?"

"Don't ask stupid questions. I enjoy all my experiences with him, and every one of them is a step closer to us growing into a relationship."

Mahzi Kane   Tea Leaves

"I had an abortion."

Everybody looks at Clarke.

"An abortion? When?"

"A few months ago, Iris. I found out that I was knocked up, I didn't know who the father was, and I decided it was best to have the procedure done."

"I could never kill my baby — that's a mortal sin."

"There's a fine line between sinner and saint, Toya. You of all people should know that."

"I don't care what you say, committing adultery and killing an innocent baby are on two different sides of the sin coin, Clarke."

"If you think so, but Toya, a sin is a sin."

"Was it really that easy for you, Clarke?"

"Not as easy as getting my nails done, but I didn't cry or whine about it. I made the best decision in a bad situation, Sage."

"I thought about having an abortion when I was pregnant with Jaden. I didn't have a job, Erik was cheating like a dirty scoundrel out in the streets, and I was living at home with my ma. It seemed like the easy choice to make, but I thought about having to answer for my actions."

"It had to be more than that. What really made you decide to have your baby, Rashida?"

"If I had to be all the way real, it was to keep Erik. It was the dumbest, smartest thing that I ever did. Nothing I could have done or said would have stopped Erik from cheating, but at least I took responsibility for my actions. Every time we lay down with a man, we know what can happen. Plan to prevent it or deal with it but Clarke, it's ridiculous to wait to fix if after the fact. That's like waiting until the last second to try to get out of the path of a runaway train."

"Rashida, I'm far from mother material. Most times I don't even like the idea of kids. It doesn't fit. I don't know what good mothering looks like so I think that I did do the responsible thing."

"My mother passed when I was a child, and I plan to be an outstanding mother. Don't use your parent as an excuse. Be real for once, Clarke."

"Ms. Ila, I am nothing but real. I didn't want the baby, I'm too selfish to be anybody's mother, I want to do what I want to do when I want to do it, and I'm not ready to stop that for anybody. Real enough?"

"You're right, Clarke, you did what was fair. A baby doesn't deserve you."

"How can you say that to me, Iris?"

"Now you know I speak the truth. You weren't ready months ago, you may never be ready and by your own admission, motherhood isn't your goal. When I add all that up, and if you look at having to give up what you want in order for your child to exist as a burden, then you aren't built for the blessing of parenthood."

I roll my eyes and drink from my cup, mad as hell that there is nothing I can come back with because Iris is on point as usual.

"Everyone's told a secret but you, Iris."

Toya is right, but I don't know what to say. I intended for this to be a silly game, but this is getting too heavy, and the night before my wedding is not the time to try to unpack and sort through years of baggage.

"My secret is ... every now and then, without even realizing it, I get this dying urge from out of nowhere to do the unthinkable."

Everyone waits for Iris to expose a scandalous chapter from her book of life that has been sealed off from the world.

"This urge makes me want to ... want to ... eat chicken."

I bow my head to exaggerate the moment, and the ladies suck their teeth and throw their hands into the air with boisterous laughter.

"Come on, y'all, I had to! There is no way we gone turn this into a group therapy session. Ain't this a party?"

Sage exits the hot tub and returns with a bottle of wine and another blunt. This blunt is special. It has North Philly super-green, purple haze, Khan bud, and the rolling paper is laced with syrup to make it burn extra slow. Sage fills our glasses and takes her place back inside the hot tub. I light the blunt, take a hit, and it goes straight to my head.

"I really appreciate each of you and thank each of you for being who you are and sharing intimate parts of your story on my final night as Iris Isan. Cheers, bitches!"

Chapter Eighteen

one + one : i r i S

THIS IS IT — THE DAY THAT I've tediously planned for over a year. The day that I've been breathlessly anticipating since he asked the question and I answered "yes." I become somebody's wife on this sacred day — and not just any somebody, but a man that I adore and admire. The squad and I wake up to a lovely breakfast brought up by room service. The morning is light and serene, even Ila and Clarke aren't their normal catty selves toward one another. The ceremony commences at 6:00 pm in the open-air theater at Longwood Gardens in Brandywine Valley, about 45 minutes away, and has 20 indoor gardens where plants are grown and is the perfect place to plant the seeds for our marriage. Three hundred and fifty acres of land are open to the general public, including palm collections, the sacred lotus flower, a lily display garden and the stately topiary elephant.

When we pull up to the garden I smile at the hardwood forests that overflow with oak and hickory trees, and the sight of golden weeping willows settle the butterflies inside. Wildflowers speckle the grounds as we amble by numerous greenhouses. The orchids seem to sing congratulations as cockscombs wish me many years of happiness. We stop to take pictures at the beautiful Italian water fountain, and I look off into the sky for a second, reflecting on the beauty of the day and the newness to come. Walking through flowered archways, we enter the ceremony and reception area. Honeydew melon green and ivory roses are far and wide. Tables are topped with wicker baskets intricately laced with ivory raffia and blooming green roses sparkling at the tips. Around the basket, a ribbon reads "Malcolm & Iris, For the Rest of Our Eternity." The tables are arranged in a half-circle, with an aisle up the middle and a throne-like table for two at the front. An elaborate ice sculpture is off to the side, along with a table for gifts. As we marvel over the splendor of the room, the engine of another vehicle is heard in the distance. The girls sweep me off in superstitious fashion, saying it is bad luck, which I tell them I don't believe in, but they continue nonetheless. I insist that Rashida check to see if Malcolm has arrived, and she confirms that he is here. Soon guests filter in through the same flowered entryway and take their assigned seats.

In my bridal suite, I replay our relationship: our first date when all we did was talk, never making it to the restaurant; the nights he sat with me and encouraged the pretty words to flow from my pen and meet the pages, and when he made love to me on the beach in the rain and I let the tears of his name fall from every part of me.

"Come on baby doll, it's time to take that walk."

I turn and it's my mother, decked out in her ivory gown, and as if sensing my nervousness she sits next to me and rubs the side of my face.

"Iris, there's nothing like being a man's wife. It's a kinship that is beyond this world. It transcends a crush and whoever happened in the past. You're joining an elite group, at least when it's done right, and baby doll, you and him, y'all doing it right. Everyone can feel the joy in the commitment you two share. The future is bright. Embrace it. Wear your love proudly. Protect it. Now your daddy's waiting for us, so let's go start the rest of your life."

The African children's ensemble welcomes us all with traditional dance and drumming. Their high-spirited reverberation take us across seas and it feels as if we are back in the birth place of civilization, taking part in a ritual that has been passed down from generation to generation. Upon completion, Devine Essence approaches the microphone and belts out the melodious notes about being ready for love. The guests are signaled to stand. My parents are on each side of me, walking through the semi-circle of loved ones. Malcolm stands at the other end of the room, and it's like I'm seeing him for the first time. He walks toward us, and we meet in the middle of the aisle where he hugs my mom, shakes my dad's hand and then takes me by the elbow. At the altar, I see a tear fall and land on his cheek. I reach to wipe it, and that's when I know without reservation that I am meant for this man.

Our officiant Mr. Grey, an esteemed elder that we've come to know and value, approaches the altar and places a hand on my head and the other on Malcolm's.

"Welcome family and friends. Today we celebrate the coming together of love. We ask them to fill each other with love and use all the jewels bestowed upon them, to employ all that is necessary to be rich and plentiful, not only in the material world but in the essence of their souls. Today, Malcolm and Iris shall exchange promises and offerings."

"Iris, from the second I laid eyes on you, I've been in love. The moment you spoke to me, I was enchanted. I listen to the things that you say in awe, impressed by the inner workings of a mind like yours. I promise compassion and protection, to nurture you, and build a place so full, so inspiring that you can't help but find things that you didn't even know you wanted to write about. I offer you time — time to flourish, to hunger after new truths and new worlds to conquer. I am your student and your teacher. You motivate and support my ambition. You calm me like nothing else. In your eyes I found home. In your words I found my solace. In your soul, every day, I find my mate. You celebrate our wins and make sure we overcome misses. I stand here a happy and fulfilled man, comforted by the knowledge that we are built to last."

"Malcolm, it is such a privilege to spend life with my best friend. I promise to experience each moment with passion, but this is far more than desire. This is value. I promise to uphold all that we've put into this relationship forever, and to thirst after our love daily. You are the hero I never thought I needed, my king with a grand standard that measures how great we can be, and the balance that feeds my peace. Our love is all our pretty words breathing life into us, us breathing love into each other. I promise to breathe deeply, as if it's my first and my last. We are bonded by our word, connected in righteousness. My words show that I chose you. My actions prove that I keep choosing you every day without hesitation. I am in love with you always and forever."

"These rings represent the eternal connection of Malcolm and Iris Bey. This cipher is 360 degrees of growing, elevating and evolving from individuals into a bonded unit. It symbolizes the unification of husband and wife. Malcolm, adorn your queen."

Malcolm places a beautiful pearl set in platinum onto my left ring finger. I couldn't have asked for a more fitting ring if I had picked it myself.

"Iris, adorn your king."

I place Malcolm's platinum band onto his left ring finger, and we hold hands. One of the children from the dance ensemble carries out the handcrafted marriage broom and lays it a few inches in front of us. We look at each other and soar over the broom, bound by our hearts, ready and eager for the newness of being husband and wife.

The reception commences and we settle in on our throne waiting for our dinner and accepting the greeting line of loved ones buzzing about the ceremony and the beauty in everything around us. Jumbo shells stuffed with spinach, French onion soup, mixed green salad, tomato bruschetta, crudités with dips and hummus, vegetable skewers, stuffed mushrooms, grilled asparagus, soba noodles, vegetable lasagna, eggplant parmesan, butternut squash ravioli, blackened red snapper, garlic mashed potatoes, collard greens, barbecued tofu and long grain rice, three varieties of stir fry, green beans, yams, vegan macaroni and cheese, and a sweet cart encompass the delectable feast we patiently anticipate. I didn't realize how genuinely excited folks are for people in love. Once all of our guests greet us, the entire African dance troupe return to perform their grand finale. Colorful stilt walkers, commanding drummers, elaborate dancing, and death-defying flame throwers amaze us and bottle the magic of the evening into an intricate fireworks display that erupts from the top of the open-air theater.

I bet Clarke is eating her words because this is worth every dime spent. Wide smiles wrap the faces of Clarke, Sage, Ila, Toya and Rashida, who are all seated at a designated table alongside a special nook for my parents, Grandma Rue and Malcolm's Aunt Faye. The wait staff serves our guests and quickly removes plates and bowls as they empty. The crowd parts like the Red Sea as Malcolm and I set out to share our first dance as husband and wife. The band gets people up out of their seats and the hits have them grooving on the dance floor. Typical of black folks, the Electric Slide filters about, and the floor is mobbed by anxious supporters eager to engage in the line dance. My dad clangs his fork to his glass, signaling that it is time for a toast. The band halts, and everyone raises a champagne flute.

"The day Iris was born, there was this thing in her eyes that told her mama and I that she was special, and while every parent says that about their child, there was an undoubted difference in her demeanor. That's why we named her Iris, because you could see straight to the purity in her soul and know that she was destined for great things. You see, it was in her eyes. You've always made your mama and me proud of you, and today you're reaping the reward of being an extraordinary woman. Malcolm, make sure you take care of my baby. It ain't gonna be a walk in the park 'cause Lord knows she can be as stubborn as her mama, but you'll make her a fabulous husband because you're a decent man who's getting my marvelous baby girl. To Iris and Malcolm."

The festive sound of celebration permeates the theater as Malcolm, the photographer and I take to the grounds for photos. Although it's customary for the bride and groom to kiss at the end of the ceremony, Malcolm and I share our passionate kiss by the angel's trumpet floral arrangement. The luscious aroma of our intimacy, flowers and the fragrance of evermore plus the sweetness of Malcolm's kiss makes my head spin with happiness and delight. We finish taking our pictures and return to the reception. Once we are at our seats, Rashida takes the altar.

"Iris and Malcolm, I have never met two people so perfectly suited for one another. Malcolm, take good care of my sister because she's been my rock when I needed her to, my good advice when I wished she would shut up and a surrogate father to my son when I felt like I was walking through parenthood alone. Iris, you have always been an excellent woman to Malcolm, and now you'll be an exceptional wife because you have the ideal example in your parents. At 12, we pricked our fingers behind Ms. Sunket's backyard and became blood sisters, and since that day I've never been by myself because we always had each other. Today you move on to explore and conquer new horizons, and with a new title that fits you so well. I love y'all and wish you two all the happiness that your universe can hold. To Iris and Malcolm."

The unwedding concludes with the final dance of father and bride. I feel like the same little girl who used to stand on her daddies' toes as he waltzed me around the dining room to Sam Cooke. My father holds me so close, not wanting the dance to end because he'll have to let go. I whisper in his ear not to worry — I'm not going to the other side of the world. He gives me a sheepish smile and kisses me on the forehead as Malcolm approaches to lead me out of the flowered archways that I had entered hours ago. Nothing compares to the euphoria as Malcolm and I get into the Rolls-Royce, say farewell to our guests and are off to honeymoon in the Fiji Islands.

Chapter Nineteen

o FF - bALAnce : r A S h i D A

THE HOUSE IS QUIET. MALCOLM AND
Iris are honeymooning and Jaden is with Erik, so
I've been filling my schedule with tons of overtime.
I took the day off to visit two apartments, one in
Northern Liberties and the other in Germantown.
It's a lovely day outside so I'm walking even though
Iris gave me the go-head to drive her car. I meet
the landlord for the first apartment at 11:30 a.m.
It's a compact version of Iris and Malcolm's. Both
bedrooms are on the same landing, and there is one
bathroom. Other families with children reside in
the building, which is a plus, but the rent is $725 a
month, which is more than I want to pay. The place
isn't screaming anything to me except overpriced. I
thank Ms. Passini for her time but tell her that this
isn't what I am looking for.

I make my way to the second apartment, and
the landlord and I pull up at the same time. Upon
entering I am impressed by the new floors and
fresh coat of paint. The kitchen has plenty of
counter space and a new refrigerator. The upstairs
has two cozy bedrooms, a spacious bathroom, and
a washer and dryer in the pantry area. The landlord
informs me that all of this is going for $625 a
month. I am thoroughly interested, but the
neighborhood is leaving a nasty taste in my mouth.
I stepped over several crack vials, and the corner
stoops are filtered with grown men lounging in the
middle of the day. I tell the landlord that I'll think
about it because I have several other places to see.
He tells me that he will keep me in mind because

he likes renting to young people who are making their start in the world.

I sit in the car, contemplating the second apartment. I don't want to jump at the first apartment that I like. I think I'll follow up on the first-time-homeowners program that I heard about at work. If I can get a house of my own for the same amount that it would cost to rent every month, that's a real prize. The only problem with that is finding out how long it takes to get into the house.

I am deep in my thoughts when something familiar makes me take notice . . . Piccolo and Clarke coming out of the apartment building across the street!

*

Over the last two days, I've been racking my brain for the best way to handle this Piccolo predicament. I really don't have any proof that something foul is taking place, but knowing Clarke, nothing good will come from this. I mean, what logical reason do they have for being together, alone, in the middle of the day? Iris comes home today and I can't wait because I need help carrying this load. I don't like hitting her with drama as soon as she returns from her honeymoon, but I'm at a loss for what to do. I can't tell Ila without proof, and I can't confront Clarke for the simple fact that I have a very low tolerance for her smart-ass responses.

I decide to leave Iris a message on her cell phone and cross my fingers that she listens to it before she gets home. I hear the door open as I remove vegetable lasagna from the oven in celebration of their homecoming. Iris has been giving me cooking lessons, and vegetarian eating isn't as boring as I assumed. I sit the lasagna out to cool, remove my apron and rush to the living room to embrace the newlyweds.

"Welcome back, y'all!"

I give hugs and kisses and then help them bring in their luggage. I hand Malcolm his list of messages and the pile of mail.

"Dinner is waiting if y'all want to eat."

"Go head, Rashida, I see you. You enjoying it here, huh?"

"Definitely, Malcolm, but I'm not getting too comfortable. I'm still on a massive hunt."

"Don't trip, girl. You'll find your place, and when you see it, you'll know. I'm going upstairs to shower and relax. I'll let y'all catch up."

Malcolm's bizarre intonation hints that Iris has heard the message and discussed it with him.

"Wassup, Iris? How was it?"

"I didn't wanna come back, Rashida, I'm trying to tell you! It was so inspiring; I wrote about 10 poems. Wait until you see the pictures I took! The water, the sand, it all was so perfect that it looked fake. We were in awe, girl. Our villa was private with a sunken Jacuzzi that got to know us personally and we snorkeled in the ocean and had a private dinner on the beach while a Fijian band played. Magical shit, I'm telling you!"

"I know you did some extra freak shit."

"Oh we had the most fun when we had on the least amount of clothes. Where's Jaden?"

"Still with his father. He'll be back tomorrow. Did you, ah, get my message?"

"Of course I did. What are we going to do?"

"I was hoping you'd have the answer to that."

Iris sits on the sofa staring into another dimension. Within seconds, she is up and grabs the telephone.

Mahzi Kane   Tea Leaves

"Who are you calling?"

"Clarke."

It's my turn to sit on the sofa as Iris paces back and forth waiting for Clarke to answer. I have no idea what Iris is going to say or how she is going to handle this. I go into the kitchen and pick up the other end to listen.

"Hey, Clarke, what's the deal?"

"Hi, Iris! When did you get back, lady? How was it? I know y'all had a ball boning on the beach and seeing all the sights. Did you bring me back a souvenir?"

"Slow down, Clarke, dag. First things first: Are you or have you been fucking Piccolo?"

There is silence on the phone, and I watch Iris' jawline tighten as she taps her foot waiting for Clarke's response.

"Why you asking me a question like that as soon as you come back from your honeymoon?"

"Answer the question, Clarke."

"Who told you that?"

"Answer the fucking question, Clarke!"

"Why are you getting upset? He's not your husband."

"So it's true?"

"Yes, I had sex with him once. Is that what you want to hear?!"

"No, that's not what the fuck I want to hear! I can't believe you, Clarke! Of all the stunts you've pulled, this is the ultimate. I know that you don't like Ila, but how could you, why would you stoop that low and sleep with her man?"

"That's not her man, and he approached me!"

"And that makes it right?! You know how that woman feels about him, and even if you didn't go after him, which I don't fucking believe, don't you have any morals? Don't you even care? There's a line that I thought even your shallow ass wouldn't cross — respect for the squad; death before dishonor, but clearly I am mistaken. All you care about is Clarke, money and dick. For all I know, you'd fuck Malcolm!"

"How can you say that, Iris? I would never do anything to hurt you, and you know it!"

"I don't know shit when it comes to you, I have no clue what you are capable of doing, or the things that you allow yourself to be OK with doing to people. You think it's fine to mistreat Ila because you don't like her? Well it's not! To be so intelligent, you are as dumb as a fucking cup. Don't you realize that by hurting her, you're hurting me! Shit, that's hurting us all! She's my sister, and up until this point so were you."

"What does that mean?"

"It means that I'm done with you! You're a fucking snake, and doing slick shit is just as much a part of who you are as shedding skin. You think the shit you do is cute when it *so* isn't and I'd be begging to get bit if I keep you around."

"Iris, you don't mean that. You can't mean that. You gonna throw away a 10-year friendship over a nigga that ain't mine or yours? It was one time damn! He loves Ila, so what's the real harm? I saw him the other day to get my bracelet, and he said that sleeping with me was a big mistake and that he wants to be with her, so why ruin whatever it is they're trying to do? Let this ride! We can lock this in the vault, and nobody will suffer. You're my closest friend, the one who gets me when nobody else understands me Iris!"

"You mean I was. I can't be friends with low-down, conniving bitches like you. And if you think I'm mad, wait until Ila gets a hold of your ass."

"How is she going to find out?"

Mahzi Kane   Tea Leaves

"I'm giving you 24 hours to come clean, or I'm dropping the dime on your ass. Either way watch your back because she is going to fuck you up."

"I can't believe that you're choosing her over me, Iris!"

"You made that choice. You failed to be who I thought you were, who I thought was hiding behind all the ugly shit other people see in you, but I was so wrong. Stay away from me, and grow the fuck up, Clarke!"

By this time, Malcolm is in the kitchen because Iris was screaming into the receiver. Iris slams the phone down and falls into Malcolm's arms in tears. Despite Clarke's imperfections Iris loves her like a sister, but the inevitable is here.

*

Lying in this in-between room, belly full, my mind racing, so unable to stop thinking about what is going to go down when Ila finds out that her arch nemesis slept with her prince charming. Malcolm yells down the hall and tells me to pick up the telephone.

"Yes?"

"Why didn't you put enough socks in the bag for my son?"

"You're calling me at 10:30 at night to ask about socks? You can't be serious, Erik?"

"What am I supposed to put on my son feet in the morning, paper towels?"

"What do you want me to do about it now?"

"I want you to pack the damn bag right, Rashida. It ain't that hard, especially for you, Miss College Lady."

"Yup, and I'm smart enough to know that you should have your own shit for your son — I shouldn't have to send one piece of nothing because as a parent you should be prepared to clothe yours."

"I'm not trying to hear that shit."

"That's your problem!"

"Rashida everything has to be how you want it to be or not at all. It's always a fight with you to get you to listen to what I think, or what I gotta say because with you I'm always wrong, I'm always the bad guy, forever the asshole! Well, you're not perfect, and all you had to say was that you forgot, but no, instead you flip it on me."

"What's the point of calling me up at this time of night to hear me apologize over a pair of socks? That's just silly or psychotic! It could have waited until you drop him off, but that would have defeated your plan on calling me up with your patented baby-daddy bullshit! I'm tired of this, Erik!"

"Well, so am I, Rashida!"

"We can't keep doing this like this. The way we communicate is a joke. That counseling that the judge suggested can help us because we go to war over every little thing, the smallest difference of opinion turns into a huge fight. Neither of us knows how to fix that, and our son needs for us to fix this as soon as possible. He can't keep seeing us act like this toward one another."

Erik is silent as he lets my suggestion sink in.

"I'ma try if you are. See you tomorrow."

He hangs up. Usually I'd run down the hall and vent to Iris about the latest jerky thing Erik has done and how much of an idiot he is, but instead I study the window and the moonlight coming in halfway, partly blocked by the shade yet still competing with the artificial light of the ceiling fan. Its draw is subtle, seeming to caress the windowpane, slowly seeping through the glass like the Earth is smiling and bringing joy to all that exists. The window feels nature's power and the moon's love. I wish that I could be that window: content with just being, existing to absorb the light instead of pointing out all that's good and all that's bad about being the window. There are so many sayings about light — come to the light, bring something to light, see the light — and in every way the light is there to illustrate, expand or emphasize what needs to be seen. Has me wondering what I need to see to make things better, to make things easier. I wish I could keep it light, but mostly I hope to be more like the light because the light seems happy.

Chapter Twenty

m Y S hitt Y F An : i L A

The majesty entwined in every detail of the unwedding was a great inspiration. For me, it's not about being a princess for a day and having all eyes on me. Nope, I've never been into fairytales, but I like the idea of feeling secure enough to give another person my heart. What's safer than having somebody take me forever, assured that nothing or nobody could separate us two? If I do get married, I must consult Iris because her wedding was the bomb, a remarkable example of black people in love. Piccolo and I are getting closer as the days go by, and I cross my fingers that this is an indication that he's going to ask me to be his in the near future. Next we'll be walking down the street holding hands, planning vacations and eventually exchanging keys, living together and existing on a level where I don't have to say it because he already knows what I'm thinking. The thought of marriage used to bore me, but who knows where this can lead? Who the hell could this be at my door at 11:00 in the morning?

"Piccolo. What a pleasant surprise! I was just thinking about you."

I hug him tight, inhaling his smell. Ordinarily I would have a fit if a man were to pop up at my apartment unannounced, but Piccolo gets a pass.

"Hey, baby, I wanted to see you. The impulsive side of me suggested that I surprise you, is that OK?"

"Boy, stop playing. You know it's cool or you would have gotten serious attitude by now. Do you want anything to drink?"

"No. I want to talk. Please sit down."

I sit down, biting at the corner of my lips.

"Ila, we've gotten tight over these couple of months, and I cannot deny that I like every bit of it. I hope that you're feeling the same about me. My life has been quite hectic, and you're the first thing that's making me want to slow down and enjoy the simple things in life like commitment and family."

Is he asking me to marry him?? As if reading my mind, he continues.

"I'm not ready to jump all in like Malcolm and Iris, but I would be a happy man if you would be my lady. I want it to be you and me, growing and learning about each other and our love. The manner in which Malcolm spoke about Iris, I was feeling that. What you think?"

I part my lips to tell him that I've been waiting for this since the day that I saw him on Wayne Avenue, but my telephone rings.

"Yes."

"Ila?"

"That's who you called, right? Who is this?"

"It's Clarke."

"What do you want?"

"I've been advised that you're gonna find out anyway so here goes: Piccolo and I slept together. It was only once. He told me that he feels awful that it happened. He really does want to be with you and only you."

And with that, the line is dead. I must be going deaf in both ears. Did she really say what I think I heard? Piccolo sees Ila's instant change in demeanor and rises from the couch to move closer to his woman, but before his touch reaches her

Mahzi Kane   Tea Leaves

shoulder she cocks him in the face with the telephone receiver.

"What the fuck is wrong with you, Ila?! Why did you hit me?"

"Her, why her?! You fucked HER! You know how I feel about her — you know I never trusted her! But I trusted you … you who sits in my face with all this 'be my lady' bullshit! Got your punk ass all in my face talking about commitment — what a joke! I hate you with every bit of woman that I am down to every bit of the man that you ain't! You low-down, two-faced bastard, if I had a gun I'd kill you dead! Get the fuck outta here, and take your lies with you!"

"Please calm down and tell me what the hell you're talking about?!"

"You know damn well what I'm talking about, asshole, unless you're screwing that many people. You slept with Clarke, Piccolo … CLARKE! That was her on my phone giving me some half-assed, non-remorseful confession about how she fucked you. YOU, Piccolo! If you know like I know, please get the fuck out. I can't see you right now, I don't want to look at you, standing there with your dirty dick, and I certainly don't want to hear anything that you have to say!"

"Let me explain, baby. I'm so sorry. I never intended to — the thing with Clarke was stupid, baby, believe me I know that. It terrifies me at times, you know, at how much and how fast I am falling in love with you, baby, but trust me I never meant for this to happen, and especially not with her. You're right, I crossed the line, but sometimes though, baby, the demons from our past make me second guess whether or not we'll work again, whether or not you'll be true to me and if we really are ready for a grown-up relationship that lasts."

Mahzi Kane   Tea Leaves

"And your way of dealing with that was to fuck somebody that I be with? Even though I can't stand the wench, she hangs with my crew — what kinda shit are you trying to pull on me, Piccolo?!"

"I know it don't make any sense, baby, but that's how love and feelings are, they don't make sense sometimes; they just are what they are, you know? I gave in to lust trying to convince myself that I'm not in love with you, but it didn't work, you hear me baby, it didn't work! I feel like shit, and I never feel guilty about anything! I don't want her, baby, I want you. Listen to me, please. We met up so I could return her bracelet, and she tried every trick to get me to fuck her again, but none of it worked, and this proves it, Ila! I want you. I LOVE you!"

"Well, doesn't that just make me the fucking world champ."

"I'll spend the rest of my life making up for this horrible mistake. Please, Ila, give me a chance — us a chance!"

Piccolo cries and my heart is mush. His plea for my forgiveness teeters on the crack in my love for him. My mind races in opposite directions, carrying overstuffed bags of my unmet expectations. We owe it to each other to be better than who we've been in the past — an improved version of who we've been to other lovers. I don't know what to think as he moves closer to me, falls to his knees and buries his face into my stomach to bawl like a baby. I rub the back of his head, mourning all the things I would have done for him up to that point. Tears, tears and more tears, but mine are not of sorrow or shame — they are of outrage.

"Piccolo, how do you expect me to think with you in my face begging me to look past something that I just found out? This is a heap of shit to process, and it's not as simple as you crying and then me saying I forgive you and then we go on as if nothing happened. I need to get out of your space because here with you, I am baffled - totally confused by who, what, how and mostly why. Why would you do some shit like this to me? But I can't even listen to the answer because I don't know what it'd make me want to do to you."

"No, Ila, let's sit and talk. You don't scare me, but losing you to this does! Let's stay here for as long as it takes and work this through. I mean, come on baby, it's not like we haven't been down this road before, remember?"

"Yeah, actually I do. I remember that you dumped my ass and never looked back! Now that the shoe is on the other foot, you wanna have all this fucking compassion and wipe each other's tears while we have some bullshit heart-to-heart? Fuck that. I thought that I'd seen it all, but nothing compares to seeing you in this moment, in this mess that you've brought to my home, into my world, turning what I thought was good into that same old gutter shit like the dog you are. The bottom line is, I need to leave, so motherfuck your conversation. I have to get away from here and away from you."

I snatch up my car keys and bolt out my front door in my pajama shorts and bunny slippers. I know exactly where I'm going and what to do when I get there. I know that bitch did all of this on purpose. This is no accident on her part; no oops, he innocently stumbled into her pussy — this was done intentionally to mess with my head, and there is nothing she can say to make me see it differently. Well, every dog has its day, and a bitch gets no exception in my book.

I watch Ila get into her car without any idea of what I should do. I could chase after her or even call Sage or Iris, but then I'll have to rehash the whole sordid ordeal and risk tarnishing my good-guy image. Rather than face my truth, I pace the floor rubbing the lump on the side of my face when the telephone rings again.

"Ila??"

"Um, no. This is Sage. Where is she, Piccolo?"

"I don't know, Sage. We had an argument, and she stormed out. It was pretty bad, and I don't know what to do."

"So she knows?"

"Knows what?"

"Don't play stupid, it doesn't suit you well."

"Clarke called."

"You asshole, that's where she's going!"

*

I screech up to Clarke's apartment building and kick my slippers off in the car to keep them from slowing me down as I run up the front steps two at a time. An inch away from the front door, my heart racing a million beats per second, and it suddenly flies open, exposing a 20-something Puerto Rican chick.

"My bad, Ma."

"It's cool. Listen, do you know Clarke Tate's apartment?"

"Here to whip her ass, huh? She stay in the middle of some bullshit and always over a man that ain't hers."

"Is it that obvious?"

"Ma, you look like you're breathing fire. It's Apartment E. I never liked her trick ass anyway."

The Boricua chick disappears out the front door, and I creep down the hallway, feverishly

Mahzi Kane   Tea Leaves

searching for Clarke's apartment. Once I find it, I cover the peephole with my hand and tap on the door. At first I hear nothing, and I start to think she isn't home, but then the sound of footsteps brighten my spirits.

"Who is it?"

I say nothing and instead knock again.

"I said, WHO IS IT?!"

Still, I say nothing hoping that curiosity and annoyance get the best of her and she unbolts the door. The turning of the lock sends an adrenaline rush throughout my body, and when the door opens a crack, I push into it like a human battering ram. I spring onto Clarke like a cheetah in the wild ripping into her flesh, clawing at each layer of her fraudulence and deceit. We tussle, struggling to gain the advantage, and in the midst of it all I pummel her face and chest with a vengeance, overpowering her with punches. My fists wield my cause to help avenge this great injustice done to me, to free me from being the pun at the end of her joke, the fool too naïve to uncover the trick. In a matter of minutes her nose is bloody, her lip busts and I work on blackening her right eye. She squirms away, attempting to scurry to her feet, begging me to stop, but I don't. I grab her leg and she falls to the ground. We wrestle until I get the upper hand and straddle her body. I use handfuls of weave to bang her head into the floor.

"I HATE YOU! I HATE YOU! WAS IT WORTH IT? DID IT FEEL AS GOOD AS THIS ASS-WHIPPING, BIIIIITCH?!"

Mahzi Kane   Tea Leaves

The hands around her neck wish to squeeze the life out of her, and they belong to me. They are mine, similar to the ones that once wrapped themselves around love, fingers gripped with his, swaying in the light breeze but now these hands are heavy and wish to destroy. Messing with my life, thinking this is another victimless crime to add to her brag bag and brandish the pin of her latest conquest on the lapel of her overpriced, low-class whore uniform as some trophy. Her eyes roll back, and I let go but am far from done. I stand up as she lay gasping for air and hurl my foot into her face first, her stomach next. She coughs — speckles of blood in a bright red tinge reminiscent of the scarlet letter hit the carpet. In my mind, I am a superhero, dismantling evil and stopping the disrespectful wrongdoings of the misguided. No need for Wonder Woman bracelets, the power lies in these hands as my theme music blares in triumph. Without a doubt, I am invincible until I feel hands restrain me.

"Get off of me, get the fuck off of meeeeeeeeeee!!!"

"Ila, it's me, Sage! Calm down, calm down! Stop fighting, it's me!"

"She slept with him, Sage! She ruined him and stole my dream! She did it to hurt me, and I'm gonna hurt her over and over again! You deserve every horrible thing that happens to your trick ass! Bitch, you crazy if you think you wouldn't pay for what you've done. They gonna carry your bloody ass outta here today! Hoe, you messed with the wrong one! Let me go!! You're the shit I scrape off the bottom of my old shoe. You can never be me, bitch, no matter how

Mahzi Kane   Tea Leaves

many of mine you fuck, you wack-ass, wannabe mistress. Take yo' trifling ass back to the clinic where you belong, tramp!"

It takes Sage, Iris and Toya to remove me from the apartment building. As they whisk me down the hall, neighbors emanate from their quarters to figure out the cause of the commotion. Clarke wails about pressing charges, and I manage to break loose and attempt to get back to her to give that bitch something to press charges about, but they get me before I can finish serving the beat down Clarke Barbara Tate bought.

We ride in Iris' car, where I rehash the entire ordeal beginning with Piccolo showing up at my door, to Clarke's unapologetic telephone confession and ending with the fight, and I use that term loosely because that skank didn't land one hit. Rashida stays behind to get my car, and we spark up a joint as we wait for her to arrive.

"Ila, you were like a mad woman! The look in your eyes was scary as shit. I thought you were going to kill Clarke."

"I felt like I was going to y'all, I'm serious — look, I'm still shaking. I have never been this angry in my life."

"I can only imagine what you feel, all the things going through you, and I know it has to feel crazy. It didn't even happen to me, and I'm still trying to let it all register in my mind that Clarke really did this. I always gave her the benefit of the doubt, and she used that against us all. I should have confronted her about her shit a long time ago, but I really did think that she was on our side."

"It's not your fault that she is a slut, Iris."

"What about Piccolo, Ila? Remember, it takes two."

"What about him, Sage?"

"We all know how Clarke is, although we didn't expect this. We can't act like this is outside of her character, but if Clarke sashayed her naked ass across his front lawn, Piccolo's love and loyalty is supposed to be with you regardless to anybody. He's the one who spent months reconnecting with you and strengthened that connection when you two made love, so it's his responsibility to keep that foremost in his mind, not Clarke's."

"Sage, I know you're not saying that she is innocent?"

"Of course not, Ila. I'm saying that I think it's typical female shit to think the answer is to beat Clarke into a coma but let Piccolo get off with a crack with the telephone. In my opinion, that's not fair at all."

"But Sage, Clarke is supposed to be squad, she's supposed to be someone we should be able to trust."

"Iris, that's a huge crock of bullshit, and we all know it, which is one of the reasons that Ila never liked her ass — lack of trust. She's fake as hell, and the only person that Clarke is loyal to is Clarke. That chick wakes up with the gimmes and goes to bed with the can-I-haves and that does not exclude us."

"I get where you're coming from, Sage, but there has to be a line of solidarity when it comes to respecting another woman's relationship because if there were no willing women, how could men cheat? The village has to respect the union of the two in order for the community to grow and remain strong. Plus Clarke has had her pick of any man from the day that I met her, so the way I see it, this thing with Piccolo was maliciously done to cause Ila pain, and I'm not pushing that off on anyone except Clarke."

"I hate to be the one to bring this up, but what goes around comes around, Ila. When have you ever been faithful? You reap what you sow, and maybe this is God's way of showing you the effects of how it feels to be betrayed."

"Toya, are you saying that I brought all of this on myself and this is karma's fucked up idea of payback? Because if you are, there is no problem with me handing out another ass-whipping today!"

"Those threats don't move me, Ila, and us fighting isn't going to solve a thing. You don't deserve this, and you know that's not what I'm saying, but don't act like you've been perfect. Learn some self-accountability."

"Moving words from an ex-adulterer. You got your conscience, what, two weeks ago, and suddenly you're a beacon of wisdom? Girl, please."

"Trying to hurt me by saying mean things won't help you. You can be mad all you want, but at some point, you have to take a long, hard look and check yourself."

I roll my eyes to holster my angry tears and spite-filled words. I am grateful at the sound of my car pulling up. Rashida enters into the living room to join the rest of the crew.

"Ila, you fucked that girl up bad! The paramedics came and all!"

"That's what she gets. Maybe she's finally learned about fucking with things that don't belong to her."

"All three of y'all have issues that need to be ironed out, if you ask me."

"Well nobody asked you, Rashida."

"Ill, stank-ass attitude. How did Piccolo take it when you gave him his walking papers?"

"Who said I was doing that?"

"WHAT?!! You're staying with him? You can't be serious!"

"Rashida, we all make mistakes. It's not like I haven't cheated on him, or every other man as its been pointed out."

"Damn near 10 years ago, and you were teenagers in high school, and fuck what happened then, we are talking about him! I fail to see the comparison."

"Rashida, so what? Who said I'm staying with him? Maybe I will, maybe I won't, but I can't make a snap decision because you and Toya say I should. I need time to collect my thoughts and put all of this into perspective."

"All of what? He crept behind your back with one of the girls in our circle. What more perspective do you need? He's no good."

"Things in general, Toya. I have so many viewpoints going on in my head and other peoples' opinions I might add, that I honestly don't know what to think."

"Let me tell you this. A smut isn't a smut by herself. Piccolo is not the man for you, and you need to suck that truth up and move on. Don't fool yourself into thinking that you two can move on from this point. If it wasn't Clarke, believe me when I tell you that it would have been someone else. I had to accept that fact myself."

I don't respond because I know that Toya is right, in fact they all are to varying degrees, but it ain't about them and what they think. I take one last tote of the joint and get up from my spot on Iris' living room floor.

"Thank you all for saving me from going to jail today. I love y'all and I'm out."

"You're leaving??"

"Yes, Iris. I have unfinished business to handle and quite frankly, I can't take any more of the advice swirling around up in here. Later."

On the drive home, I try to come to grips with being alone, but it isn't sitting well. I'm desperate to be the type of woman who could still be with Piccolo, gullible enough to do all that it takes to please him. Reconciliation is possible, but can we build something solid on "I'm sorry"? I did what I was supposed to do, managed my urges and followed the rules despite our unofficial relationship status and still turned down all the fine brothers that approached, yet he couldn't seem to resist Clarke. What a slap in the face. I should have cheated, but instead I changed for someone so undeserving, further proof that I am too full of him, too full of myself to notice the fallacy in my fantasy. I miss the thought of us already, but how a thing starts sets the tone, and the salty, bitter taste of getting played is not how this was supposed to turn out.

I pull up on my block and notice Piccolo's car out front of my place. My heart races, fully aware that the results of this moment are permanent, knowing that whatever we say here determines if we will continue, and I want to back off this street and run from our uncertain future. My daddy's words echo, urging me never to settle just to claim I'm chasing love or because I think I'm getting what I want. He told me to always remember that I'm a winner. Feels like I lost, and I hate losing. Begs the question what am I really fighting for? What do I hope to win? His devotion shouldn't come with a question mark.

Piccolo sees me pull up, leaps from his car and rushes over.

"Where have you been? I've been worried sick. Oh my god, are you OK?"

"You weren't that worried because you sure didn't follow me."

"You told me you needed me out of your face. I thought I was giving you want you wanted."

"I also wanted to be with you in an exclusive relationship, but I guess that wasn't high on your list."

"We can work it out, baby. I guarantee that it will never happen again. Give our love a chance."

I ponder the notion of accepting this offer to be his ladylove. On the one hand, I would get to be with him. On the other hand, I would never trust him and would second-guess his motives and actions. Most importantly it eats up my insides to think that Clarke would get exactly what she wants if I decide not to be with Piccolo, but it sickens my soul to think of having him inside of me, knowing that he's been with Clarke. I don't forgive easily, and I surely don't share.

"Piccolo, you know that I've always loved you. In high school, we were young and dumb, and yes, I messed up what we had. When we found each other I thought it was a sign, and I gave up a really great guy on the premise of our bullshit love, so don't talk to me about giving it a chance — I did! This is our second chance — the long shot, our one-in-a-million, life-changing event where we'd fall in love, and it'd be so fast and consuming it'd be like the inside of a tornado funnel. You'd get all of me, and I'd get all of you, and you know why? Because we're adults got-dam it! Grown-ass people who know better so we do better. Of all the things I envisioned for us, betrayal never crossed my mind. I didn't think you would do this to me this way and then have the balls to call it love. But I do love you. I mean I looooove you, you hear me? But I don't have the kind of love that it takes to fix this. I don't know how I will live without you, but I still have to let you go."

That being said, I walk up the front steps, enter into the sanctity of my apartment and break down into a river of tears. I want my daddy — he will make me feel better, help me lick my wounds and pull myself together. I dial his telephone number but get his machine. I hang up rather than leave a weeping message and upset my father, when really all that I suffer from is a broken heart and shattered ego. To think that after all these years, I am in a position where I feel like I need a man. Me! This scared, punk-ass boy who pandered his dishonorable action, overstepped the fundamental boundaries of a relationship and squandered exceptions that I'd made all in the name of loving him. Him! I'm independent even when I'm in a relationship, so for this to happen with the first real commitment I was prepared to make is sickening. Before I can even think about what I'm doing, I dial numbers and soon the soothing inflections of Justice's voice fill my soul.

"Hello."

"Hi, Justice, it's me."

"Long time, no hear."

"I know. How have you been?"

"Better than you sound. What's wrong, Ila?"

"I think they call it karma."

"What?"

"Nothing. Just wondering if we could, uh, get together and talk."

"What do we have to talk about?"

He's making this hard. I want to tell him that I am a fool for letting him go. I want to beg him to come back and promise my heart and hand, if only he will have me.

"We can talk about us, Justice."

"Ila, there is no us — there is you, and there is me."

"I've been thinking that maybe we could, uh, you know, rekindle what we had."

Mahzi Kane   Tea Leaves

"I don't know if I want that. You change direction like a fart in the wind, and I don't have time for your childish games."

"I'm not playing any games, Justice. I'm realizing the error of my ways, and I'm fighting to make it right."

"Or a bad decision could have you seeking my comfortable predictability that had you bored out of your mind."

"Time is teaching me about myself, Justice. Please give me a chance to show you what I'm learning."

"Ila, I've been out of school for a long time, and I have no intention on going back. You think I don't know about you and old boy running around town like the happy couple? Then you call me talking about "us"? And I'm supposed to believe you've learned something? You take care, Ila. Goodbye."

If I didn't have reason to wail before, this is it as I crash and burn. Being alone. Feeling lonely. I have no idea what those look like on me or how to function in a space deficient of testosterone. These foreign concepts close in fast, strangling the air, knocking me off the high horse I ride on draped in over-confidence and seething with the arrogance necessary to fuel a hyper-sexualized handling of men. The years of macking and two-timing mean nothing as I sit by myself, in the corner of my living room wondering how I'm going to face another day.

L Aughing L ASt : c L A r K e

TALK ABOUT A TRAUMATIC EXPERIENCE! I have never been in a real fight and had no idea of how to defend myself against the likes of Ila, the self-appointed brawler of Iris' little crew. I'm not ashamed to admit that I got my behind kicked, but as long as Ila ends up without Piccolo, it's worth every bruise, ache and stitch. I'm not going to lie, it was mortifying in the emergency room to look into the mirror and see that the trauma patient staring back was actually me — my lord! My eyes are black, stitched up lip, nose swollen, and the attending nurse says that I'm lucky that it isn't broken. Imagine that, I look like an extra from a zombie movie, and this peroxide-bottle blonde is telling me that I should be grateful. Helpless is more appropriate, unable to prevent the consequences of some shit that I chose to start. My chest and stomach are covered with black and blue bruises, and the doctor said they will be there for weeks. Dr. Nguyen asked if I wanted to press charges, but I declined. I just said that to make the mad bitch madder. The damage that I've done outweighs any sentence that a judge can render.

Who still fist fights over a man? True mean girls fuck with your mind, they don't get caught up in that same old jealous woman's script where I play the villain. She blames me because she was too dumb to notice their fake-ass love affair. I am so better than this entire situation and the one-sided mob mentality that decided my fate. What made Iris sacrifice me to Ila? Is our friendship this trivial?

Mahzi Kane   Tea Leaves

It's maddening really, the thought that she's cutting me off over something so petty. If anything, they should thank me for uncovering the real Piccolo. He ain't shit just like every other man and besides, I seduce — it's what I do. Why should I feel guilty? Why hate me for shining light on the dirty spots of her thrift-store china? She should take it as a free lesson.

On the ride from the emergency room, for a quick second I think of swinging by Iris' house to plead my case and confront her face-to-face about this rash and biased reaction. Maybe if she witnesses for herself what her friend did to me, she'll reconsider. How could she choose Ila over me? I mean, she's known me longer, and we lived together for goodness' sake. Has she forgotten the late nights we spent planning our futures, and all the support and positive feedback I gave when she read her stories and poetry? If it hadn't been for me, she might not be the great writer she is today. But do I get any thanks?

I need familiar territory. A scene that is void of any ill will directed toward my very existence. My apartment is exactly where I need to be despite the doctor's concerns about my attacker's return. Here I can relax in a tub of bubbles and put my pain at ease. I walk into the comfort of home smelling like ointment and rush to my answering machine with hopes to find a message from Iris to at least make sure that I'm not dead. Deep sighs full of disappointment attach to the ring of murky emotion swimming around my head, then the neck-turning drip of water from the bathroom and the squish of wet carpet underfoot welcome me to my nightmare: I was preparing my bath before the attack, and with the excitement of the melee, no one thought to shut off the running water. See this is just the type of by-myself shit that begs the question: Where is my support system? What about me?

After notifying the super of the flood and him alerting the landlord, it's best that I leave the premises. They claim that whenever there is an altercation or upheaval in the peace within the complex, my name is in the middle. My only option is to go, without my security deposit and with half of my things ruined. At least I avoid a lawsuit. I've accepted a position as head buyer for a major department store in Manhattan anyway so they have his wack ass apartment. I need a change of scenery because Philly is old news with nothing here but fair-weather friends and tired men. Everyplace is better than this, and a fresh start is what I need to leave this ugliness behind.

I'm down but I'm certainly not out even though my damsel-in-distress thing is out of gas. Time to switch back to the career-minded, eat-bitches-for-breakfast-and-fuck-their-daddies-for-dinner go-getter who makes shit happen. All of a sudden my hoes are too busy to help me out, and of all people, Peanut turns into my hero in shining armor and picks me up. So much for my fake-ass sponsors and their hollow pledges. When it comes down to it and you really need them, men generally prove not to be worth shit. Iris can stay stuck on the same block with them regular bitches living mediocre lives while I'm going where I can play to my strengths and do great things. So done with trying to bring them up to my level, done with tolerating the artificial relationship with Ila, and done with Iris' bogus consciousness. Clarke's moving on. Take notes, bitches.

Chapter Twenty-Two

o utSiDe i n : t o YA

I WORRY ABOUT ILA. I CALL, but there is no answer, and she's not returning messages. We contemplate going to her place, but in times like this, some people want to be left alone. I've always been in awe of the fighter in Ila, never backing down, but you can't bully love. Always getting your way can get messy, and it's hard to make moves in the mud that results from the dirt you do. I resign to leave another message letting her know that if she needs anything, Sage and I are waiting by the phone to help.

Once again, and against my better judgment, I let Danielle convince me to go out with her on a double date. Quincy is her latest flame, and Sam is his cousin visiting from Delaware. With nothing else to do and tired of waiting to hear from Ila, I agreed to go. Worst decision ever. Sam had nothing to say, and he spent the entire date saying it. His head was the size of a cantaloupe, and his sleepy eyes made him look like a Basset Hound. The three of them picked me up in Quincy's Chevy Coupe de Ville. Sam and I shook hands, and his awkward gawk undressed me until my cutting eye indicated that it was not acceptable. The icing on the cake was the 20 minutes we spent riding around looking for an ATM that dispensed 10s because Sam only had nineteen-fifty in his savings account. We ended up stopping for pizza and going back to Quincy's poorly furnished apartment. There was a folded-up card table in the dining room, a weight bench in the living room and a television set propped up on an empty milk crate. My mind raced with speculation as to what the upper floors looked like. I knew for sure that I was in a nightmare when Sam popped in a Jerky Boys cassette tape. Danielle was too busy in Quincy's face to notice the crooked eye I gave her, and just when blood seemed to drain from my eardrums, freedom from the torture chamber arrived and we left. That date drove home a moot point: I need a change.

Nobody knows, but instead of getting a new job, I enrolled in a study-abroad program. While submitting resumes, I saw an advertisement about the IT International Language School. I took a tear-off postcard, sent it away, and a week later received the brochure and scholarship information. Besides learning a new language in the yearlong program, I will do community outreach and get to see the world. I leave in four days for Spain, and I'm struggling to make up my mind — should I share the news or simply disappear? Should I at least make Sage aware of my plans? Will they chalk this up as another stupid decision? I don't need their disapprovals tampering with what I think. I think this is going to be an adventure, a blessed miracle where I get to be still and reassess my life while I don't have anybody else to worry about. I can't survive life without my own identity. I'm leaving so I can hear me in a space where I can turn up the volume on what's in the inside. I'm truly looking for a timeless experience because I am so bored here. I want this to rock my spirit and push me to get to a point where I'll spit on the next person trying to come between me and my joy. Some might say I'm running, and I might be, but all I know is wherever you are in life, you should be able to live out in the open. I've been living scared — afraid to lose love, worried that the mask would be removed, petrified of the truth. I want to be the type of woman who holds up well under the pressures of life and not be so desperate to have love and happiness that I lose who I am trying to get it. In that moment I decide that if I want to be ready for that type of growing then I have to be confident enough to tell the people who are important to me that I'm going.

I walk into the living room, and Sage flips to the next page of the latest hair magazine. I take a seat next to her on the sofa. "Hey, Sage, feel like talking?"

"Sure. I'm still on edge. I so wish Ila would call. It's not like her not to have contacted me by now. This is shitty. I know my best friend feels like crap, and I can't find her, let alone watch her favorite movies, listen to sad love songs, eat pizza and talk shit about the best sex we've had to take her mind off the heartache. She gotta get over this. On another note, I heard that Clarke's trifling, lying ass has left town. Philly ain't need that trash hanging around any damn way."

"I have to tell you something, but I need you to keep it between me and you."

"OK."

"I'm serious, Sage. When I want others to know, I will do it in my own time and my own way."

"Alright, already. I won't say a word. What's up?"

"I'm going to be going away for a year."

"You about to do a bid?"

"Be serious, Sage."

"OK, to where and for what? What are you gonna do with your stuff? Leave it here? This ain't public storage, you know. What about finding a job?"

"You really should look into detective work with all these questions. Let me explain: I enrolled in a travel-abroad language school."

"Why wouldn't you want people to know that?"

"Because everyone will think it's stupid and pointless, and act like I yanked it out of my behind and that it has no real promise."

"Who in our squad will react like that to news like this? We not talking about a married man here — you're taking control of your life, breaking free and opening up a new world like a spiritual awakening."

"My mom and sister won't understand. Neither will my church family. And I know Pia will think I've lost my mind."

"Forget what they say. Anybody who knocks your self-improvement ain't about shit anyway. I'm proud of you, girl! Where are you going?"

"Spain."

"Oh my god, I am jealous! Do you know how many fine men there are in Spain?"

"Sage, I'm looking for insight. Life has to be bigger than Philly, men and a steady paycheck."

"True that. What kind of job will you get with this?"

Mahzi Kane   Tea Leaves

"The program trains you in community development, so I'm thinking of working in a neighborhood recreation center or in a safe haven for victims of domestic violence when I return. I'll know more as I get acquainted with the curriculum, but definitely some kind of outreach to help others. I'm anxious at the thought of everything being new and far away, but mostly I'm excited to give myself this time to grow from the inside out."

"You should be. I'm excited and I'm not going a damn place. I'll get the herb and the wine 'cause we got shit to celebrate!"

Chapter Twenty-Three

g Ame o ver : r A S h i D A

EVERYONE'S UP IN ARMS BECAUSE
ILA hasn't made contact with the outside world.
Not trying to be mean, but I have real problems,
and when Ila is ready to come out of hiding, she
will. The earth don't fall off its axis every time a
woman's heart gets broken. On a less dramatic
note, I've met a man. Vance Harper. He's the agent
assigned to my case, and we met when I attended
the initial consultation for the first-time
homeowners program. When I walked into Vance's
office, his perky eyes and straightened shoulders
mirrored my own twinge of intrigue and attraction.
As Vance educated me on the home-buying
process, I learned that he has a 6-year-old daughter,
Kyrah, is a top graduate from Swarthmore College
and owns a home in the northeast.

Three sessions and two dates later and I 'm
digging him. Vance is smart, funny and down-to-
earth. For our first date, he arrived with a dozen
pastel-colored roses and then whisked me off to a
fairytale dinner at a blues lounge. On our second
date, he surprised me with a trip to a random movie
theater, where we saw the first thing listed on the
marquee. He actually had me watching a movie
with subtitles. Our conversations are like foreplay
— provocative, tense and leaving me wanting
more. In a short time, we've debated everything
from parenting, religion, history and politics, to
relationships, happiness and sex. I think he might
be one of the good guys, like he cares about who I
am, what I think and how I feel. Now his claim not

to expect sex right after meeting a new woman raises my eyebrow. He said that while it's true that nothing is more divine and pleasurable than the flesh, he's content with waiting until he's intimate with a woman's mind. He claims to be an eternal lover of the dating process. By that, he said, you can acquire a pool of data about an individual and examine what's there and more importantly, what's not. I'm waiting for Vance to pick me up to go buy a gift for his sister and brother-in-law's first anniversary. We're gonna check out a few of the boutiques and specialty shops downtown. I'm not a gold-digger, and I sure don't mind struggling a bit with a brother, but there's nothing like a fine Blackman with money. Especially when he ain't afraid to spend it.

As I come down the apartment-building stairs, Vance posts up against his black sedan, looking casually fine in a pair of black jeans, matching T-shirt and sandals. Clarke hates men in sandals. She said that a real man would never wear his feet out. Vance's locks hang past his shoulders, and the cut of his shirt shows off his sculptured frame. I walk over to the car, and his gaze sings to me as I sit in the plush interior of his ride. His oil invites me to lose myself in its exotic fragrance. He leans over and kisses me on the cheek, and I think I am going to faint.

"You look nice, Vance."

"As do you."

"It's a great day for shopping, I have to say."

"Every day is a shopping day as far as a woman is concerned."

"True, oh so true."

Another thing that I dig about Vance is that he has a preset on his car stereo for talk radio, a surefire way to dodge the monotony of the same

Mahzi Kane   Tea Leaves

five songs every hour on all three major stations and the annoying DJs as the rotten cherry on top. Back in the day, the radio was the place to hear all the new hip-hop and R&B jams that would one day be classics, but now it's filled with bullshit. Don't get me wrong, I love good music, and that is why I buy CDs, so I can hear what I like.

Vance parks in the lot on 15th and Sansom Streets and holds my hand as we stroll to Walnut Street. Erik never wanted to hold hands, hug or display any affection in public. He said it made him feel uncomfortable. What a chump.

"Were Malcolm and Iris upset when you told them that your house won't be ready for six months?"

"Naw, they're cool. Shocked, but they both assure me that it's not a problem for Jaden and I to stay there until my place is done."

"What a coincidence."

"What?"

I turn to see a gorgeous woman and an adorable little girl coming in our direction, but they haven't noticed us yet.

"Who is that?"

"My daughter and her mother."

"Daddy!"

The little girl's face lights up as she runs and jumps into Vance's arms.

"Daddy, daddy! What are you doing here? Mommy and I went shopping, and I have a new doll."

"That's nice, pumpkin. Hello, Theresa, how's it going?'

"Fine, Vance, how are you? What brings you to Center City?"

"Shopping for Tiffany and Terrance's anniversary gift."

Mahzi Kane   Tea Leaves

"Wow, it's been a year already? Be sure to send them my love."

"I will. Theresa, this is my friend Rashida."

"How nice to meet you, Rashida."

"And I'm Kyrah."

I smile at them both and say "hello." Theresa is stunning — skin like peaches and cream, body of a top model and the perfect French braid swept to the side. Her spirit is warm and inviting — not filled with attitude. Impressive.

"Well, Vance, I'll see you this weekend. Enjoy the rest of your day. It was nice meeting you, Rashida. Hope to see you again."

We wave goodbye and proceed into a quaint gift shop and emerge with a handcrafted time capsule for the loving couple to fill with mementos as their life together unfolds. Meeting Theresa set off a firebomb of questions in my head and my curiosity eats away at me because I want to know more.

"Theresa seems nice."

"She is nice."

"How long were you two together?"

"Almost seven years."

"Shit, that's common law."

"A very long time, indeed."

"She's beautiful. We've talked about our pasts in general but not about any one relationship, and I have to say, it seems like you two were the perfect couple."

"Not hardly. I'm family-oriented and she's focused on her career. I wanted her to stay home and raise our daughter, and she wanted to jump from red-eye flights to express trains for board meetings and bigwig parties."

"Why is it that a man always wants a woman to give up her hopes and aspirations? Being a mother doesn't mean that your life stops."

"Having a life doesn't mean that being a mother stops either. It's not like I wasn't going to provide her with every necessity. I wouldn't make such a demand — rather, suggestion — if I wasn't in a position to make it happen. Children are only small for a short period of time, and there is plenty of it left to fulfill one's dreams."

"Yes, but it seems like women are expected to make the sacrifice and push the pause button while y'all go full speed ahead. Whether in a relationship or as a single mother, the brunt of parenting falls more so on us than y'all, and that bugs me out."

"I understand but that's why mothers get the best gifts, and daddies get the big piece of chicken."

Vance's sense of humor takes the edge off of a delicate subject. I decide not to berate him because of my experiences with Erik — who let his desperation to control me outweigh his rationale and destroy our family before it started.

"At least you two can still be cordial. Me and my son's father can't seem to agree on anything except that we can't agree."

"Fortunately, Theresa and I didn't end on bad terms. It became apparent that we had two totally distinct outlooks on the way we viewed our future. That's why I take my time getting to know a woman before I go and make life choices like having a baby."

"I hear you. Erik and I start our counseling sessions on Wednesday. This is the last go at trying to get us over the hump we're stuck on."

"Good luck. At least you both can admit when you need help before it's past the point of no return."

"When you start arguing over socks, it's time to call in outside forces."

"I'd say so. Why do you think the relationship is this way?"

"I haven't let go and neither has he."

"What does that mean?"

"We still hold on to who the other person was when we were together."

"And that's not good, I assume?"

"Not one bit. After plenty of drama, I opened my eyes and realized that he wasn't good for me, and that no matter how much I loved him, he wasn't ready to give it back the way I needed or deserved. I want to be appreciated and valued by the one I love."

"You were seeing him for a while then?"

"Two long years. And it was then that I learned that people turn on you and as great as people make it appear, love can destroy everything when it's in the wrong hands."

"Not all love is manipulative, Rashida."

"I know that, but I lived something else. I felt tricked into loving him more than I loved myself. At times I couldn't tell if he loved or hated me. I feel like he expected me to be the greatest woman ever while he used my emotions against me and made me feel obligated to give into all his selfish needs . . all in the name of being his good woman."

"I hear that. My concern is that you harden and say fuck love, when it's really fuck the person who did that to you."

"Understand that when I look into the future I do see love, but it's not a man trying to tame a woman and take her fire. It's a connection based on balance, sacrifice and compromise. I need a man who'll get my favorite cupcake on special occasions, not play me and give away what's supposed to be ours."

"Infidelity leaves a scar."

"You can't undo what you've seen, and you damn sure can't un-feel what you've already felt. Unforgettable can't even begin to describe what it's like having him jeopardize everything, break my heart and waste my time."

"Try to remember that even though they say all men ain't shit, that's not true."

"That remains to be seen, sweetheart."

*

Sunday morning I wake up and do something I haven't done in too long: go to church. The soulful sounds of the choir send chills through my body, the harmony overshadowing whomever Brother Jones is cheating with and what scarf Sister Jackson shoplifted. Gripes ignored, every person in one accord, thankful for being alive. That's why I go, not for the sermons, because I can read the Bible at home or turn on any cable preacher, but for the fellowship and the oneness of people.

I get my dose of joy and take it with me on Wednesday afternoon into Dr. Rollins' office. He specializes in counseling couples, has been practicing for 10 years and has been married for 23. Surprisingly, Erik is already seated at the mahogany table in the center of the room. I take a seat across from the doctor and next to Erik. I'll give it to him; he still looks good.

"Good Morning, Rashida. How are you?"

"Fine, thank you for asking Dr. Rollins. Hi, Erik."

"Hey."

"I have the background on you two from when we spoke Rashida and have been talking a bit with Erik. I think the issue is you two are divided. It is the result of your individual grievances, which

Mahzi Kane   Tea Leaves

can skew your perspective on how to work together as a whole. The only way to fix a problem is to identify it first. Erik, would you like to start?"

"I guess. My whole beef is that I don't understand why we can't try to make it work and be a family. That's the problem with the chicks these days; they bail at the first sign of trouble. My moms stuck with my pops through thick and thin. I'm man enough to admit that I was a little misguided in my younger days, but she trying to punish me for the rest of my life."

"Erik, do you want to be in a relationship with Rashida simply for a family environment for your son, or do you love her?"

"Of course I love her, she has my son. I never stopped loving her. And I don't like that she's dating other dudes and bringing them around Jaden. I don't need another man playing daddy to my son. And on top of it, she's dating some old dude!"

"Rashida, rather than respond to what Erik said, voice your individual grievances. You'll have an opportunity to address what he said in a minute."

"I don't understand why he's so concerned and worried about who I date. He had his chance, and he wanted them nasty, stank freaks out running the streets — not me. Sometimes there is no such thing as second chances, so it'd be best for him to worry about being Jaden's father. He's preoccupied with this sitcom family life he's trying to concoct, but you know what, I'm a 25-year-old single mother who's finally putting her life on track. I don't have time to experiment and see if he's ready to be the man that he should have been."

"How did the things that Erik said make you feel?"

"Mad. Who does he think he is to question anybody I date? I could care less about the skeezoids he goes out with. And he talks about I'm trying to punish him? After all the heartache and grief he gave me and the way he continued to disrespect me, he has a whole lot of nerve. If he was true to the heart with this "wanting us to be a family" thing, why isn't he working toward it? Why hasn't he gotten his own house? What, me and Jaden supposed to come stay with him and his hoe cousin? I don't think so. Erik talks a good game, but when it comes to stepping up to the plate and swinging, he's seriously lacking. I don't know if he's working a legitimate job, and the last time I checked, he didn't even have a driver's license. There are too many uncertainties with him, and I can't promise my future to that. Jaden will always be his, but he's under the misconception that it's a package deal."

"OK, Erik. Respond to what Rashida just said. How did it make you feel?"

"Look, once you have a man's baby, y'all are connected. Some women were meant to be sluts so that we can get rid of all this sperm. One woman can't take all that penetration. But the special women, the one that you are meant to be with, you give them sons. Rashida gave me everything, and I want the chance to give it back. She talking a house and all this and that, but why should I when she got a man?"

"Erik, you have some jacked-up views when it comes to women, and then you wonder why I can't up and be with you again?"

"What did I say?"

"God, you can be such a jerk! You are totally clueless."

"See what I mean, Doc? She be tripping over nothing!"

Mahzi Kane   Tea Leaves

"Let's settle down. I'm going to throw a suggestion out there, and you two tell me what you think. Erik, at this point, Rashida isn't willing to try to be in a relationship with you. The focus should be on being the best parents to Jaden. Why not try to do things as a family unit such as trips to the zoo or taking him for pictures, you know things that aren't romantic? What do you think, Rashida?"

"I don't know. Erik might have a hard time telling the difference between that and being my boyfriend, and I don't want any unneeded headaches or misunderstandings."

"I'm not slow or stupid, I get it. You ain't all that for me to sweat you after you say you not with it. Go 'head and kick it with old boy if you want to."

"Old boy got something that you want."

"That something can't stop old boy from catching a bad one either."

"You're an idiot, and I wish I could sew your mouth shut."

"Rashida and Erik, take a minute to stop talking and breathe. You two are operating off of anger, and not only is it counterproductive, but it's immature."

"I apologize, Dr. Rollins, but he thinks being a thug is the answer. You can't beat everybody up, and even if you could, why would you want to when you're supposed to be a grown man?"

"Doc, my bad. The thought of another man dropping my son off at school and tucking him in bed at night doesn't sit well. Going out on trips is cool, but what about the unplanned stuff? What about sitting down at the table for dinner, watching his favorite cartoon with him and the stuff that you can't pencil in on the calendar because it just happens as he grows up? I miss all of that because of her."

"You should have thought about all of that before! This is NOT my fault!!"

"I think that this is enough for the day. We've covered enough. I'm going to send you home with a two-part assignment. Number one, come up with ways for you three to not only spend quality family time, but also find ways to implement Erik into Jaden's daily routines. Number two, come up with three things that occurred in the relationship that caused it to end and your part in those things. It's time for self-accountability folks."

We jot down the assignments and schedule an appointment for next Friday. This is the beginning of an interesting journey. I'm going to have to look at those ugly times where I put Erik first. I'll have no other choice but to free myself from the habit of punishing Erik for what he did in the past, giving him hell for the shit he does and doesn't do in the present, and being frustrated that he doesn't get it yet. He seems to think that the fact that he still cares about me makes up for my struggle as a single parent when he's very much around. How can I believe in him or any man when he's not giving me any reason to? Trusting a man is complicated, but trusting myself to pick a good one is damn near impossible.

Chapter Twenty-Four

i K neW me : S Ag e

TIME FEELS LIKE IT'S DRUDGING ALONG, forcing itself to proceed to the next second. I've had clients back to back to back. I haven't had a break or bite to eat since breakfast. With no men to keep me busy, I've put all my energy into work and have made an extra $3,000. I'm learning to check all of my cravings, and I came to the conclusion that men and sex are too big of a distraction. At the end of the day, I was still lonely, wishing for love from another when I wasn't loving myself the right way, yet expected a man to shine his light on my world. I was pressed and obsessed with having a man have me when I'm still discovering who me is. I am thinking of planning one of those mother-and-daughter pampering days at the spa around the corner. I want to clear the air with my mother and try to form a friendship. I have to believe that eventually even the bad things turn around and change for the better, and this relationship should not be the exception. I deserve the maternal guidance that a daughter is supposed to get. No matter what people say, I won't let go of how I know a mother should treat her daughter. She needs to know my heart and open up to me. I want to be able to call my mother and talk about the man in my life and hear excitement rather than contempt. I want to go on Saturday shopping sprees, get manis and pedis, and dine at fancy restaurants like in the movies, and sip tea and eat scones while I tell her my troubles. Why can't she be my best friend? Why won't she be my safe place? Life is too short to drift away from people because we're boggled down with too much crap. This can be our turning point, our chance to take the time to stop running and let our real feelings show, and yes, it's hard to let go of the past, but holding on is in our way.

"Sage, pick up line two."

"Oasis, this is Sage."

"You sound awful."

"Hello, Mother."

"What's wrong with you now?"

"I'm tired."

"You being lazy at business, but I bet you go all night with them men you lay up with."

"Not today Mother, I'm past not being in the mood. What do you want?"

"I was wondering if you could treat me to a cruise. Not the whole thing, I only need $300. Me and Ms. Edna wanna go on a five-day cruise to the Bahamas to celebrate our golden years."

"Mother, you aren't even 60 yet."

"Look, are you gonna give me the money or not? It's the least you can do, I did give you life."

"That is it! I have had it with you!"

"Hussy, who you raising your voice at?!"

"You, and for once you are going to be quiet and listen to what I have to say! I don't owe you shit! You're supposed to be taking care of me, you're the parent, remember? You do everything with everybody else, and I know it didn't cross your mind to ask me to go with you! You don't do anything except beg. It's not my job to make up for the past. It's not my fault that bastard beat you, and it sure as hell ain't my fault that you stayed. I'm tired of being punished for it and being juiced. I'm not your sugar daughter! You make me feel like shit, like I'm nothing, and I'm tired of it! I'm not taking it anymore."

"I don't know what to say except that I ask the Lord for help."

"That's not good enough."

"I don't know why I am the way I am, Sage. I love you; you're my first-born, my only daughter. I'd be an animal if I didn't love you. You just came at a bad time, and it got worse every day after that. I haven't meant to blame or punish you for it, but I guess in trying to shut out that period of my life, I shut you out too."

"All I know is that we can't go on like this. I can't keep running into the brick walls you put up. If you want to be by yourself, then so be it. One thing is for sure, don't call me when you're on your deathbed and expect a soft moment of sentimental reconciliation and forgiveness. Do me a favor and stay away from me if you're going to continue to be the mean and bitter sea hag who's come to represent everything painful and evil. If you want to work toward a real relationship that's built on love, caring and support, then give me a holla. Goodbye."

The receiver hits the base and all eyes in the shop are on me — unpoised and vulnerable with shaking hands, watery eyes and heaving chest — but none of that matters … at all. I needed to do that, and place of business or not, I couldn't miss the opportunity to be free. The on-the-scene-witness details aren't relevant. She can no longer erode my self-esteem and make me feel unworthy of her love and attention. I have no more time or space for her misplaced regrets. We have to talk if the wedge between us has any chance of disappearing, but I can't deal with easy cop-outs and a victim mentality — I am the child.

Mahzi Kane   Tea Leaves

"Sorry everybody. I didn't mean to disturb you. Please, excuse my rudeness."

I finish out the rest of my day feeling like fresh air. I decide to go to my yoga class to untwist the knots of the day and channel the energy through my meridians. Waiting for me at home is a letter from Toya. The others were stunned when they found out she went abroad. I guess a new place and people will help her see the world differently. This is the first letter she's sent. The back of it reads: "Don't open until you're with the squad." I call over Iris' to see what she and Rashida are up to and tell them about the letter. Iris ushers me to come over, and on the ride there, I call Ila so she can meet me there. Ila finally turned in her recluse card after weeks of being held up in the house listening to sad love songs and eating every piece of chocolate that she could find.

The door is unlocked so I walk in, and Iris, Rashida and Ila sit at the dining room table looking at old pictures. I lock the door, take off my shoes and approach the table.

"Oh goodness, whose idea was it to pull out the photo albums?"

"Ila's. Look at Iris' stacks in this junior prom picture!

"Turn the page, please."

"Don't be shy now, you were hot shit then. Where's the letter, Sage?"

"Here it is, Rashida."

They move the pictures aside and focus their attention on me as I remove the pages from the envelope and unfold the letter:

Dear Sage, Iris, Ila and Rashida,

Almost a month gone but it seems like I was there yesterday, right? I know all of y'all are doing fine. All is well with me, so much has happened. I've been taken through every human emotion —

Mahzi Kane   Tea Leaves

anxiety, fear, homesick, excitement, gratitude, and inspiration. There's so much to say but I'll start with now. I'm sitting on my balcony listening to the disquiet of the town. The sun has just come out. It rained all day yesterday and all last night. There is a breeze blowing and the trees are swaying. My clothes are drying on the line. I'm still in my nightclothes and it's a Saturday morning. There are sweet plantains baking in my oven. Esteban just finished oiling my hair. I know your question … who is Esteban? Esteban is my new friend. We met the first day on the train ride to the airport and we've been kicking it ever since. He's a twenty-four-year-old student from Brooklyn who enrolled in the program for the hell of it — for the experience. He's insightful and smart. He's peaceful and serene and oh God he is so funny, profoundly funny. He's an abyss of useless information and he spits bits and pieces of it in the pause of conversation to see what kind of reactions he's going to get from people. He's showing me a different slice of life and he's bringing out the good in me. He's gotten me into running y'all, yes exercise! And I got the nerve to enjoy it. I feel better about myself, I feel healthier and I've lost five pounds. Esteban is fine as hell, y'all! He is Puerto Rican and Black, husky and he has straight hair. I like him and he likes me but we agreed not to take things to the physical level until we get back home.

I'm learning so many new things; it's unbelievable! Spanish, a bit of Portugal, gardening and I'm learning to throw down on every Spanish dish that I can. One of the girls, Marguerita is teaching me to cook in exchange for me braiding her hair. Sage, you would be so proud of my hair! It's grown past my ears and I haven't had a perm

Mahzi Kane   Tea Leaves

since before I left. It's getting healthy and soft like you said. I've given out food to hungry kids, visited a children's Sunday school, volunteered at a shelter and helped a teen mother find housing. I finally feel like a person - not a shell wandering around being destructive. Danielle has been writing me letters every week but my mom still won't talk to me. She'll come around when she sees the better person that I become. Well, Esteban and I are going to get breakfast so until next time, I love y'all!!!! Tiene un dia' bueno. (That means have a good day.)

    I Love My Sisters.

    Toya

Chapter Twenty-Five

h eArt broKen : i r i S

SASHA CALLS TO INFORM ME THAT in two weeks, I'll have a few appearances to publicize my book. I love meeting people, particularly those who have been touched or transformed because of something that I've written. Hearing from Toya is a great end to a good day. I knew that she could find a way to grow into herself, and on top of it, she has met a man. She's finally on her way.

While driving down Broad Street getting information for my next article, I decide to surprise my Grandma Rue. She had such a nice time at the the unwedding and I want to let her see the proofs before we send them back to the photographer and tell her about the honeymoon. I pull up to her house and ring the bell, but she doesn't answer, so I use my key. In the quiet of her living room, I call out her name but get no response. She may have walked to the fruit truck, so I sit, but the sound of a television prompts me to venture upstairs. From her bedroom doorway, I don't see her, but as I walk to turn off the television she must have forgotten about, the corner of her foot catches my eye. I run to the other side of the bed and my grandma is sprawled on the floor. I scream her name and fall to my knees to see if she is breathing. Tears blur my vision as I start CPR, but nothing happens. I grab the telephone, dial 9-1-1 and give them the address. I toss the telephone aside and bang my fists on her chest.

"No, Grandma, no! Don't leave us, please! Breathe, Grandma, I need you to breathe! Please don't go!!"

I collapse over her as I realize that my grandma is gone. I sit up crying, and I feel the golden locket around my neck that she gave to me on the day of the the unwedding. She pulled me to the side and reached down into her huge pocketbook, and this lovely locket emerged. She said that it was my great-greatgrandmother's and that it was tradition to pass it down on the day one of us takes a husband. She cried as she put it around my neck, and then she kissed my cheek, and told me that no matter the what, and no matter the who, I would be happy.

As the paramedics attend to my grandma, I sit downstairs on the couch breathing but not moving, seeing but not speaking, living but not feeling. I haven't had the strength to call my parents or Malcolm, but luckily my grandma's neighbor Ms. Janice came over when she heard the ambulance. I gave her the telephone numbers to my parents' home and restaurant, and Malcolm's work number. I am waiting … more like dreading re-telling this story because I will be forced to relive the day I lost my sunshine.

Making the funeral arrangements is harder for my father than I expect. He doesn't make a sound on the ride back, torn from the inside out now that both of his parents are deceased. The day of the funeral I am in a daze, seated in the pew replaying the pictures that I have of her in my head, and the memory of who she was and how she looked the last time we were together. When they lower her into the ground, I faint. I come to in Malcolm's arms as he fights to keep my body from hitting the ground and my father is throwing himself onto the casket.

*

Everyone reassures me that as time passes so will my pain, but I can't tell. Since she returned to the essence of all things, I haven't left my house. I don't care about writing, deadlines, nothing. None of it can bring her back. Today I have no choice but to leave my cave so that we can go to the reading of her will. Simon Rosenberg has been my family's attorney for years, and considering his history with us, he's coming out to the house as a courtesy. I turn the key to her house, and silence smacks me across the face. No Al Green, not her humming or the smell of good cooking. Only cold, dead silence. I promised myself that I wouldn't cry, but that was lie when I made it.

Much of my growing up took place with her in this house. I will always remember the time she gave my cousin and I a royal ass-whooping for stealing the change from her bank and spending it on penny candy. On Saturday mornings, she would take us to Wanamaker's department store for shoe shopping and lunch. The best was when she and Aunt Kathy would have us over for the weekend, and we'd eat junk food and watch Michael Jackson do the moonwalk on *Motown 25* like we hadn't seen it a million times. My absolute favorite was when we'd go on bus trips to English Town. It was like going to another world — everything was outdoors, and there were so many diverse people, selling these wonderful things that I had never seen. I always thought that she would be around to let my children lick homemade lemon icing from the bowl, devour her dollar pancakes made with perfection and teach them how to sew with love. Who else but her could wrap them in her wisdom and tickle them with her laughter while they laid on piled up blankets on her bedroom floor on hot summer nights when the fan in their room just wouldn't do? I never thought about my life without her, despite the knowledge that death is a part of living. Why did she leave us so soon? Will I miss her forever? Can I be happy with her gone when she has been a fixture in all of our lives since I can remember being alive? My life's adventures remain, and I can't bear the thought of not sharing them with my grandma, the anchor of our family, the link to our roots and the keeper of our traditions.

An hour later we sit with my parents, Uncle Wesley, and cousins Cindy, Cicely and George at the dining room table my family has gathered around for countless holiday dinners and anniversary celebrations, and that has hosted out of town relatives and finally the last wishes of our matriarch.

"To my one and only son, Martin, I bequeath all savings and checking accounts, totaling $23,000."

My dad sits dumbfounded, his hand on his cheek as my mother rubs his shoulder.

"To my loving daughter-in-law, Queen, I bequeath my entire jewelry collection. To my brother Wesley, I bequeath all paintings and artwork left unto me from our beloved father."

Uncle Wesley throws down his napkin and sucks his teeth. My mother squeezes my father's arm to caution him that this is not the time to put Wesley's ungrateful ass in his place.

"To my nieces, Cindy and Cicely, I bequeath unto you the residence at 1600 North 11th Street in Philadelphia."

My dad interrupts. "Simon, are you sure? I think Iris gets her house."

Mahzi Kane   Tea Leaves

"Everyone, let's all relax. This is what the will reads — and there's more."

"I should be getting my house, Martin, and you damn well know it like everybody else sittin' 'round this table!"

"Wesley, shut your ungrateful mouth, you old asshole. This ain't about you and your jealous bullshit!"

"JEALOUS?!"

"Martin and Wesley, PLEASE!!"

My father and uncle retreat to their corners as calm and logic fight their way back into the room and Simon continues.

"To Iris, my kitten and my very special granddaughter who has grown into an exceptional human being, I bequeath my entire stock portfolio, all investment returns and dividends, CDs, all remaining personal property and the residence at 59 Westview Street."

"What? There's another house?"

"Yes, Iris."

"Simon, how did she do all of this? How did all of this come about — you've been our legal counsel for years, you have to know something."

"Martin, this is a substantial estate due to the inheritance she received from her parents and her sister, Kathy."

I am stuck in a daydream of knotted memories — the smell of Jean Naté, Murray's hair pomade and Old English furniture polish that tangle in the pit of my soul. I feel them looking through waiting eyes for me to do something, anything, but I'm lost in the puzzle of his words, struggling to find my own. Have I lost the power of speech?

"Iris, are you OK?"

Mahzi Kane   Tea Leaves

"Mom, I don't know … what I am … I … "

I need space to breathe, like a comma between the air and my tears so I can formulate my words into meaning and make this make sense.

"I am shocked that she never said a word about this other house. And it's … it's …mine?"

I break down, too full of loss and gain, too overcome by the contradictions of grief, joy and gratitude. All I've ever wanted was her company, yet she's giving me so much more, and I thank my Grandma Rue for the miracle she is, even from the grave.

*

Malcolm and I plan to see the house this morning, but instead of excitement, I feel drained from losing two major women within the last six months. They say death comes in threes, so I'm waiting to see whom else I love that is taken. I don't even want Malcolm to leave the house because I'm terrified that something dreadful will happen. On top of being paranoid, I can't eat, I'm tired, and I feel yucky. He thinks I'm depressed and should see a doctor. Sage wants me to take herbs because she says I'm stuck in a low energy field. Rashida suggests I let it all hit me in full force and cry like a crazed fool until I don't feel anything. None of them realize that I don't want to be better and I don't want to go back to my old self. Can't they see that I will always carry this grief? How can I move on like everything is the same when it's not?

On our way out of the apartment, I notice a stack of mail and shuffle through it without a care until I see familiar handwriting — Toya's. I tear open the envelope to find a greeting card with a despondent woman being comforted by another black female on the front. The words read, "Holding you together," and on the inside, "When you're falling apart." I manage a real smile for the first time since this whole ordeal began. Toya goes on to say that she is sorry for what has happened and even sorrier that she can't be here in my time of need. She promises to keep me in her prayers, regardless if I believe or not, because I need the Lord's grace to help me see the life left to live. I can do without the religion, but I so appreciate her acknowledging my loss and the truth that this hurts and I need healing. I am fragile, and this cruel reality is unfamiliar enough without forcing myself to do things I don't want to, so I cherish any support that's not trying to fix me or make me experience my pain differently.

Malcolm and I turn onto Westview Avenue and the historic charm of Chestnut Hill's single designs, each home with its own personality — a two-car driveway, winding hill or secluded entryway — is an instant change from the monotonous row homes of the north side of town. We pull up and park in front of the stone colonial marked "59," and as Malcolm opens his door, he notices that I don't move.

"It's going to be OK, Iris, I promise you it will. You'll never forget her, not ever, so don't think that if you stop feeling sad, it means that you don't miss her. Baby, I know you can do this. Falling down is a part of life, but getting up makes the difference."

I take a bottomless inhale of air in hopes that it will propel me from my seat, and it does. I get out of the car, and we approach the pale-yellow house with white shutters and a paired chimney. Flowerbeds line the walkway leading to three steps, a porch with a white swing and three potted plants in need of water. I hand the key to Malcolm, as mine are too anxious and unsteady. He opens the door, and we enter into a stunning vestibule. I stand a few inches from the stairs landing in awe of the high ceilings, gilt mirrors and elaborate wall sconces. The red brick fireplace stands out against the stark white of the living room, and there is the faint scent of pine on the hardwood floors as we meander through to the formal dining room complete with crown molding and wainscoting. Under the natural light, I feel at home, my nerves evening out as we marvel at the expertly carved oak wood of the kitchen cabinets. I shift focus to the wood tones of the exposed ceiling beams and the granite countertop of the two-tiered island with pedestal seating. This is like waking up and trying to remember your dream: foreign but familiar because this feels like her, down to the enclosed porch with wide-paneled windows and old screen door that opens up to a small but functional dark brown patio. We follow the slightly sloped mulch and gravel path to a spacious backyard of fruit trees, tomato vines, shrubs, bushes and tall blades of grass surrounded by stone — our very own private retreat great for lovemaking and stargazing. We return inside and take the back steps to the upper levels, guided by snazzy bannisters like those of a 19th-century hotel. The sparkle from the cut-glass doorknob of the master bedroom casts golden bits of sunshine against the bare walls of the adjoining foyer and full bath. We turn the corner and pass a cozy bedroom on our way to the third level, where we find two larger rooms. Outside the half bath we find pull-down stairs in the hallway that lead to the attic, which Malcolm finds packed with boxes and old furniture. Back on the main floor, we stand facing the bay window, and I place my head on his chest.

"Iris, don't cry."

Mahzi Kane   Tea Leaves

"I'm not sad. These are happy tears. Grandma Rue took care of both of these houses alone, and I am so honored that she chose us to continue the job. This is our home, Malcolm, can you believe it?"

"Only because I'm standing here with you."

There with him, I imagine my tiny hand wrapped inside hers, smooth brown and sturdy, and I feel her in me, the warrior that never let the harsh ways of the world break her or turn the sweet in her sour, even on her bad days. Hers is a true showing of a good life and how to leave some of it behind, and I realize her greatness can't be diminished — not even by death.

*

Malcolm informs our landlord that we will move in 30 days. He lets us out of our lease, considering the circumstances, and won't penalize us with any fees. Rashida and Jaden are coming with us until their house is ready. She refused at first, saying that they'd rent a room but Vance and I said that would be foolish. She wants Malcolm and I to establish our life in our home alone, but I remind her that we are never alone — we always have family, and that includes her and Jaden. I am pleased that she has met Vance. So far I think he is good for her, and while I don't know if wedding bells will ring for them, I do know that he is resuscitating her faith in men and love, and I love that. Why shouldn't she have a partner who is honest and transparent, one who will respect her heart and be real with her at all times, even if the truth might hurt? All any woman wants is a man that won't abuse her trust and who doesn't force her to walk away with another scar. At the end of the day, I want all my sisters to experience love because they each deserve someone who they can relate to, who gets them and who is qualified to be their king.

I finally agree to take Malcolm's advice and see my doctor. No more crying episodes and I'm out of the house as usual, but I am tired all of the time, so here I sit on this metal table in this blue and white polka-dot paper gown waiting for Dr. Franklin to return.

"OK, Iris, I think we've discovered the problem."

"Am I crazy, depressed or anemic?"

"You're pregnant."

"Pregnant? Who?"

"You. Your last period was well over two months ago. Didn't that strike you as odd?"

"I thought it was stress. Pregnant? How far?"

"I'd say about nine weeks or so, but we'll schedule your first prenatal visit with Dr. Klein, and he'll tell you all of the details. Congratulations, Iris, you're going be a mommy."

I put on my clothes, the whole time repeating the words "I'm pregnant" out loud. With everything that's been going on, pregnancy didn't cross my mind. I hadn't pictured our new house with a nursery.

*

I walk into the apartment and find Malcolm packing up the office.

"What are you doing here?"

"I decided to leave work and come home to give you a hand. How was your doctor's visit?"

"I think you should sit down."

"What is it, Iris? What's going on?"

"I'm pregnant."

"You're what?!"

"Pregnant."

He picks me up, spins us in wobbly circles, my arms around his neck as he covers me with slobbering kisses until he puts me down and places his face on my belly.

"A baby, Iris! You're having a baby, OUR baby?!"

"I'm almost three months, and my first prenatal appointment is in two weeks."

"I'm going to be a father! Me! And you're going to be a mother. We're going to be parents! This is insane."

"We weren't planning to have a baby. I didn't mean for this to happen, Malcolm."

"Woman, I'm thrilled and I can't wait to meet my boy!"

"A boy? Slow down, sir, this is a girl."

"Boy or girl, this child is our chance to bless the world with a miniature version of us — smart, conscious and fly. I love you so much, Iris!"

He pulls me close, puts his forehead to mine and cries. I cry too, and we stand together, basking in the glow of bringing forth life, and there is a calm in my heart where there was once noise and the loud gruff of a troubled soul.

Chapter Twenty-Six

t he **e** nD iS **A** LWAYS the **b** eginning

THE DAYS GO BY, AND EVERYTHING keeps changing — my expanding belly and matching nose, sudden heartburn, uncontrollable emotion and strange cravings. My parents have begun a college fund because my dad is predicting his first grandchild to be a genius child prodigy – his words, not mine. We don't know the sex of the baby, but that hasn't stopped my mother from buying dolls and snatching up every piece of pink baby furniture that she can find. We're all moved in, and decorating is an adventure that makes me miss Clarke and her keen eye for style. I hope time heals this rift between us and our paths cross again. I look forward to life's experiences making her into a better friend, and if it doesn't, I feel bad for her and worst for the people that have to put up with her bullshit.

This has been a tumultuous journey of questions for my squad. Turns out that Sage's best move is a slow one, and she's getting in sync with her natural rhythm, steadying her crown so that she can wear it straight up as a love goddess, not a sex slave, and select a suitable man. She is safer in her relations with men and can hold out for exchanges that last longer than an orgasm, confident at setting boundaries and making decisions that preserve her bodily treasures. I think that she's content with relying on herself for her happiness for now. Toya is getting more out of her life, having overcome the trap of believing that second is her place. Instead she is defining her role and embracing being number one, and discovering the true value in being herself, and because of that, she is able to vibrate her joy on a higher level. Rashida understands that sometimes it's best not to get the life that you plan and that you can make order out of whatever mess you've made without being rigid and cold. Harnessing her powers of forgiveness and compromise is a breakthrough in emotional maturity that has mellowed her out, and she shines with an optimism that's helping her find the things that encourage her to laugh, and seeing that in her smile in phenomenal. Her laughter is such a wonderful complement to her strong will, and it's great to see her use all the shit that she's been through for better communication with the men in her life. She's learning that security comes with the discomfort inherent in trusting someone to do the right thing. Ila's deflated ego, regret and the realization that she can't run from how she treats men are the things that still keep her awake some nights. It's hard to accept when you get back what you've put out. She's in upgrade mode, learning to care more and play less, deciding what it really means to win while aligning how she acts with what she wants to receive. She is trying to understand that equal consideration and loyalty work both ways and being independent doesn't mean being a bitch. And Clarke just didn't make the cut.

Finally, I've grasped the knack of not owning other peoples' problems, issues or bullshit. As if watching what I say and how I say it isn't work enough, these days I listen, empathize and support, but I've turned in my savior card and no longer make excuses for the destructive habits of women just because we're cool. Instead of grieving, I glorify my grandma's life and carry on her legacy because this is a time for renewal, and it's powerful to think of a piece of her manifesting in my child.

Motherhood is a new dimension, and in it I recognize that I am not perfect, and that's more than OK. I'm a real person with cracks and bruises and mistakes, not to mention some shit that just can't be undone. But within the things that I thought might break me, a new sparkle of joy blossoms, and I am refreshed. I beam with the promise growing inside, encapsulating gleeful moments in prose, and I delight in my creativity, reveling in my potent mastery of words. Here in motherhood I have found freedom.

See, the unknown can be a scary place, so we act like we know what to do all of the time and that there aren't any regrets, but that isn't true. We look for indicators of the right time for something to happen — in stars, cards and numbers — anything that might interpret our patterns and tell the meaning of the inexplicable. Trying to predict things based on little bits of scattered information is like trying to tell the future by looking at the tea leaves left in the bottom of a cup after you're done, after you've drained away what was heavy. We peer at the remnants of our interactions with others and try to access the inner and outer circles to determine who's not in the right position. Most times we get it right. Sometimes a good decision slips by us, but we don't really need a magic ball to tell us where to go look for peace in everyday moments, or search for comfort when times are turbulent. We have to have the courage to admit when we victimize ourselves, and accept when it's

Mahzi Kane   Tea Leaves

time to deal with the consequences when the telling isn't what we foresaw in our expectations. I've learned that the real messages come from the insight that tells us what to do when patterns of action say everything we don't want to be true. Life's glitches can occur quickly or lay in wait off in the distance. The trick is trying to be ready. Hindsight contains the teachings of the past which can hold some of the answers for the future so that when shit happens, I have an idea of what to do. Intuition and flaws can work together. Trying to decipher the sometimes cryptic messages of life is hard but using all of who I am opens me up to discover reasoning that is deeper than the surface meaning. The real gem is that most times, life just requires us to use common fucking sense. Why be foolish, childish even, to wish for some kind of guide to destiny, a map of every safe move from any fixed point in time to the obscure future? Would life be easier with a guarantee of coming events, or is a better person made through growth and adaptation? When life's troubles get stirred up, the only question that matters is whether or not I am standing in my truth.

ABOUT THE AUTHOR

Mahzi Kane is a Philly native, wife, mother and entrepreneur. She enjoys writing fiction and is currently working on her next novel, Selfish. Visit her website MahziKaneBooks.com

TEA
LEAVES